Total Business Management (TBM): Practices
For the 21st Century

Achieving Sustained Substantial Profitability,
Operational Excellence and Growth in a
Hyper-Competitive Business Climate

James K. Lim

Order this book online at www.trafford.com
or email orders@trafford.com

Most Trafford titles are also available at major online book retailers.

Note for Librarians: A cataloguing record for this book is available from Library
and Archives Canada at www.collectionscanada.ca/amicus/index-e.html

Printed in Victoria, BC, Canada.

ISBN: 978-1-4251-8907-5

*We at Trafford believe that it is the responsibility of us all, as both individuals
and corporations, to make choices that are environmentally and socially sound.
You, in turn, are supporting this responsible conduct each time you purchase a
Trafford book, or make use of our publishing services. To find out how you are
helping, please visit www.trafford.com/responsiblepublishing.html*

*Our mission is to efficiently provide the world's finest, most comprehensive
book publishing service, enabling every author to experience success.
To find out how to publish your book, your way, and have it available
worldwide, visit us online at www.trafford.com*

Trafford rev. 7/23/2009

 www.trafford.com

North America & international
toll-free: 1 888 232 4444 (USA & Canada)
phone: 250 383 6864 ♦ fax: 250 383 6804 ♦ email: info@trafford.com

Total Business Management (TBM): Practices For the 21st Century

Achieving Sustained Substantial Profitability, Operational Excellence and Growth in a Hyper-Competitive Business Climate

CONTENTS

Acknowledgement

The processes include time-tested and/or innovative ideas and practices all of which work together supportively to foster substantial, sustainable growth and equity. Nothing succeeds like success and the proof is in the pudding. Lessons of cumulative experience are influenced directly or posthumously from the thoughts and experience of phenomenally successful and proven corporate leaders of world caliber: Stanley Shih (Acer), Jeff Bezos (Amazon.com), William Verity (Armco), A.P. Gianini (Bank of America), Jim McNerny (Boeing), John Browne (British Petroleum), John Chambers (Cisco), James Stillman (Citicorp/National City), Sanford Weill (Citigroup), Michael Dell (Dell Computers), Roy Disney (Disney Productions), Paul Oreffice (Dow Chemicals), Frederick Smith (FedEx), Jack Welch (GE), Alfred Sloan (GM), Lewis Platt (HP), Lou Gerstner (IBM), Andy Grove (Intel), Ralph Larson (Johnson & Johnson), Ray Kroc (McDonald's), Bill Gates (Microsoft), Paul Galvin (Motorola), Ken Iverson (Nucor), Christopher Sinclair (PepsiCo), Sol Price (Price Club), William Danforth (Ralston Purina), Al Dunlap (Scott Paper), Herb Kelleher (Southwest Airlines), Howard Schultz (Starbucks), Fred de Luca (Subway), Morris Chang (TSMC), George David (United Technologies), Tom Freston (Viacom), etc. It helps to pull back the curtain to see how the magic is done.

My confidence has increased over the years as I delve ever deeper into the marvels of management theories and methods. Regrets have been remarkably few. There is a wide body of books and articles written about business management including autobiographies of movers and shakers from within and outside the hallowed halls of Ivy League schools. I am awed by the prolific writings, zeal and profound insights of management legends such as Peter Drucker, Michael Porter, Tom Peters and Ken Blanchard. Quality gurus W. Edward Demings, Joseph Juran and Phil B. Cosby, with energy of great magnitude have added new landmarks in the quality arena. Crème de la crème of marketing, Philip Kotler and Theodore Levitt have made profound impact in marketing of which we are deeply indebted. Forward thinker and innovation expert, Gary Hammel provided new insight into the innovation agenda. Distinguished production management experts William J. Abernathy, Kim B. Clark and Alan M. Kantrow have added new trajectory to production know-how. I have been particularly privileged to have interacted extensively with high technology professionals in Silicon Valley and in the international arenas.

And to those eminent leaders and thinkers who worked outside the public spotlight, I also say heartfelt thanks for their contributions of incalculable value.

Many people, including those who supported behind the scenes have contributed to the preparation of this book, a culmination and encapsulation of more than five years of time consuming, laborious but enjoyable effort. It has taken me a lifetime to learn. This book, in readable prose has been influenced by an enormous numbers of authors, business leaders and managers (including those aforementioned) and it would be impossible to cite them all. I also relied on the books listed in the bibliography and a wide range of professional articles. It is gratifying to witness advances in the body of business management literatures including a respectable body of scholarly opinions, contributed by renowned and talented scholars and practitioners, both classical and contemporary. Both personally and professionally, I owe a debt of gratitude and applaud the remarkable authors and organizations referenced in the bibliography and in other sections of the book for their immense individual and collective intellectual contribution in stimulating new thinking and better understanding of the art and science of management. Their profound insights, penetrating and thought provoking vision with occasional doses of harsh but inescapable facts are eminently presented in their books to the benefit of the business community. The ever-changing business landscape, fascination over the panoramic business opportunities and urgency has provided an impetus to write this book. This is also my first foray in book writing but a long-standing aspiration to add my voice to the pursuit of business excellence. It would be mea culpa if there were shortcomings in this book.

The thoughts in crafting this road map to industrial revival and boundless prosperity were refined during many hours of invigorating discussions with friends, colleagues and experts in the field. Some segments are based on thoughts and fragments during times of contemplation. I am fortunate to have the assistance of many exceptional people with their treasure trove of knowledge and experience. I am and continue to be intrigued by the many facets of evolving management theories and practices, articulated so well in various forums. While many of the ideas are not original, they represent a consolidated set of practices, when suitably applied will contribute to success in business. Although this book is focused on U.S. companies, the principles, theories and practices can be applied in other parts of the globe with astonishing results. Whether you are an executive, manager or business professional, this book will help you gain valuable insights in your quest to lead the pack and achieve Total Business Success in a complex and daunting landscape. Readers may be spurred by this book to study closely and in more detail some of the aspects presented herein. I hope that you will find this book worthy of the effort. I also hope that you will refer to this book over and over again, enjoy and benefit as you embark on this remarkable journey.

I apologize to countless numbers of people who contributed to the book who go unrecognized.

This book is dedicated to the happy memories of my departed father and mother. In their own ways, they have made the world so much richer. Last, but not least, I must acknowledge with great pleasure my wife Joyce and daughters Olivia and Vanessa for understanding and support and in enduring my countless hours of preoccupation from inception to conclusion of this project in addition to long hours at my full-time job with a high tech company. The efforts have proven more laborious and time consuming than I anticipated. Long form composition is demanding. They have endured my long hours of toil, writing and rewriting the manuscript. They have provided a balance among divergent demands and daunting workload. They are a source of joy and satisfaction.

Feel free to contact me if you would like to discuss or have questions on issues relating to Total Business Management. I can be reached at jameslim@totalbusinessmanagement.com.

James Lim
Silicon Valley, California
July 1, 2009

Introduction

⌘ The measure of a man (or woman) lies not just in the scale of challenges he faces but how he handles these challenges. ⌘

Success rarely comes easily... and this is hardly a novel thought. It requires more than ability and motivation; and clearly, there is no single road to riches. The road to broad and enduring success may be long and circuitous, especially in a business landscape that is rugged, transitional and in a permanent state of flux. Simply stated, there is no mystique and uniform answer surrounding Total Business Management (TBM). There is no simple, rigid, mechanical formula that can predict successful performance with certainty. It takes time, resilience, hard work and leadership coupled with executive capabilities grounded with solid understanding of business crosscurrents. It tests the ingenuity of leaders in mastering technology driven strategy, competent workforce management, heightened understanding of the domain of sales and marketing, customer and quality orientation with efficient and high quality production.

Merely imitating past successes alone is grossly inadequate. Managerial theories and practices must not be embraced willy-nilly. Many companies that are successful now whether achieved by luck or foresight may not be as successful in the future. Some successful companies, including those with strong brand names and sound financial base will undoubtedly fall on hard times in the years ahead. Companies that are successful in one aspect of their activities may not be successful in other aspects. Those who are successful in the old system have to change their priorities and behaviors to be successful in the new system (Nicholas Imparato and Oren Harari, 1994). Achieving growth and market leadership is difficult. Of greater difficulty is to stay on top once you have reached there. The process of attaining and maintaining total wide-ranging and long-lasting success in business poses many challenges of Byzantine proportion.

People are always looking for panacea for failures. Explanations regarding reasons for failures are more often oversimplified. Management fads come today and go tomorrow. Many old assumptions no longer apply. New mantras must withstand the test of time. "To each according to his ability, for each according to his needs." Isn't this utopian theory sounds familiar and good? Except; it does not work. All mantras, however attractive, must be tested before releasing for mass consumption. In the business parlance, there is no "one size fits all."

Simply put, to succeed in the new era, each company needs to weave its own tapestry of business strategy and tactics with never ending quest for excellence, using both conventional and unconventional means.

Thomas Aquinas observed that if the primary aim of a captain were to preserve the ship, he would leave it in port forever. William Fulner (Shaping the Adaptive Organization, 2000) also pointed out quite interestingly: "There is more to survival in business. After all, sharks have survived much longer than human beings, but they are far from being the most interesting species in our planet." The underlying thrust of a corporation is to create long-term value and wealth that are sustainable, though it does not mean that other factors are unimportant. Business is a powerful force in the world. It is a force that transforms human, social and environmental conditions into harder coinage: jobs, trade and money. **Total success in business means achieving and perpetuating outstanding organizational, managerial, marketing, technological, finance, quality, customer service and every other measure of corporate excellence in good as well as rocky times, in charted and uncharted territories.** As the legendary Jack Welch noted in his book (Winning, 2005), "Winning companies and the people who work for them are the engines of a healthy economy, and in providing the revenues for government, and they are the foundation of a free and democratic society."

Over the years, many books and articles have been written on the subject of how to achieve excellence in business management. In their own ways, these authors with the sharpest minds have brought forth views and reservoir of knowledge that cover almost every aspect on how to manage business successfully. While some of the concepts are based on proven age-old practices - putting old wine in new bottles, others have been battle-tested and breaking new paths. Cumulatively, these authors have spawned influential and matchless management ideas over the last three decades. Business practitioners and scholars have benefited from the wisdom and valuable information on how managerial capabilities can be embellished to improve competitiveness in business. While there are innumerable works of originality, nevertheless successive books and articles are built on the works of the preceding ones, each with its special emphasis, clarity and wit. There is a need for on-going valuation of the basics, concurrent reassessment and renovation of our management system and capabilities to cope with ever-changing business conditions and secure competitive edge on a global scale. As Andy Grove (1996) pointed out on the importance of coping with groundbreaking business trends, "a strategic inflexion point is when the balance of forces shifts from the old structure, from the old way of doing business and the old ways of competing, to the new."

The Reality

Organizations worldwide, now and ever before are faced with fast-changing markets, changing demographics, higher level of customer expectations and more demanding shareholders. U.S. companies must understand and cope with the new mode of competition in the midst of increasing rigors in order to stem slippage in global business dominance. Managerial theories, assumptions and practices must keep pace with societal and economic advances by proper application of new and well-used tools. Heightened understanding helps plant the seed for renewed commitment to managerial excellence in ever expanding frontier. The chasm between the realms of academia and industry must be bridged. Companies must overcome the inertia of precedent and tradition; embrace vibrant innovation agenda and lead performance gap against the pack over a wide margin.

We don't have to look far to witness the information and communications revolution that has collapsed the information and financial float. The multidimensional possibilities for further advances are staggering. These historic advances hailed in the U.S. and abroad, have been made by the cutting edge generation. While many of the early claims during the dot-com era about the online economy turned out to be grossly

4

exaggerated, nevertheless information and communication technologies are force majeure and have dramatically changed how organizations work. As Kirk Cheyfits (Thinking In the Box, 2003) aptly stated: "Technology is the tool that enables solution; but is never the solution." The impact of information technology (IT) is felt in every industry: computer, consumer, media, broadcasting, communication, financial services, chemicals, aircraft, defense and so on. Business is rife with examples on how information technology and Internet revolution have reshaped the way of doing business. IT is an invaluable tool that delivers information at the fingertips of corporate executives. And there are vast ocean of possibilities and a plethora of benefits that are yet to be tapped. The overwhelming challenge is the connection and creation of relationships between poorly or unlinked internal and external systems. There is a need to have an open solution that will enhance the investments already made by corporations and bring new value from the system already owned.

Formulae and Choices

This book is a culmination of years of practical observation, research and analysis on management practices in large corporations and small company scenarios, from the shop floor to the executive suites. It is benefited from working in the trenches in high technology companies for 30 years and my association with professionals in industries spanning automatic test equipments, defense electronics, computers, telecommunications, professional audio equipments, image sensors, graphics, core logic chipsets, programmable devices, semiconductors and component services. It is based on a lifetime of opportunities, challenges, experience and good fortune. It is derived from lifelong study of companies in the trough and belle époque of business and economic cycles. It blends key concepts that are used to develop winning strategies, create products, shape the market and manage the creative energies of all employees today and tomorrow. It explores the ingredients for highly successful companies and provides a unified, broad-base and balanced prescription towards managing healthy organization that promotes perpetually increased profitability, operational excellence and growth. It paddles on the edge of a vast sea of opportunities waiting to be claimed. It is my hope that this book will persuasively convey key concepts, practices and new paradigms to a wide audience of business leaders, managers and others who are interested in achieving total, substantial and sustainable success in business. Hundreds of published articles and books were reviewed, underscoring the immensity of this worthwhile project. A fascinating variety of strategies, people, processes, methodologies and organizational structures were studied.

There are those who maintained that large companies are stumbling giants that cannot innovate but they can and some do, time after time. Why do powerhouses such as Adobe Systems, Amazon.com, Bechtel, Caterpillar, Charles Schwab, Chevron, Citigroup, Dell, eBay, FedEx, GE, IBM, Microsoft, Nokia, NTT DoCoMo, Proctor and Gamble, Royal Dutch/Shell, Sony, Southwest Airlines, Staples, Starbucks, Tesco (British grocer), The Home Depot, Toys "R" Us, United Technologies, UPS, Wall-Mart, Yahoo!, 3M and various others thrive in the face of on-going competitive and adversarial conditions while many others (Arthur Anderson, Bethleham Steel, Burroughs, Compaq, Coors, Enron, Global Crossing, IBM PC Division,

LTV, Lotus, Lucent Technologies, Osborne Computers, Pan Am, People Express, Pets.com, Qwest Communications, Sears, TWA, Tyco, US Steel, WangLabs, Webvan.com, WorldCom, Zenith, and the list goes on) languish in obscurity or fade away? How do these companies deal with posing issues in adaptation, coordination and execution... like adapting and navigating many legs of the centipede in rough terrain? How do companies achieve outstanding organizational management, marketing, technological, finance, quality, customer service and every other measures of corporate excellence in good as well as rocky times? How do mature as well as stagnant companies embark on organizational reinvigoration from deep-rooted practices to unexcelled competence before they are compelled to act after the situation become irreversible? How do companies tap into the wellspring of the American system and apply it successfully year after year, across businesses and borders? How do companies address the unprecedented global business agenda? What are the key elements and linkages that contribute to Total Business Success? These companies achieve operational and financial success by a wide margin through appropriate application of a combination of structured and creative managerial, administrative and technical processes. At the core, corporate leaders who have thorough understanding of the underpinnings of companies and are adaptive to changes in business environment run successful companies.

Lessons from failed companies and leadership can be instructive. There is no mystery at all why some companies are eclipsed or face terminal decline while others, through managerial acuity, experienced renaissance. Many leaders have lost their moral force, lulled by excesses of the glorious past, got their eyes off the ball, the result of not knowing or adhering to sound managerial principles and practices. They failed to listen to wake-up call to take immediate corrective action to recover lost ground. They are sidetracked, loss the footing, felt the weight, made ill-fated miscalculations or failed to adapt to the complexity, pace and dynamics of business enterprises. The levels of demands and complexity beyond their capabilities overwhelm them. Some bite off more than they can chew while others are one-trick ponies that over time have lost their competitive edge. I am certain that all the ill-fated companies have poor grasp of some, if not many of the drivers of operational excellence indicated in this book.

What are the most admirable choices and actions fueling business today? Organizations must not rely merely on pragmatism and pure business. There need to be balanced concerns with noble aspirations, vision, values and skills with data and balance sheet. Companies can ill afford to be estranged from a rapidly changing global business interest where there is greater premium for trust, integrity and high ethical standard. They must move away from cold, impersonal and inhuman practices. Just as importantly, organizations need to forge relationship to a higher plane, from one that goes beyond competitiveness or just making money to one for the greater good. The modus operandi should include examples of honesty, loyalty and friendship and so forth for guidance in how to live and work in addition to drive, energy and competitive savvy.

There is much to be learned about the vast business opportunities that lie ahead. There are grounds for cautious optimism. On the aggregate, I remain upbeat on many U.S. companies for their capacity to reexamine, relearn and rejuvenate their organizations in order to stem the decline in fortune. For these companies and many with unsung success stories, the future is radiant and promising. The implications are obvious for those companies who are unable to do so. Obituaries for U.S. industrial competitiveness though are premature.

I have included a chapter on "Wall Street" as its activities have significant bearing on decision and actions of public companies.

Chapter 1
Good Leadership is Pivotal to Business Success

⌘ Truly successful leaders manage and perform well not
only in good times but also during turbulent times. ⌘

It is irrefutable that leadership is central to business success
and begins from the top. Leaders are responsible for lives,
jobs and fate of companies. They know how many of their
decisions, attitudes and actions affect others. A leader will not
have self confidence unless he is convinced that he can do the
job. Evidently, this is not a new finding, but a tried and true
source of achievement. The success of an organization,
however, does not only depend on the quality of leadership
from the very top of the organization, but also requires skilled
leadership from all managers and individual contributors who
are responsible for operating results. First-rate leadership
can elevate a business from mediocre to exceptional: leaders
with business acumen will most likely succeed where others
have failed. In fact, authoritative leadership models must be
articulated and understood by managers if organizations are
to improve productivity. As Warren Bennis and Burt Nanus
(1985) wrote in "Leaders" which emphasizes the role on
visionary leadership in business success, "A business short on
capital can borrow money. One with a poor location can move.
But a business short on leadership has little chance for
survival. It will be reduced to the control of, at best, efficient
clerks in narrow orbits." John C. Maxwell, author of "The 21
Irrefutable Laws of Leadership", also noted, "Leadership is
about influencing people to follow, while management focuses

on monitoring systems and processes." Now, more than ever, we need leaders who are committed to building enduring organizations. Great leaders, from Henry Ford to Steve Jobs and Warren Buffet, leave lasting marks long after they depart from their organizations. *"I've reluctantly discarded the notion of my continuing to manage the portfolio after my death – abandoning my hope to give new meaning to the term "thinking outside the box,""* said Warren Buffet.

The long-range staying power of any organization depends on the strength, width and depth of the management organization. One does not have to be a manager to be a leader. Enlightened leadership plays an imperative role in shaping a group of people into a force that proliferate a common competitive business advantage throughout the value chain. Managers can maintain direction but leaders can influence and change it. We need seasoned leaders who are capable, pragmatic, and resolute and have both an unexcelled reputation and successful track record. They must be energetic; goal focused and an agent of change. They must possess idealism and realism as well as a firm and visionary purpose with which to focus their goals. Unmatchable leadership wattage is burnished by long years of navigation and tempered by fire. A leader must be authentic, bold and decisive. A leader must also work with people and help them transcend the appeal of the comfortable mode of inaction through forcefulness of persuasion. In essence, leaders will help you achieve your goals if you help them achieve theirs. It is essential to develop strong management, vision and resilience that inspire and unify a company. Cultivate the quality and depth of leadership with a human touch in order to sustain growth and commanding market dominance. There should be a mixture of competence, passion, compassion, savvy and strength.

Though leaders should be ultimately accountable for an organization's performance, they should not overshadow their subordinates. As Jack and Suzy Welch aptly stated in their book "Winning", "Leadership is not about you. It's about them." Delegation of responsibility assumes greater importance when issues are technologically complex and should be decided by those who best understand the issues concerned. It is important to remember, however, that a corporation is not a democracy. There are some jobs that a leader should not delegate. In other words, they have to do them themselves. One should not confuse between delegating and abdicating. Delegating work assignments requires assessment skills.

There is a wide repertoire of leadership styles and strengths. Organizations are facing individualized problem, as a result need specific types of leaders at the top. One company may need to grapple with issues on technological shift while another may need to address issues dealing with fast growth. Yet another may need to deal with lumbering, giant organization. As Jeffrey Pfeffer (Managing with Power, 1992) noted: "Your success in an organization depends not only on your intelligence, industriousness and luck, but also on the match between your political skills and what is required in the position you occupy." It is crucial to perfectly match a leader's skills and experience with the needs of the organization. It is worthy to note that generally it is difficult for tradition-bound leaders to see the warning signs. Furthermore, a leader may reach a level of competence wherein his hat no longer fits him.

1. Qualities of Astute Leaders

⌘ **The man who does not have imagination has no wings.**
                                    - **Mohammad Ali**   ⌘

What are the unique qualities of leaders required to lead
organizations of today and tomorrow? What makes leaders
tick? What does it take to lift companies to the top? What are
the common threads in good leadership? Contrary to familiar
notion, we should value capable leaders not only for what they
know, but also more importantly for who they are. What they
are endures but what they know become obsolete. We also
need leaders who have stature, grit and related experience.
Leaders cannot be effective if they cannot sustain themselves;
who have proven themselves again and again and powered
through adversity throughout life. Authentic leaders should
not be afraid to be open and transparent. They should be able
to handle sport-light well. They should be trusted to tell the
truth. If a leader lacks authenticity and moral sensibility,
then he/she will be afraid to be transparent, and it shows.
Courageous and impassioned leaders know what it means to
hold clear convictions. Some call it a high calling. While
executives and managers have a lot in common, every
executive or manager has his or her own style of leadership.
But every leader must be clear headed and have the ability to
manage continuity and change. A leader must be able to
handle all kinds of pressure, stay cool and calm even in times
of uncertainties. There is a need for clear thinking, face tough
realities and make tough decisions. A leader must be
prepared to fight hard but be prepared to accept victory on the

terms than can be won even when they are short on perfection.

Leaders can be successful by observing or spending time with people who are successful. It is essential to "walk the talk." Leaders are highly visible and therefore set examples (Peter Drucker, 1995). Instilling confidence is one of the key responsibilities of a leader (Jeffrey Kames, 2002). Leaders require imagination, optimism, sensitivity, knowledge, rigor intensity and depth. Other qualities include the ability to think at multiple levels and articulate, making the right tactical decisions at the right time whilst keeping the strategic view. Leaders must differentiate between the time to force the issue or letting it germinate. A leader must be careful not to misinterpret what he sees in the horizon, be bold and decisive, must take risk to invest in new technologies, requires courage grounded in common sense to implement his principles and learn to expect the unexpected. In critical or highly sensitive matters, he/she must differentiate prudence from paranoia. He/she must have the ability to make good choices when the payoff is not immediately apparent. There is a need to deal with the present but plan for the future at the same time. He/she needs to be awash with the ability to reconcile competing sectional interest by managing the tensions among various camps whilst being determined and forceful. Negotiation skills and diplomacy are important but a leader must be prepared to use a strong hand if reason does not persuade. As former president Nixon said: "A leader is one who leads the people to where they ought to be, not to where they want to go." A demonstrable skill in making decisive, proactive business management decisions is at a premium today. There is a direct correlation between these traits and the long-term success of a leader.

Leaders have oversight responsibility to assure that companies are run ethically based on sound business principles and practices. Leadership decisions range from the profound to the trivial, complex to the simple. Leaders must be willing to take the heat, accept risks and make difficult decisions under fire. A leader must take responsibility of the mission and get it accomplished. Leaders need followers who are not docile. Instead, they want responsible and forward-looking associates. They must have the ability to judge loyalty and talent. They want performers who are as committed as they are to the success of the enterprise. Leadership is about fielding the best teams, putting the best people in the field and covers the ground with grace and insight. The essence of leadership is to be comfortable with persistent ambiguity, understand human nature, remain engaged, tactful and tap the best in people. A leader is generous towards other people's possibilities and lenient towards their limitation. A battle-hardened leader who is capable of galvanizing and transforming a corporation is highly needed in today's business environment. A leader of transformation needs to understand the psychology of individuals, groups, society and change. Healthy leaders require work-life balance. In the drive for success, it is easy to lose compassion for the other person. It matters to care more than the next person. In other words, a leader needs to be caring and commanding.

There are slim ranks of world-class leaders today. There is little argument that effective leaders are both preachers and doers who foster collective determination in the organization to succeed. The bigger the company, the more likely the chief executive has lost touch with the front lines. Chief executives must go to the front lines to actually see what is happening. As Peter Drucker stated: "I'd been telling them for thirty years that management is a practice, not a science... They need to get their hands dirty." They have a crystal clear objective and willing to develop new ways of winning the race. They must have a broad view based on hard facts and are flexible enough to connect the past, present and future. Emotional maturity, the ability to forecast future social and economic trends and deliver results will be advantageous. People need to be led so that they can manage themselves. You bet on the jockey and the horse. Leaders recognize the importance of creating and cultivating a pool of managerial talent and take steps to promote creativity, management development and succession planning. Secure leaders give power to others. Every leader has a season. Poorly handled management succession can cripple a company. Leaders must be rational and logical in estimating the magnitude of the task. They help people in developing their ideas and implementing new approaches to solving problems. It is built on the bedrock of trust, listening, staying in touch and respect for the dignity and creative potential of everyone in the organization. It blends vision, passion to excel and constancy of purpose. A leader's behavior is a symbolic communication to people down the line. Thus, he/she must project clear, concrete and consistent message about values and what is important for the organization. Integrity is a must, for without it, the entire enterprise is at risk. The current business environment has raised the performance bar for all corporate leaders. The wave of corporate scandals has sparked renewed dialogue about the importance of corporate leadership. In a survey of more than 750 Chief Executive Officers, Wharton School Center for Creative Leadership (CCL) found that CEOs believe good leadership is critical to a company's success. Nearly 79% of the respondents ranked leadership as one of the five most critical factors in achieving a competitive advantage.

Some of the key findings in the study were:

> People management and other "soft" skills were viewed as critical to effective leadership. This includes personal characteristics such as flexibility and adaptability.

> Nine out of the ten CEOs surveyed saw the development of leaders as an important personal responsibility.

> CEOs who said they were outperforming their industry peers financially were more likely to say that their company supported learning and development of leaders.

2. Seasoned Leaders Create and Nurture Stimulating Work Environments

⌘ **The mountains are high and the emperor is far away.**
- Chinese Saying ⌘

The role of a leader is to create and nurture an environment that stimulates people to produce extraordinary performance. He/she creates a working environment with depth, texture and richness, one in which people are clothed in dignity and deserving of respect. He/she is able to reach deep down within and bring out the best in him/her and in others. This includes the capacity to listen and to have people of high caliber around him. A stimulating environment is one where employees see others grow and are entrusted with responsibilities that would stretch their potential. Develop leaders within the organization's ranks. In the process, people discover strengths that they may not known they had. A leader is a change agent. He/she leads by example, keep up the drumbeat and share the credit of achievement. It is hypocritical to expect others to change if you are unable or unwilling to change yourself. A leader leads the band by setting the direction and tone and inspires excitement about the company's future. Power is distributed rather than concentrated. Everyone has a degree of creativity. Proper environments foster creativity and innovation that resonate throughout the organization by unleashing human potential. It will help inspire people to take a combination of individual responsibility and collective actions. The work environment must be nurtured which makes people always want to come to work, love their jobs and reaching for the best. Comity of employees takes drudgery out of the job. It provides a balance between the colliding demands of family and career.

It is the leader who sets the rules with clarity and forthrightness, creates the culture and determines the values that guide the organization. As a teacher, a leader nurtures the seedlings, builds second echelon of leadership and teaches those under him/her the nuts-and-bolts of managing a business in a complex environment. He/she primes, encourages and rewards those under his/her jurisdiction. Employee involvement provides a sense of ownership and pride thus encourages them to be effective in utilizing their knowledge and experience in accomplishing given tasks.

Team members feel that they own their jobs and have meaningful roles to play without their initiatives being stifled; limiting the oxygen and sunlight it needs to thrive. He/she must avoid demoralizing people by demanding too much too soon. He must lead transformation from dispiriting efforts into ones full of energy.

3. Watch How They Perform, Not Just What They Say

> ⌘ It is the province of knowledge to speak. It is the privilege of wisdom to listen.
> - Oliver Wendell Holmes ⌘

In today's complex society, keen judge of character is essential for success. Though this is not a new revelatory, this quality is important. It is essential to know and understand the people who work for you and to have a reasoned view of people you interact with. In many situations, on the surface and in more substantive ways, there is a significant gap between what people say and what they are capable of doing, resulting in disenchantment. Leaders must be able to distinguish dolphins from sharks. It should be the leader's business to find out and assess people fairly, objectively and honestly, without denying them their rightful place. Past conduct and current behavior can be strong indicator of personality traits. Personality traits cannot be trained. If leaders are unbalanced and hypocritical, that will be reflected in their judgment and performance. It may also be the result of jaundiced filter. Simplistic ideas can often get many people excited. More often, actions speak louder than words. We

19

need leaders who stand on moral high ground, who are clear-minded and determined to solve the woes of business. As important, we need people who can willingly share their knowledge with other people. We need leaders who are unifiers, not dividers. We need people who get results in addition to being great to work with. Leaders who lack style can make up with substance. We do not need people who are ambitious, self-promoting and do not benefit their associates. We need people who are sincere with moral passion instead of rhetoric and flair. Words are cheap and can go so far. While form and style are as important as substance, ultimately you have to get the job done. Let accomplishments speak for themselves instead of surface appearance. Separate facts from "PR" spin. It takes more than a spin-doctor to deceive people for long.

4. Equanimity

⌘ **A happy life consists in tranquility of mind.**
- Cicero ⌘

Finding a sense of peace in a growing turbulence is not an easy task. Today's competitive environment creates great anxiety in all of us. Anxieties are the result of competing forces that clash with the human desire for stability and certainty. Equanimity is a skill for self-awareness and taking the middle ground through good times and bad. Self-awareness is the ability to recognize our feelings. Unlike other creatures, one of the human endowments is to be self-aware. In business as in life itself, there are high and low points, triumphs and setbacks. There will always be critics and detractors no matter how good we do or how well we perform. There is no surefire way of doing things. There is growing rift between managers and the managed for a multitude of reasons. Sometimes, power may override common sense. It is essential to maintain a balance of thoughts and feelings when facing events of exhilaration, intense workload, and calamity or when making tough decisions. Shroud of uncertainty permeate business conditions, placing an enormous strain on the mind and thus causing anxiety. Anxiety and distress must be rebalanced, even in situations where the outlook may be as bleak as it seems. Anxieties will be significantly minimized if we do or say things that are believable and unassailable. We must be sober and realistic, even under stress. We must master the discipline to do so before the event sweeps you along.

Equanimity is often misunderstood with apathy. In essence, equanimity is not the same as indifference. In "indifference" there is "I do not care" attitude; the person does not want to understand. Equanimity smoothes the path with evenness of mind when facing situations that is as frustrating as it may be. It is sustained by continuing optimism even under the rough and tumble of business activities. It keeps you steady instead of being swayed with the trends. More often, it involves efforts to find the balance in the midst of chaos and sail serenely onward. It involves being a wonderful listener and being genuine. Even under supercharged or bleak situations, equanimity can change negative behaviors such as anger, violence, alcohol abuse and so forth. It helps keep your equilibrium and perspective intact in spite of turmoil around you. It can enhance a person's conviction, confidence and gives solace.

21

5. Grace and Magnanimity

⌘ In War: Resolution;
   In Defeat: Defiance;
   In Victory: Magnanimity;
   In Peace: Goodwill.

                              - Sir Winston Churchill ⌘

By most accounts, people's actions are governed by quid-pro-quo. Admittedly, human activities are based on mercantilist relics. Truly altruistic deeds are rare. Sad to say, one can easily succumb to greed and worship of false deity. Today's business and social contours have become fairly clear as people are more aware of what is going on in their workplace and socio-economic environments. Leadership involves stewardship, accountability and toughness as a linebacker. A selfish leader reaches the top and leaves everyone behind. Magnanimity denotes stretching the mind to do great things, not being petty, radiating goodness and benevolence. Leaders who epitomize such quality are in great demand today and in the future. Broadly speaking, magnanimity and unity are strengths of lasting importance. The experience can be liberating.

Contrary to commonly held beliefs, magnanimity toward others, the strength of conviction, cooperation and generosity of spirit bring about results. It enriches you and everyone it touches with a new broader vision. While it is easy to say but hard to carry out, the more you practice it the more you get better at it. It casts a new light into a troubled world at large, with its ups and downs, with deep seated insecurity. Grace and composure open doors and helps keep you going day after day without losing heart. It provides a template of possibility to do good and righteous cause that enriches the communities beyond measure. Personal experiences with grace and magnanimity are uplifting and will remain major landmarks in people's memories.

There is a compelling argument that if you dwell in bitterness over people who did you wrong, it will just eat you up. It stunts your capacity for growth as you get trapped in the debris. It narrows or closes your mind. In many cases, rapprochement will be slow and uncomfortable. It makes you unable to be generous. You just deal with it and move on.

⌘ **As it was once said: managers try to do things right, leaders try to do the right things.** ⌘

Chapter 2
Honesty, Trust and Integrity – A Timeless Principle

⌘ Do well by doing good and we should not fear the Truth. ⌘

Honesty, trust and integrity represent the foundation, the trinity of business leadership. Good leaders adhere to the highest ethical standard. As Harold Myra and Marshall Shelley (The Leadership Secrets of Billy Graham, 2005) noted; "Those who observe leaders soon conclude that talent and character are measured separately. Talent can take you far, but the accomplishments that talent brings also produce great temptations." I whole-heartedly agree that leaders and companies should be measured not only by their accomplishments but also by the strength of integrity that is consistent with the personality and character. Old values still matter. Man's knowledge and capacity has outstripped his moral capacity.

It is no secret that the moral and social dimensions of business are very real. In a time when Enron, Lehman Brothers and other financial scandal looms large, it is important to remember that honesty, trust and integrity are essential virtues in a field where people are easily seduced by the opportunities for personal wealth. Aside from fame and fortune, business leaders must examine the ethical standards that they hold for themselves and over their employees. As Socrates said, "The unexamined life is not worth living." Truly successful companies are fortified on solid ethical foundation. Every action a corporation takes represents what it stands for. Companies must proclaim and adhere to professional code of ethics, truthfulness, loyalty; respect for law, self-discipline and social responsibility. People may disparage such talk as naïve and out of touch with reality, but corporations must realize that longstanding business principles such as superior customer service, productive employees and technological innovation fall apart without the tenet of honesty, trust and integrity.

The fact of the matter is; people don't like to be duped. Employees today are increasingly concerned with corporate character as well as moral and ethical issues. As Scott McNealy, Chairman of Sun Microsystem said; "Business school ethics course are trying to teach something that the parents are supposed to teach (page 3E, Mercury News, January 1, 2007.) There is increasing nexus between integrity and superior leadership. Trust makes possible one's ability to influence (Charles Watson, 1991). It cannot be demanded but is a commodity that must be earned. Every leader knows the value of relationships and networking, necessary threads in the fabric of business. Trust is the lynchpin that makes such relationship possible, with positive ripple effects that eventually permeate the entire organization. It adds spice, spirit and invigorating qualities to life and should be an integral part of the corporate culture. A leader is subject to many conflicting desires and financial trappings, but courageous leaders face such conflicts head-on, exhibiting the highest quality of character, managing his or her team with the guiding vision of higher standards. He pursues his objectives along the high road, enforces humane policy, is led by the enduring guideposts of honesty and integrity and refuses to entertain temptation of quick and easy personal gain. He makes reasoned judgments concerning the relative importance of various desires and commitments with the aid of honesty, scruples, astuteness and balance. One might question how might one become such a leader, one who exhibits this kind of moral fiber? These qualities are not in good supply in many companies and thus, never before has there been more cause to ask it.

Though it is easier said than done, a leader's job is to instill a culture of fair play and honesty across the board, while advancing business standing. Leaders play a custodial role, must shoulder the responsibilities and move away from behavior that makes them disreputable. They are bound legally, by duty and by moral commitments, free of hidden agendas. Leaders can set the tone for ethical conduct with an unambiguous message from the top. Invite people to speak the truth. Talk the talk and walk the talk. Win cleanly and by the rules. There exist a disingenuous assumption that good reputation can be created through mere public relation stunts and manipulation. However, a good image and reputation in the marketplace is actually established through years of dedicated pursuit of high ethical standards with consistent reinforcing signals. It is a heritage built up slowly over time, the product of well-formed habits. A pattern of honesty accumulates through many small actions to display a strong message that eventually reaches the multitudes. Trust, like a tree, takes a long time to grow but can be cut down fast. In some organizations, the traditions fashioned by their founders have been rooted in praiseworthy principles and therefore leave an indelible imprint. Business dynamics across the board require trust for long-term survival and effective organizational performance.

Is the leader trustworthy and credible, as he or she appears to be? Is there a dearth of trust in the organization? Employee cynicism comes from superiors who are bad examples, untrustworthy managers who have also been disillusioned by past experiences of widespread greed, selfishness and violation of trust. People look up to honest and competent leaders and managers. No one likes to be manipulated. A leader lacks integrity if he or she fails to act on core commitments through a weakness of will and self-deception. Create a culture where people are treated right, where the "open door" policy is not an empty phrase, but a reality. We need to have an unflinching look at our own behaviors and make necessary corrections. If we want to hold our employees accountable, they must feel that they can trust management and not suspicious of the motives. Contribute to a meaningful work environment by doing everything with honesty and integrity. Consistency is a vital shaping force and conveys the key to credibility. Avoid teaming with unsavory characters. There are unprecedented pressures on today's managers and employees to achieve, and there are always temptations to use unfair or illegal tactics to gain unfair advantages. It is crucial to foster personal and professional integrity at all levels to admit failure and correct mistakes. In the crucible of life, mistakes will occur. Deal with failure openly and immediately even if fixing it may cost considerable amount of money to fix it. Shining the light on the truth is more sensible than trying to keep it hidden. It is better to be up front deliberately than it is to hide something. A sensitive leader is aware of human frailties and traps that befall all human beings. Moreover, someone who does not feel right about what he is doing will probably not exert his optimum efforts toward the task. Though it is difficult to precisely quantify the advantages of moral fiber, it is obvious that preservation of a company's good reputation and stewardship inspires admiration and attracts talented and noble employees. Morally bound leadership builds a positive relationship with stakeholders and helps reduce the cost of doing business over the long run. Almost everybody recognizes honesty when he or she sees it. People are able to ferret out superficial promises and overstatements, detecting them instinctively. On the flip side, people look up to leaders with integrity to elevate their own conduct to a higher standard. In turn, inspiring with such credibility depends on a good image built through real ethical conduct. Concrete examples of goodness from the lives of successful people serve to inspire and encourage. Genuine goodness should be privileged over legalistic righteousness as any aspiring leader's guiding star.

As Bill George, former Chairman and CEO of Medtronics said, "If we select leaders principally for their charisma and ability to drive up stock prices in the short term instead of their character, and we shower them with inordinate rewards, why should we be surprised when they turn out to lack integrity." In business as in life itself, the tension between money and integrity is ever present now as in time in memorial. There is a faulty belief that success in business requires greed, deception and unfeeling ruthlessness. Corporate leaders should do more to deflate the myth that excellence and competitiveness are incompatible with honesty and integrity. Unethical activities do occur in business and seem to result in material gain, at least in the short term. As appealing as it may be, stay away from pernicious influence of questionable and unprincipled behavior. Many leaders and firms never learn the lessons until it is too late. Dishonesty and deception are simply wrong and will be discovered early or long after the smoke has cleared. There are too many contact points inside

28

and outside a company to weather scrutiny. Today, the speed of Internet communication makes it harder to hide deceptive practices and bad news. Deception and soiled reputation will ultimately take a toll on the health and wealth of the organization. Honesty is a vaccine that assures a good night's rest. Once a reputation is sullied, it is hard to redeem, no matter how hard you try to shake it. All of these appear to be obvious and yet many have succumbed to the pressure of quick profit and its debilitating effects. Too much is at stake for companies to risk not playing by the rules of fair play and ethical conduct. Businesses must deal fairly with customers, employees and suppliers. Companies must be sensitive and not to have even the appearance of impropriety in their business activities. Though profit is the lifeblood of business, it is not the point of life.

There is a need to have a system of increasing openness, authenticity, check, balance and accountability of corporate behavior from top to bottom in the financial and other arenas. These are principled aspirations. While recent United States (US) and foreign media have highlighted various corporate financial shenanigans and avarice, US companies for the most part are ethical, moral and open, though the ranks are being thinned. While many people bemoan the decline in corporate integrity, there are several bright spots. In fairness, it is gratifying to note that many companies, run by leaders of distinction have established policy of zero tolerance for unethical conduct, though in some aspects of doing business there are fine lines in defining what is unethical. The facts still remain however that we cannot rest on our laurels but need to maintain integrity in the uppermost rung of our corporate agenda. The lessons are sobering and yet immensely exciting. Ethical virtues are worth preserving. If past is prologue, there will be immense challenge for corporation to improve public perception of business leaders not only in the US but also globally. We must constantly be on guard against ethical lapses, managerial blunders and complicity in perpetuating financial scandals. Failure to do so will weaken the technological and financial pillars that propped up the business. Corporations should not do business with people they cannot trust and corporations must be driven by the desire to do decent and moral things. He must be on guard whenever there is moral misgiving about certain practice. Companies who deal with untrustworthy people are set for the fall. Deeply held principle of honesty and integrity must be preserved and reinforced. Practicing solid values however does not guarantee results unless there is commitment to high performance.

⌘ A good life, as I conceive it, is a happy life. I do not mean that if you are good, you will be happy – I mean that if you are happy you will be good.
                                            - Bertrand Russell ⌘

Chapter 3
Walk the Talk

⌘ The devil can cite Scripture for his purpose.
- William Shakespeare ⌘

We live in a world of seemingly shifting values but corporate leaders cannot simply toss aside the underpinnings that create a company's solid reputation. Companies must be run with an undeviating noble purpose, dedicated to certain business and ethical principle, not solely concerned with growth and profitability. This is a new corporate currency for breakthrough companies. It is not my invention nor is it new. Leaders must not only be philosophical and theoretical but must rather be practical. They can vary in detail but never waver in principle. They must be a student, perpetually studying, not be shortsighted and ahistorical. They must not be stampeded into making decisions that cause them to regret later on. It is not uncommon for leaders to choose caution and calculation in place of principles.

It is abundantly clear that a business must be run on its record, not on unstable rhetoric and a penchant for publicity. Actions speak louder than words. Think long and hard about your promises and obligations. Make good on agreements. Personal and company reputation are at stake. It can be easily undermined by inconsistency and hypocrisy. True values are ingrained, not programmed nor ephemeral. Development of this view does not automatically entail inflexibility in dealing with complex and tough situations. Abuse of trust and manipulating employees not only indicate a lack of ethical and moral substance, they are also short sighted and ineffective. This is not a healthy way to live. People can see through decisions that are self serving and manipulative. Subordinates have an amazing ability to "figure out" the boss. Ultimately, such actions will result in lost appeal for both the company's workforce and customers. If business commits ethically questionable actions, it diminishes its moral standing and disaster is not far away. Do not attempt to build your company's reputation by throwing empty words at the public – demonstrate a commitment to integrity through your actions. Equally important, do not be seduced by fast-talking sophisticates. If the messenger is credible, people will believe that the message has value. A businessman with an ethical compass and unassailable character will be respected. We must stand more forcefully and stir policy makers against corporate greed. Remember to stay away from marginal practices, albeit legal ones. It is not uncommon for people to have the mistaken belief that marginal practices can be rationalized. Action is demanded in place of philosophical platitudes or cute rhetoric. We have come a long way but we have a distance yet to travel in this regard. The journey will be excruciatingly long and arduous.

Chapter 4
Simplification & Clarity

⌘ Do not use a hatchet to remove a fly from your friend's forehead.

- Ancient Proverb ⌘

When a gardener cultivates a bed of roses, he cuts the stems back, and they grow renewed, luscious and more beautiful than before. Similarly, the notion of simplicity is vital to all businesses. This is hardly a new idea. *Al Shugart, the highly successful pioneer of the disk drive industry who brought the price of disk drive and technology down to earth has a plaque in his office that reads: "Keep it simple."* It is essential to transform the complex to the comprehensible and to clarify the abstracts. To be rich and lean, companies need to be aware and rethink legacy mind-set to find new ways to simplify overall processes and procedures including the following:

➤ Set goals and objectives that are clear and understandable
➤ Avoid lengthy chains of command
➤ Minimize redundant bureaucracy
➤ Lower excessive administrative burdens
➤ Reduce pointless ceremonies
➤ Eliminate turf battles
➤ Reduce waste
➤ Remove unnecessary restrictions
➤ Increase user friendly products and services

Set Goals and Objectives That Are Clear and Understandable

⌘ Everything should be made as simple as possible, but no simpler.

- Albert Einstein ⌘

Simple and clear goals can be powerful. Be sure that the objectives of any project are clear, continually reinforced and linked to the purpose of the organization. Make sure that clarity is rooted in values and expressed in explicit programs. It is easy to equate simplicity with superficiality and stupidity. Goals and objectives should be polished and re-polished until they are easy to comprehend. Avoid cluttering goals and objectives that feature fancy languages and biases. The logic here is simple. It is as easy as breathing. Cut through the jargon and fads and get to the heart of things. There are times when plain talk is necessary. Avoid confusion with mere following of process rather than reaching the right outcome. The goals and objectives must be verified by measured facts instead of assumptions. Confusing goals, objectives and buzzword-filled management process blur a business' ultimate vision.

In setting of goals, remember not to over-focus on individual functional goals but bear in mind the over-arching importance of delivering value to customers. Avoid goals that are short on definition but long on motherhood and apple pie. Avoid fragmentation of functional goals as they will result in fragmented objectives.

Avoid lengthy chains of command

⌘ Anyone can carve a goose if there is no bone.
- T.S Eliot ⌘

Companies need a wake-up call to realize that they can ill afford to do things with business as usual. Nowadays, many businesses are less stable and less predictable. Rather than being wedded to habit and protocol, organizations must rapidly respond to a fast changing and competitive marketplace by being in tune with the times. Make the chains of command systematic, purposeful and directly accessible with periodic checkups. It is especially hard to run large organizations flawlessly. Lengthy chain of command causes immense and unwarranted physical, political and psychological stress in an organization. It increases the depth of a company's disadvantage. People in established hierarchies usually do not appreciate people who try to leapfrog the chain of command. This has an unintended effect of making some employees feel that they are marginalized. Able and creative people are hamstrung to effect positive contribution. Therefore, it is essential to minimize vertical hierarchy by restructuring and flattening the organization to make it less insulated but practical and revealing. Further manifestation to counter the tide of competition is the lean organization. In addition to be a great to work with, lean organization makes it harder for people to hide. It will help magnificently to ameliorate problems besieging your organization. Replace the amount of time for making decisions with good planning and realistic thinking. The objective is not to cut corners but to become efficient.

Rather than being mired if over-complicated deliberations, managers must first have a clear understanding of what they want to achieve. If it works, do it.

Minimize Redundant Bureaucracy

⌘ **Our greatest growth industry is the Civil Service.**
                                        - Lord Lucas ⌘

As the legendary Alfred Sloan stated: Good management rests on a reconciliation of centralization with decentralization or decentralization with coordinated control. Large organizations are able to get large projects done. Tiny companies and lumbering conglomerates have something in common – bureaucracy. Bureaucracy connects people through hierarchy, division of labor, rules and procedures. German sociologist Max Weber originally championed the bureaucratic culture. When it functions well, a bureaucracy can accomplish a lot economically though thick bureaucratic structure provides form that decreases flexibility. However, one needs to be politically astute to lead bureaucratic organizations.

On the other hand, people in stolid bureaucracies complain about gridlock, rampant politics and maneuverings to advance one's interest. These are symptoms of giantism. Many large layers produce low measurable returns. It also impairs business flexibility. People become mere functionaries instead of stewards. Bureaucrats have much to lose but little to gain by taking risks. Huge and unwieldy bureaucracies are not easily changed. For some companies, the benefits of economies of scale are robbed by bureaucratic turf battles. Redundant bureaucracy results from unbridled organizational expansion during period of growth when resource is abundant, when there is not sufficient competitive pressure. Companies may start small and focused but over time can balloon into independent departments that lack accountability. As companies grow, more employees are added to the payroll, the organizations grow and business processes become more complicated. The organization may be aligned at one point but the policies and procedures may derail people and steer them in the wrong direction. Broadly speaking, a bureaucracy is the enemy of productivity and can cripple a company.

Bureaucracies emphasize process over accomplishments. Multi-layers of bureaucracy are cumbersome and inhibiting. The problem with a bureaucratic system is that one must penetrate a number of layers before translating plan into final action. When the arteries of bureaucracy are hardened, they produce red tape. Red tape stymies information flow, impedes the process, clouds minds and slows decision-making. Bottlenecks can be created if people have to wait for approval or guidance from overworked senior executives. Oftentimes, it adds political content to the process and seriously eroding corporate competitive performance. Instead of putting the business first, bureaucratic employees mold jobs and the system to suite themselves, form the internal structures of business and then cling on when anyone tries to change the architecture (Nigel Nicholson, 2000). Some even purposely avoid action that may benefit the company because such actions might step on the toes of another in the bureaucratic web. There is inherent tendency for people not to storm the citadel of bureaucracy. To eradicate such nonsensical problem, insulating layers of management must be cut. Layers add costs and slow things down. The yoke to the beast that drags business down a company must be restructured, repositioned and forged into a simpler framework. Companies need to take a close look at how to keep bureaucracy to a bare minimum. In the words of Jack Welch, "bureaucracy cannot form, just as ice cannot form in a swift moving stream." Bureaucracy that serves no good purpose must be eliminated.

Lower Excessive Administrative Burdens and Process Steps

⌘ I have little interest in streamlining government or making it more efficient, for I mean to reduce its size....my aim is not to pass laws but to repeal them.
- Barry Goldwater ⌘

In a hyper-competitive business environment, companies can ill afford excessive administrative burdens and bloated operation. Every relay doubles the noise and cuts the message in half. It is not uncommon for people in large organizations to spend inordinate amount of time doing work that do not add value. It is essential to review regularly administrative and process steps in a new light. Managers must be imaginative and unencumbered to eliminate unnecessary burdens. Identify key processes and make them lean and efficient with quick surgery. Minimize thick binders of documents and charts, wherever and whenever practical. High administrative cost is a thing of the past. Go through administrative processes with a fine-toothed comb. This applies to sprawling as well as smaller organizations with long and convoluted administrative and process steps.

Companies must trim down; get in shape and do more with less. Process steps can be reduced, as many steps exist for no good reason. More often, they exist by tradition or by formal procedures, which may be outdated. They may also be the result of the amalgamation of disparate organizations, particularly in large companies. At every level in many companies, there are so-called teams that are historical hangover that are no longer necessary. Eliminate them. These committees and groups may have been set up for political or faddish reasons. They are a drain on the company's finances. It is not uncommon for medium and large companies to be populated with brokers and paper shufflers. Eliminate them as well.

Reduce Pointless Ceremonies

Habits are hard to break. The best way to do things is to get things done now, not with a committee that can get things done after a meeting that takes two hours to organize and two hours to conduct. While most meetings are unavoidable, some can be extremely vexing. Pointless ceremony cripples a company. Therefore, keep meetings as small and as quick as possible unless there are clear and distinguishing benefits. Meetings and presentations must be kept simple and to the point. Regular programs meetings or irregular ad-hoc/mission meetings should be spent as efficiently as possible as a means of face to face encounter to accomplish managerial tasks. Reduce the number of sign-offs, reviews and task forces that add work but do not add value. Eliminate old rituals and fanfare that make meetings a waste of time. These can be ponderous and inefficient causing products to market to be years late.

Eliminate Turf Battles

Even when customers will benefit and money is saved, turf battles prevent change from happening and leave lasting scar on the organization's psyche. Stable relationship is in everyone's interest. Factions are dangerous and debilitating to the muscle and sinew of an organization. A serious issue like this should not be treated dismissively. They contribute to the most insidious effect on organizations including causing polarization and logjam. Results are underscored by the facts that turf battles in whatever guises and forms can be ferocious and the fallout can be inestimably devastating. Organizational cohesion will be fractured resulting in anguish and alienation. These corrosive forces contribute to indiscipline and chaos, fouling the business. For business to thrive there should be a degree of unity and cohesion instead of provincial bastions that are at odds with each other. Internecine squabbles must be stopped before they become too strong to turn back.

Reduce Waste and Misguided Regulations

It is a common recognition that waste and misguided regulation proliferate in society and in organizations. This is the antithesis of progress and particularly burdensome during period of economic crunch. These are common habits that beset most businesses and are hard-to-break. Unnecessary paperwork is a waste and evidently on the rise. Be wary of thick reports and regulations that require reams of data. Work processes must be refined and continually updated, lest they are asphyxiated by the complexity. Some people may not understand the business but use process and procedure as a crutch. Eliminate wasteful and repetitive steps in the work process by comparing the relative worth of activities. Examine microscopically and deftly dissect activities that do not add value, in ways large and small. Move quickly and decisively by cutting through the labyrinth of regulations.

Remove Unnecessary Restrictions

With the emerging trend towards financial control and accountability, there is an inclination for erecting restrictions under-written by processes, procedures and watchdog agencies. There are benefits and drawbacks with processes and procedures. It is possible to have too much or too little of it as well as gradation between the two. The line between necessary and unnecessary restrictions may be smudged. Employee may perceive "structures" as boundaries that inhibit innovation. Look for crazy quilt of contradictory and complex provisions. Simplify or eliminate them. Some regulations are strict for no practical reason. Or, some organizations may be overly strident in implementing them. There is certain amount of reluctance to change existing regulations. To a certain extent, restrictions provide protective strata and exist ostensibly to enhance bureaucratic power and political gain. Processes and procedures must be continually revised based on a pragmatic view and in the light of new experiences. Some processes and procedures may have outlived their usefulness and therefore must be scaled back. Elaborate forms and piles of paperwork must be cut back. It is important to remember that although removing restrictions can make a company leaner and eliminate bureaucracy, the flip side is obviously the risks that lifting certain restrictions entail.

Proliferate User-Friendly Products and Services

Companies need to make it easier for novice as well as experienced customers and users to purchase and use their products and services. This is hardly news. With distractions from other priorities, it is easy for companies to be oblivious to user requirements. In working towards this goal, companies must establish listening posts to understand what users want and need. User inputs must be treated deferentially. Companies must inculcate insatiable thirst for improving products and services with respect to end-user perspectives and ones that are distinguishable from competitors. These must be rigorously tested and energetically promoted until they take root and spread. Once established, they can be a showcase for other groups in the company to emulate. It is not without its costs. There should be increased capacity for users to access information promptly and cheaply. Companies bear some responsibilities for the way they are being perceived by customers.

Clarity and Focus

Abstractions abound in the high technology and financial industries. Sometimes it may not happen by intent but occur due to a variety of reasons. Discussions and debates sometimes tend to obfuscate. Avoid distortion and double-speak. In an era of sound bites and short attention culture, we need to be plainspoken and candid about the objectives and expectations. We fear that people we do not understand may be concealing something. Clarity inspires trust. Focus your energy and fuel your success. Forcefully articulate with reasoned views. Avoid goals and pronouncements that are of questionable quality and also those that point vaguely in generalized fashion. Use concrete, straightforward and unambiguous terms for communication that allow your people to visualize what you say or write. Aim at the target and be able to set mid-course correction. Get the people to talk to each other. Cut through the jargon and fads and get straight to the heart of things. Avoid being overly theoretical and philosophical but rather be more practical with serious thoughtful deliberative ideas. Replace abstract and disconnected processes with ones with high degree of precision. Lighten up murky areas and substitute it with the presence of clear strengths. Bright and hard working people may not be effective if they are not focused on systematic and sustained effort to get things done. Clarity and focus will contribute mightily to whatever goals and objectives that you set up to accomplish.

Chapter 5
Five Key Reasons for Corporate Failure

⌘ Integrity without knowledge is weak and useless, and
knowledge without integrity is dangerous and dreadful.
                                      - Dr. Samuel Johnson   ⌘

Companies must be built to withstand recession and financial
earthquakes if they are to remain standing for long. Genetic
weakness appears when organizations face difficulties that
they have not seen before. There are five key reasons for
corporate failure. These are unforgiving mistakes and are
fatal, especially with businesses that are proceeding at Mach
speed.

#1 – Choosing the Wrong Leader

This is a common malady that afflicts failed companies. It is
imperative that to lead your company well you must make the
right choices, and in particular, choosing the right people
whose personality, experience, reputation and capabilities are
in congruent with the needs of the organization and the types
and size of the business in which the organization operates.
Having the right leader is the lifeblood of any business
enterprise. The logic behind this is compelling: the higher the
position, the more devastating the consequences if the wrong
person is hired. It is therefore imperative that you use right
judgment to choose leaders that fit the needs. At times you
may need to choose a field general compared with one who
thinks strategically. A clear illustration of this statement was

Ross Perot's ill-fated selection of former Admiral James Stockdale as his presidential running mate. While Admiral Stockdale was eminently qualified in other arenas, he was ill suited for high profile politics where serious missteps can damage careers. Who am I? Why am I here? While these may be logical in themselves, they appear to be too simplistic, not something people expects of a presidential running mate.

As stated above, the right leader must have the right fit for the company and for the particular position. It should not be the result of chance or lack of thorough consideration. For large companies, it will be unwise, to choose leaders who are inexperienced and unseasoned to take on the responsibilities associated with a company of considerable size, complexity and stature.

It is important to recognize that leaders change and so do their capabilities and reputations. Corporate life can be quite difficult. He/she must have the fortitude to handle very tough and complex situations. Examples of failed business leaders who proved to be a wrong fit for their companies abound. In retrospect, Mark Hurd was a right fit for Hewlett Packard who dealt with business turbulence and a feisty Board with polish and deft. Another poignant example was the apt selection of Lou Gerstner who saved IBM during its perilous period and laid a strong foundation for its recovery. Other leaders rose to positions by being in the right place at the right time but ultimately failing the tests. Yet other reach a position higher than their abilities warranted. There are many stories of inept executives too well known to be worth repeating here.

Though the task may appear difficult, there are a number of things you can study before you determine which leader is right for your business. Firstly, take a look at his/ her track record. What has he/she accomplished? Has he/she earned the stripes with years of great results? Secondly, it is imperative for a leader to have experience in the same or a relevant field. What industries has the potential leader worked in? What can that experience bring to your business? Also, keep in mind that the right leader should have a leadership style and personality that befits your company. Ensure that he/she will blend seamlessly with the company's business culture. Finally, take into consideration your company's particular place in the business cycle. If your business is in its infancy, its leader should be one with vision, who will take risks and embolden employees. During a time of growth, a leader must not fall into complacency and continue to make wise decisions that enable further growth. Similarly, a business in maturation must have an appropriate leader at the helm. In short, finding the right fit is key.

But how can you differentiate between a great leader and an imposter? How will you find leaders who will live up to its billing? Astute observation of lifestyles can present early hints of leadership style. Leaders with stable personalities and a well-developed value system can handle crisis and tough situations. On the other hand, power in the wrong hands will lead to boardroom turmoil and executive power struggles, in turn contributing to failed companies. It is critical to find out whether the leader is the right fit and take immediate corrective actions early on rather than suffering with dispiriting realization later on. These issues confound the short and long term prospect of many corporations: ensure the right person leads.

⌘ **Pragmatism without principle is cynicism, but principle without pragmatism is often powerless.**
                                        - James A. Baker III ⌘

Fatal flaws are constitutional defects that, if ignored, will result in your company's ultimate downfall. They cannot be simply airbrushed. They include a lack of integrity, unscrupulous business practices, disgraceful conduct, staggering debt, unsound organizational structures, poor judgment, carelessness and problematic succession from one leader to the next. In spite of the fact that these fatal flaws are obvious, it never ceases to amaze me that companies succumb to this conundrum, time and time again.

If business integrity is questionable, the business will not endure. It is a simple equation – legal issues will be found out and will result in grave and perhaps deadly repercussions. If your company is labeled as unethical, others will not join you in business ventures. Partnerships fall apart without trust.

The structure of a company must be sound. If there are gaping holes, not only will weaknesses be made utterly visible, but also, the business will function like a punctured pipe, with water pouring out of its every weakness. The leaders must have laser-sharp priorities. Provide mechanism that will help uncover gaping holes whenever they appear. Remember to avoid selecting men of unbending resolve in a business that demands flexibility. Also to avoid are people who are tactless but masquerading as men of honesty.

Finally, historical records have shown unmistakably that unworkable successions represent a fatal flaw to any company. If entrenched leaders obstruct a business – i.e. founders who are unwilling to give up leadership, that business has effectively ended. This is a serious pitfall companies must avoid. Without smooth transition from one successor to the next, a company will be clogged with office politics and petty kingdoms instead of focusing on what matters. Invariably, sound succession is the ultimate test of any leadership and institution.

#3 – Fatal Mistakes

⌘ We must cross the river by feeling the stones with our feet.
- Deng Xiaoping ⌘

It is acutely important to learn from mistakes others made in situations that do not work. Clearly, mistakes will be made, but fatal mistakes are mistakes that you can only make once.

Fatal mistakes differ from fatal flaws in that they are not constitutional – they do not represent a part of a company's self, but the wrong choices by its leaders. We know too well from history and experience that most corporate failures are attributable to wrong hiring, fatal misjudgment, political wrangling and misguided efforts with business running on the wrong track. For example, Concorde was a technical success but a misguided business effort and an expensive economic failure. Perhaps we know of people we have considered leaders

48

and friends who have made terribly wrong strategic decisions. It is one of the common excuses in books to scapegoat competitors and economic cycles for a largely internal problem. The real problem is that these decisions were made within a plausible but dubious framework until they loomed large and become painfully clear later on. Corporate failures may be due in small part by accident but mainly by design.

One fatal mistake is to make the wrong merger or acquisition decision. Mergers and acquisitions require a lot of thought and evaluation. A profitable one requires a good fit between the companies, a relevancy between them that will result in a larger market share. Moreover, the businesses must not react hostilely or defensively to the impending merger or acquisition – they must blend seamlessly together. The wrong merger or acquisition could lead to your company's downfall, so think long and hard before taking such a step.

Power can go to the head and cloud judgment. A great portion of fatal mistakes can also be attributed to leaders taking high risks without seriously considering their consequences, rolling the dice as they say. For example, if a company attempts something beyond its capabilities, it will flounder. Another fatal mistake is when a company cannot extricate itself from protracted publicized legal battles.

On-the-job training for a CEO or president can be a dangerous thing. Corporate failures are often the tragic consequences of a lack of planning and preparation and failure to recognize pitfalls and bear traps. Some of the actions are colossally shortsighted. Key decisions are made by leaders who do not possess a broad range of experience and who lack clear perspectives. Moreover, remedial measures are employed only as an afterthought, after the damage has been done, after the fatal mistakes have already been made. Plan carefully, and make important decisions with thought, cutting through complexity. Pay heed to wake-up calls. Avoid fatal mistakes.

#4 – The Eyes Got Off the Ball

For any business to work in the long run, you have to go and stay with it wholeheartedly. It requires long-term commitment. There are many examples of companies that have failed because their eyes got off the ball. One noted example is Silicon Graphic Inc. (SGI). Once a highly successful company, SGI eventually became sidetracked. In 1998 it collaborated with the US government to build "Blue Mountain" considered as the fastest computer in the world at that time. Instead of focusing on this project the company should have paid attention to the myriad of challenges arising from the competition. This has resulted in SGI accumulating loses after loses to the point of near bankruptcy. Companies can be sidetracked to take on grandiose projects that make no economic sense. White elephant sucks up cash.

Companies should not try to eat more than they can chew. Nor should they worship the wrong idols. Instead, they should learn to submerge their egos, remain focused on their core competencies and have a clear view of their business environment, even under pressure cooker. Handling too many projects, especially glamorous ones, can prove tempting, but business must recognize the financial implications of jumping headlong into such ventures. Exploring risky technologies and spreading themselves too thin will result in an inability to respond to shifts in the business environment. It may not accurately reflect the underlying business realities. Once companies are too entrenched in numerous ventures, they will not be as sensitively attuned to their specialties, and will quickly slip against their competitors. On the other hand, companies must be careful not to be focused on narrow concerns but consider wisely areas that have broader business potential. They should keep their eyes trained on the present problems and also on future potential ones so that medicines can be administered early on before the illness becomes chronic and incurable.

#5 – High Turnovers of Top and Key Personnel (especially for small and medium companies)

Some companies have fallen due to high turnover of top and key personnel. There is mobility of talents, knowledge and capital in high technology industries spanning information technology, database development, electronics, biotechnology, pharmaceuticals, etc. Business know-how is generally not taught in schools and cultivating it is difficult. There may be a misleading belief in some circles that high turnover is inconsequential. The consequences of high turnover can be far grave than the company may assume. A company will lose its vitality and strength when important employees defect. It will also affect the morale and allegiance of many of those who remain. There will also be significant negative effect in tangible and intangible financial terms including loss of time, experience and relationship capital. Worst yet is to lose top and key personnel to competitors and increasing danger of customer dissatisfaction and defection. In the immediate aftermath, it will sap the boldness which is once characterized by growing companies. It contributes to loss of synergy,

Keeps the company out of balance and is a foreboding of worse to come. Employees leave when there is ineffectual and indifferent management, a gap in trust, not coming through with commitments, lack of clear objectives and expectations, unfair standards, lack of respect, overworked, flawed ideas, rigid strategies, under or over-supervision, lack of feedback, lack of consistency, mushrooming problems, bleak growth prospects and so on. Under such circumstances, it is hardly surprising that sunny optimism and practices that served the company so well in the past may no longer be tenable.

In a wider sense, managers are accountable for the outcome. It is a manager's failure if he/she is incapable to navigate the rough waters of high employee turnover. In some situations though, it may be hard to prevent certain employees who leave because of their unrealistic and unfulfilled expectations. Or, they may simply be exploring other vistas.

Chapter 6
Continuous Improvements and Radical Change

⌘ The assumptions on which most businesses are being run no longer fit reality.

- Peter F. Drucker ⌘

Continuous improvement has been in public discourse and a business philosophy for a long time. The influence of changes is widely felt in various arenas: economic, societal, technological, political, demographic, philosophical and world view. The linchpin to business growth is productivity and continuous innovation. Corporations must recognize the unchanging fundamental rules that make business tick. Organizations need both evolution and revolution. While permanence and predictability provides an anchor, continuous improvement and path-breaking changes should be an extension of a company's long-term strategy and practices. Each model carries with it certain strengths and drawbacks. However, the two systems essentially are complementary and thus each should be applied depending on the circumstances.

Companies must be free of the shackles that inhibit continuous improvement and rejuvenation. These limits may be self generated or imposed by others. It may require changing the natural order of things. Organizations must continuously renew focus on products, profits, tasks, people and relationships. Situations change, people change and companies must change as well. Companies may be content by using tried and true formulas, thinking not only on results but also job satisfaction. As it takes time to apply new ideas, it may be financially prudent to use proven technology rather than taking slow step-by-step effort to advance cutting edge technologies. In doing so, they must not be out of touch with modern techniques and changing markets. Continuous improvement is cumulative, akin to evolutionary change and is more commonly adopted by many organizations, though it is not necessarily the natural order of things. Take small, slow but steadfast steps. Protect what you've built. Smaller accomplishments lead to bigger accomplishments. Evolutionary change involves new brand of thinking, of discovering the company's growth potential and changes in basic attitudes of individuals and organizations. It is like continuously polishing a jewel that has not been polished complete. It requires new approach and mentalities in dealing everyday business activities. It builds on small and large improvements including completing routine jobs creatively and productively. Look around; look carefully. Learn not only from your mistakes but also the mistakes of those before you. If things work well, replicate it. One must make it happen...in small or giant steps. A company must build new capabilities on an on-going basis and stimulate creativity in improving existing products, processes, procedures and practices. Failure is a large price to pay. Continuous change should be pervasive, and involve every employee from the bottom to the top. If the entire company is committed to gradual change, eventually, drastic improvement will be reached, and the business will soar to new heights. The nemesis is that continuous improvements usually come slowly, piece-meal and often go unnoticed.

In the case of rapid paradigm shifts in business, economic environments and technology, radical change is necessary. Radical change may also be necessary if the company desires

54

to grow by leaps and bounds. In such situations, companies must be ready to challenge some of the fundamental beliefs by "breaking the mold," by an iconoclast. It may be necessary to "rock the boat," so to speak. Merely fine-tuning and small incremental improvements may prove inadequate. In such circumstances it is essential to blaze new trails with radical departure from established thinking. This may include taking initiatives that are outside-the-mainstream. Companies must keep pace with the shift in the locus of innovation because failure to do so will result in devastating consequences. Apple Computer, under the guidance of Steve Jobs, is one example of a company with a phoenix-like ability to reinvent itself. However, care must be taken to assure that radical change does not cause turmoil instead of achieving new levels of improvement. Radical does not mean thoughtless or spur of the moment - reckless experimentation should be avoided and careful planning is still key in successfully implementing radical change. Remember, also, that only leaders should be involved in radical change — such drastic change requires initiative on their part, and will begin only with their resounding calls for improvement.

It is also important to note that for either evolutionary or radical change to be properly executed in a company corporate culture must permit such change. If the business culture is too stiff or rigid, even gradual, evolutionary change will be met with stubbornness and an unwillingness to entertain new ideas. Moreover, during times of major paradigm shifts, radical change would be nearly impossible to implement. Clearly, then, it is essential for a company to build a culture that is flexible, providing yeast for transformation, one that can adapt to change, as the business environment is often too fast-paced to allow for an inflexible and unmoving structure.

Corporate culture should encourage people to offer on every issue the wisdom and intelligence collectively and individually.

Chapter 7
How good do you want to be?

⌘ Do not hire a man who works just for money, but hire
him who works for the love of it.

- Henry Thoreau ⌘

There is a lot of truth in the statement that people have the
power to choose how good they can be though some highly
successful individuals are hardwired by DNA or comes from a
certain pedigree. The outcome of our lives depends on the
choices we make in combination with the desire to succeed
and the willingness to sacrifice and persevere. It is not merely
by the policies one proposes but more importantly by the
principles one stands. In part, it is continually forged in the
furnace of life. People are influenced by their own beliefs and
histories. Having surmounted the foothills of business affairs
great leaders such as Andy Grove, Bill Gates, Gordon Moore,
Jack Welch, Steve Jobs and Warren Buffet, to name a few are
drawn magnetically to the peaks of achieving business
excellence. Competence is not just a matter of training but a
question of believing in what you are doing will make
significant contribution. It is a way of life and by no means a
bed of roses. It derives from the human core where a person's
deepest beliefs about himself and the world around him
reside. There are no shortcuts to be a powerhouse, whether in
business or in other fields. You have to demonstrate your
bona-fides, combining inspiration with perspiration. It is a
timeless and universal truth that you have to be lucky and
ready. Luck matters, as the outcome of our endeavors may not
be determined by our actions alone. To a certain extent, you

have to be in the right place at the right time. You need to recognize the rhythm and pulsation with regard to your business in relationship with the business and economic environment. It may require a rigorously programmed life. You need to develop the capacity for personal growth and change and distinguish yourselves from the others. What you don't know, be eager to learn. An effective leader is one whose influence is felt in every organization and region and whose views are highly respected. These are rare qualities.

Know what you are good at. Have a deep understanding of your strengths, limitations and motives. You need to find the style and method that suit you. Do what comes naturally. However, you need to get and stay in the job before it can be used to do good and to pick the lavish fruits that ripen in the garden. You can and should go as far as hard work can take you and capitalize on the changes ahead. Rosy projections and good ambitions alone aren't enough to generate success. There need to be a vision and the fortitude to make the vision a reality. You need to find new meaning and project your vision with unmatched clarity and authority. Stay the course with intellectual suppleness and tactical dexterity. But do not wait at the sidelines for someone else to take action when action is demanded. Bystanders do not make history. Do a good job and do good when no one is watching. Attaining and maintaining success in business can't be an end in itself. While there is nothing wrong to enjoy the trappings of leadership position, success is its own reward. There can also be a lot of fun. To a great extent, you need to have immense drive, energy and stamina coupled with a vision that is forward looking and forward thinking. Our thoughts and feelings about the issues we face can become internal obstacles that hinder our progress.

A positive attitude that is infused with a purpose is one of the keys to enduring and endearing success, one that leaves profound legacy and imprint. It stimulates. Leaders lift people up with drive and dexterity. There should be renewing focus on self improvement and a sustained commitment to make the company better based on short and long-term view. It is easy to spot someone with a bad attitude unless it happens to be us. Be aware of your emotions and attitudes. Do not dwell on your weaknesses. Instead, concentrate on your strengths, finely honing your natural abilities, taking the time to learn new skills and act on advancing the work already done by you and others. When we make mistakes, we need to fix it. Time is of the essence. In today's competitive business environment, all employees from the executive suites to the office corridors, from the mailroom to the loading dock, must relentlessly strive to achieve excellence, organizationally and attitudinally.

Recognize the power of ideas to increase effectiveness and reaping bountiful profits. Rethink creatively and constructively instead of remaining docile employees, packed into a recognized pattern of doing things. Encourage a clearinghouse for ideas and permeate these ideas in the organization with a collective mission. Show up in meetings when your presence is important. It is fondly observed that 80% of life is showing up. Build people up. Look for ideas from off the beaten track. One must be forward thinking and embrace ideas even if these ideas are not our own. Put intellectual consistency and principle over expediency. Remember not to disparage opposing ideas even if the ideas are unsound but provide concrete criticism and practical advice instead. Rather than taking plain-vanilla approach, be prepared to take the organization to a new level of achievement with a marvel of managerial ingenuity and renaissance. It requires travel on several different and distinctive paths. It encompasses managing with incomparable tact and virtuosity. Achievers need to think and act at the same time and a refiner of ideas. Avoid creating management just full of good, with little feel for risk-taking or for what makes a company grow. At times, one must do things that run counter to common beliefs, exuding creativity and capturing details that often elude others. Be ready to take on the challenges of seemingly intractable issues. At times, thoughtfulness must not be sacrificed in the interest of expediency. One must work with high speed and precision, fully utilizing the capabilities to reach their full potential. It is crucial to create and maintain the right cast of team members who possess unquenchable competitive fire. One must work together with burst of enthusiasm rather than at cross-purposes. One must manage work with gusto and realize that their work has high impact and lasting value. In a nutshell, the pursuit of excellence is all encompassing and endless. Moreover, it is the hallmark of global champions. Global champions become magnets that attract capable people and will reach a level of accomplishment beyond the wildest dreams.

In large measure, unearthing new ideas, may, at times require defying the rules of traditional practices. Unfortunately, many companies do not have the knowledge to differentiate between good and bad ideas. This may be due to a lack of foresight and commitment. Or, it may be blind response to command mechanically and impersonally. A lot of bad ideas are not weeded out when they should. We must listen to the alarm going off when bad ideas do not pan out. One needs to be aware that one's fascination for the present may keep one from thinking about the future. One must know which end of the spectrum you should be. Remember to retain your bearing at all times, maintaining on-going dialogue with yourself and those important to you. It is possible to achieve excellence in all aspects and areas of business. What you need is the will to rise up to the challenge. In the grand scheme of things, companies can develop mechanisms by which dominance is achieved.

A major key is to open up a whole new vista in the area of understanding and strategizing the use of corporate financing to power business excellence. The proportion of revenue a company spends in each area depends on and determines the company's priorities. High percentage incurred on technology, research and development imply that the company values the importance of technology in the overall business scenario. High proportion of spending on quality indicates the value the company places on quality. There is a reason why people demand others to "put your money where your mouth is." If your company wants to gain a favorable reputation in a certain sector, spend enough and at full stride to ensure high-performance work in that sector. Sometimes, you have to spend money to make money. Obviously, these actions must require timing, calculation and risk taking.

Discernment

Top rate leaders draw considerable strength from unique quality of discernment, which is the ability to see what is not visible and understand what is not said. To be top rate, you must have a firm set of guiding principles and the ability to anticipate and spot potential problems, large and small. These include instincts and common sense, the ability to recognize multiple perspectives and understand underlying agendas. Another exclusive preserve of leaders with discernment is the ability to reveal, understand and the discretion to deal with a profoundly different side of a complex relationship. As important is the ability to think clearly to solve unclear problems. Leaders with discernment, at times make decisions that go against the grain. Discernment coupled with introspection can be a powerful combination. In the grand scheme of things, they may deal with crisis by taking routes that are less traversed by others.

⌘ I became quite successful very young. It was mainly because I was so enthusiastic and I just worked so hard at it.
- Francis Ford Coppola ⌘

Chapter 8
The Allure of China

⌘ Asia is not going to be civilized after the methods of the
West. There is too much Asia and she is too old.
- Rudyard Kipling ⌘

Today, no writings of business management will be complete
without acknowledging the ascendancy of China with its
intensity and global reach. We are at such a moment.

Though the traumatic financial crisis of 2008-2009 has stalled
China's breakneck growth, I believe that China will overcome
this international crisis of epic proportion just as it overcame
other major crisis in the past: Tangshan earthquake (1976),
massive restructuring of state-owned enterprises (SOEs), the
Asian financial crisis of 1997-1998 and the SAR epidemic
(2003). During the last 15 years, China has significantly
improved crisis and emergency management, though much
still need to be done. The road ahead isn't going to be easy.
GDP growth of 13% in 2007 will most likely be reduced
significantly in 2008 and 2009. Unprecedented upsurge in
unemployment has significantly risen for migrant workers
and new college and university graduates, creating concern
that it will lead to social unrest. Big ticket investment in
foreign financial institutions has failed miserably, the result
of overconfidence and lack of coherent plan, specific goals and
control. Overall, these problems will be cushioned by $585
billion economic stimulus package announced in November
2008 followed by a reported $125 billion health care insurance
extended to 90% of citizens over the next three years. This is

made possible through high savings rate and USD 2 trillion of foreign exchange reserves (2008). There are signs that the Chinese government is encouraging domestic consumption, particularly in the rural areas. Capital availability can be liberalized with improved lending practices and lowering of bank reserve requirements. With cost of labor and materials under check, it's time to take advantage of this opportunity to further develop infrastructure to include rural, Central and Western Regions. There is plenty of scope to develop public works, communication networks, improving social welfare and safety net, the environment, forestation, food safety, health awareness and response, affordable housing, education, space and scientific research and improved mining standard, product and service quality, customs procedures and legal system. With the potential to be the largest car market in the world, it is essential to extend and improve roads and highways across the nation, including rural and outlying areas. (Growth in car market in China has moderated in 2009 after years of double-digit growth). To move upstream in the technology ladder, China should increase to 3.5% of GDP from the current 1.4%, though it was higher that 0.8% from a decade ago. (In comparison, R&D as a percentage of GDP was 4.7%, 3.4%, 3.2% and 2.7% respectively for Israel, Japan, South Korea and the US.) Agricultural outputs can be enhanced via improved land management, reducing the cost of fertilizers, providing farmers with sufficient asset base through flexible, dynamic and innovative subsidies. Improved handling of citizen protests by security personnel will assure that public disturbances do not careen out of control. China must take steps to work with the West to stem protectionist pressures and to work hand in hand to weather this economic storm. These actions, aided by massive economic stimulus, will contribute to helping the world pull out of this economic doldrum.

With more than a decade of stunning economic advances, China has already become one of the global centers of commerce and an economic juggernaut. In spite of economic difficulties in 2008-2009, the nation is gaining influence and a tour de force in international business with its booming economy, massive markets; untapped pool of talents and development of new enterprises. In a few decades it has moved from the periphery to the epicenter of international commerce. This seems inconceivable many years ago. China now manufactures more steel than US, Europe and Japan combined (2006). Fueled by economic vibrancy, its impact on international business is unprecedented. It is no wonder that until the economic downturn in 2008-2009, many international companies of all persuasions are making the beeline to this new business frontier with the expectation of garnering high economic returns. China's achievements seemed inconceivable many years ago. While skepticism exists and that history reminds us that nothing endures forever, there is a forest of evidence that the country will continue to glow and have a profound impact on the world economy in the next fifty years. Businesses that fail to understand and interact with China are missing key opportunities for China's vast business power. Foreign traders and investors can profit handsomely provided they stay ahead of the curve in taking advantage of the opportunities from these transformations.

The emergence of China and other major countries implies a greater part of the world population is more engaged than before. There are many arenas where the growth of China and the economic interest of many countries intersect. It is now widely accepted that China has driven manufacturing cost down significantly due largely to its built-in advantage of an inexhaustible supply of capable, docile and disciplined labor pool. Because goods are made cheaply in China, a lower product cost has helped to reduce global inflation and has made such products within the reach of numerous societies. Reliance on low cost Chinese inputs helps companies remain competitive.

Up till the economic downturn in 2008-2009; with one fifth of the world's population China consumes half of the world's cement, one third of its steel and one quarter of its aluminum. According to UBS AG, China accounts for consumption of 59% of the world's iron ore production, 40% of aluminum product and 29% of copper by 2012. In turn, this has increased the appetite and fueled the search for more raw materials, energy and air, sea and land transportation. As the largest manufacturer of steel, China imports large quantities of iron ore from Brazil, Australia and India. This is especially good for producers of these raw materials, including Africa. China is the fifth largest oil producer. The country is now importing more than half of its oil in less than 15 years from the time it was self sufficient. Since it failed attempt to purchase Unocal Corporation in 2005, Chinese companies have been active in pursuit of securing natural resources abroad. The $14.3 billion joint investment by Chinalco with Alcoa of a 9% stake in Rio Tinto in February, 2008 is one such example. This is on top of the $4.1 billion purchase of PetroKazakhstan by China National Petroleum Corporation (CNPC) in October, 2007 and the $3.5 billion purchase of Udmurtneft OAO by Sinopec in June, 2006. Shipbuilding tonnage increased to 19 million tons in 2007, holding a third place position behind Republic of Korea and Japan. This accounted for 23% world market share. In terms of gold, China was the largest producer, ahead of South Africa, Australia, United States and Russia respectively. Nonetheless, US gold holdings are the world's largest.

The refrain was a familiar one. Evidently, China is changing the face of global business in a lot of ways. It is essential to recognize this economic power shift and provide effective response to the wave of this century. The implications for the world must also be understood in terms of China's effects on global interest-rates, inflation rates, commodity prices, wages and profits and housing prices to name a few. Moreover, with high personal and national savings rates, China essentially finances the U.S. government and consumers by purchasing Treasury bonds. China's foreign exchange reserves reached a record high of US$1.85 trillion as of 2008. This increased exchange rates risk and added pressure on continuing Yuan appreciation. Increasing wealth will stimulate consumerism and lower savings rate. Decisions made in China will increasingly drive global macro and micro economic factors raising a host of issues.

The completion of Beijing Capital Airport's new wing in February, 2008 makes it the world's largest airport in terms of floor area. The extended airport is expected to accommodate 90 million passengers by 2012; supporting increasing air travel by China's swelling middle class. Added to these achievements was the successful hosting of the Summer Olympics and spacewalk (EVA) in 2008.

Opportunities exist for China to play a responsible and catalytic role to pull poorer countries upward. Because the world is so small today, the allure of China with its high-octane economic performance, is something all businesses, even those in the United States, must take into heavy consideration as well. Companies with factories in China or those that outsource to China will benefit from its ability to manufacture products at low cost. With pricing power, businesses will be able to compete with companies that continue to manufacture in the United States and other high cost locales. China's 2001 accession to WTO facilitates reduction of tariffs and provides greater access to China by foreign firms. It has provided a catalyst for global expansion of trade.

It is difficult to undertake the task of changing a political and socio-economic system. China has achieved an enviable level of stability in spite of its large population and national political preference that are different from developed countries. In this striking and unusual period, China has successfully combined communist political system with new economic system. According to Robert Shapiro (Futurecast, 2008), Its unique brand of popularly based authoritarianism provides the political capacity and social discipline, unique among large nations, to press forward, wit modernization regardless of the wrenching dislocations it causes for hundreds of millions of ordinary people and what freer countries would constitute powerful interest groups. It is a towering achievement to overcome the inefficiency of state-owned enterprises. Rather than shutting down state-owned enterprises, it grows the economy around it to reduce its proportion, thereby lessening their negative effects. It is important to note that Chinese companies recognize that they cannot continue to grow by dint of hard work alone. They are striving to increase home grown technological content of their products with formation of key industries, moving up on the technology ladder, thereby posing profound challenges to companies competing in this sector.

MA60 (Xinzhou 60 or Modern Ark), a 52-60 passengers turboprop manufactured by Xian Aircraft Industry Company Ltd (with Pratt and Whitney PW engine) has already made its debut exporting more than 11 aircraft to Bolivia, Zimbabwe, Angola, Laos and other developing countries. MA60 will be followed by MA70, a seventy passenger turboprop in 2008/9. China's ability to compete in high tech sector is demonstrated by the roll-out in Dec 21, 2007 of a homegrown 90 seat regional jet, ARJ21-700 (Advance Regional Jet for the 21st Century), with a range of 3700 km. Delivery is expected by the end of 2009. It is projected that 30 ARJ21 will be manufactured yearly by 2011. A follow up 105 seat jet ARJ21-900 is expected to boost its reach. ARJ21 and the 50-seater turboprop MA60 are manufactured by China Aviation Industry Corporation (AVIC I). In addition, China is embarking on pooling of resources of two aviation companies (AVIC 1 & AVIC II) to form a giant company to assemble large airplane which can carry up to 150 passengers. AVIC II is the company that manufactures military and commercial helicopters. It also manufactures the 50-seater ERJ 145 jet in partnership with Brazilian plane maker Embraer. AVIC 1 and AVIC II have been supplying components to Boeing and Airbus. It is expected that this consolidation will be established in March 2008. The aircraft will be assembled in Shanghai with the nose, fuselage and tail sections manufactured in other provinces. In May 2008, China Commercial Aircraft Company received initial funding of $2.7 billion to build 150 passengers commercial aircraft with commercial production in 10-20 years. The company was formed by a consortium comprising state controlled Asset Supervision and Administration Commission (30%), AVIC I

69

and AVIC II (25%), Baosteel, Chalco, Sinochem, etc. With time and as it gain traction, the company will pose a challenge to Boeing and Airbus which currently monopolize the aircraft industry. Chinese commercial satellite business is thriving. It has launched more than 78 satellites including 10 in 2007.

With the passage of time and prodded by ever-expanding globalization, these breakthrough companies with their new breed of business entrepreneurs will learn to negotiate the speed bumps and pick up steam. Conditions now exist for them to gain more experience with its turbo charged drive and intellectual fire-power in the world stage. To be global suppliers, Chinese firms must improve their management, technology levels and develop quality systems that are robust, practical and dynamic. Improvements in the skills of managers and workers; evolve over time; will add to the growth momentum and business transformation. The country will build on its existing strengths in low cost production by using the efforts of developers and engineers from around the globe. China's rise will never be wholly without controversy. However, Chinese companies cannot be aloof from the critical issues in a fast growth, high impact business environment with high experience curve. Also, in practical terms, personal relationships with a dose of cultural sensibility will make a lot of difference for businesses in China.

This is the environment in which today's businesses have to operate. It is inevitable that China will continue to rise in importance and remain a global economic locomotive ushering in sustained prosperity. It will want to receive international respect to comport with its status and aspirations as a great economic power. An ascendant China will use its growing influence to reshape the institutions and rules on the international system in consort with its spectacular economic gains and use its gravities to pull countries into its orbit. Companies must wake up to this new reality and not go against the grain. This is not a zero sum game. The emergence of China as a heavyweight must be embraced and not ignored. Bickering will not help. What is needed are patience and acuity in dealing with issues which will pop up from time to time. Companies can enjoy co-prosperity through commercial dealings with Chinese companies. Some people may challenge the wisdom of compromise with China which seems to have different values and institutions; seeing China's political system as illegitimate. China's continuing economic growth requires a stable world that makes China to be more committed to world stability. Companies must not delay in recognizing the shift and not fail to keep the eyes open to the wider world and stake their claims. Countries must recognize that relationship with China is multidimensional and that doors cannot simply be closed on Chinese products for this will be counter-productive and ineffectual. There are temptations to succumb to protectionism in the face of growing trade frictions with respect to growing trade imbalances, valuation of Chinese currency, intellectual property protection and competition for access to raw materials. The global economy is becoming more and more interdependent. It is dangerous for countries to take unilateral actions that could lead to trade wars. These actions will smother the chances of global economic prosperity. Instead, they will unsettle world markets and international landscape. Instead, countries must keep China globally engaged through greater incentives and guarded optimism.

On the other hand, with its well earned economic achievement, China must avoid the pitfall of unbridled arrogance, especially under the hot glare of media scrutiny. Its business leaders will need to develop skills to navigate treacherous economic waters. It will be tested by periodic hurdles and occasional threats, such as the 2003 SAR scare and the 2008 earthquake disaster in Sichuan. With its new-found importance, China is saddled with the responsibility of establishing and maintaining sound ethical, social, environmental, judicial, political and economic practices. These also include respect for intellectual property, increased maturity in sound business practices, transparency and predictability. What is particularly striking about these set of forces is that they come about as the nation is increasing in prosperity. In 2007, coal contributed to more than 70% of electricity generation. With its heavy reliance on coal, China has surpassed the US as the world's worst emitter of greenhouse gases. The overriding strategic concerns should be to establish a reputable national identity and image and maintain peaceful coexistence with the international community. It is a moral imperative that business advancement and nation-building must not be sacrificed at the temple of profit. To assure that success is sustained it is essential to maintain geopolitical stability, sound financial system, controlling corruption, managing aging population, preventing degradation of the environment, strengthening rapport among disparate elements of society and continuing upgrade of education, infrastructure and workforce skill. For its economic growth to be sustained over the long haul, China growth must be seen as contributing to overall global growth including those of US, Europe, Japan, Korea, Russia, India; together with the developing and under-developed countries. The burden of managing this shift, building a foundation that is deep and enduring, rests with the political and business

leaders. Being media savvy will go a long way in improving
the image.

Chapter 9
Drivers of Operational Excellence

⌘ Leaders need to do what the people they supervise can't do for them at the present moment.
                                    - Ken Blanchard   ⌘

An executive must respond not only to a firm's internal activities but also to the challenges posed by its external environment. The external environment includes shifting customer preferences, demographic changes, competitive factors, technological developments, choices of suppliers, government regulations, etc., all of which must be assessed as part of decision making. Basic goals and primary policies cannot be delegated; top management must set them. Short-term results are vital and must be assessed and balanced against long term potential. The company's values and formulation must be complemented with performance objectives, free from political atmospherics. Companies must learn from lessons of success and failures.

Each of these drivers of operational excellence is interlinked supportively as connective tissues in the construction or reconstruction of companies. They serve as vital functions to extend the reach in every aspect of the business scenarios, widening global footprints and enabling unparallel success year after year. Considered and executed collectively, these drivers of excellence will place every arm of the company's body in good posture for far-reaching influence and to face the daunting task ahead.

9.1 Strategic Initiatives

⌘ Everything of importance has been said by somebody who did not discover it.

- Alfred North Whitehead ⌘

As Lou Gerstner, former IBM CEO concisely captured, "Good strategies start with massive amounts of quantitative analysis, hard, difficult analysis that is blended with wisdom, insight and risk taking. Truly great companies lay out winning strategies that are believable and executable. Good strategies are long on detail and short on vision." Paradoxically, it is prudent to avoid paralysis by analysis.

The crux of the matter is that strategy is a business' road map to execute whatever it plans to accomplish. Mission defines strategy and strategy defines structure. Strategy is not a goal; it is a direction with a long view. Where you're headed is more important than how fast you're going. A coherent and effective strategy must be backed up by superior operating capabilities and continually fine-tuned. Strategic plans communicate to the people what the company's priorities and its direction. A well thought-out plan can act as a business' gateway to economic survival and success, though it takes time to work their effects. They must not be long on theory, but short on performance. It is important to remember that sometimes, the devil is in the detail, so keep business strategies to the point, although processes for formulating and directing strategic initiatives may vary depending on the size of the business. Moreover, while a plan should be followed through deeply and consistently, a strategic process should allow for midcourse corrections based on new circumstances and information. When successful companies grow, a strategy that worked well before will likely no longer fit. Strategies must change as market conditions change and the value of resources shift with time. A company's mission and direction is top management's responsibility and must not be delegated. Top executives must provide final approval to every strategic decision because such decisions have great impact on a company.

Building a successful corporation takes time. Identify the economic forces at work. Be fully in tuned with your competitive position, strategic direction and allocate resources strategically. Good intentions alone do not move mountains. Companies must differentiate among long and short-term allies, opportunistic partners, present and future competitors. Good teams spend a lot of time studying competitors and themselves; determining what they did wrong and what they did right, and finally devising a winning game plan. According to Harvard Business School professor Michael Porter, a business has a robust strategy when it has strong points of difference from that of their competitors. Know your strengths, weaknesses and core competencies. Strategic thinking involves insight about the present and foresight about the future. Convert strategic thinking into a cocktail of usable strategic building block with realistic short and long-term goals. The more closely the strategy is aligned with reality, the more effective the implementation will be. Stay focused when your strategy is working. If your strategy is not working, you must devise a new one. Ask yourself, how is the company's strategic fit? Strategic fit determines how your products fit the strategic direction of the business. Strategy must be linked to a feedback loop that inputs information about what is and is not working so that major strategic decision are changed accordingly. Thus, strategies will be altered in the face of shifting economic, technological and competitive conditions. While designing your strategy, remember not to challenge your competitors in their areas of excellence and strategic capabilities. Though successful strategies are often imitated quickly, as pointed out by Professor Philip Kotler (1999), it is one thing to copy particular aspects of a new strategy that apply to your business, but quite another for any imitator to copy all aspects of the strategic architecture, which would likely achieve mixed results

The primary goal of any business strategy should be gaining market share. A company with the largest market share usually becomes the market's victor. Recognize each opportunity as it comes and rapidly and assess its relative costs and benefits. Create a steady stream of new business concepts in concert with employment of strategic leverage Stretch the perimeter of products and services to benefit multiple market segments, but also remember to evaluate the strategic fit and difficulty of implementation. To quote George Day, the Geoffrey T. Boisi professor of the Human Center for Global Competition and Innovation at the Wharton School of the University of Pennsylvania, "Some companies have become "customer compelled," jumping to meet every customer whims without a clear strategy." Instead, a successful business identifies and nurtures valuable customers and discourages customers that drain profits.

Explore strategic alternatives. Re-deploy assets and resources from areas of low productivity and yield to areas of higher productivity and yield. Building buggy whips faster is not the answer.

Professor Michael Porter eloquently stated that there are essentially two ways to prosper: be a low cost producer or have a powerful differentiation strategy. Cost savings from improved production efficiency and economies of scale are passed on to customers via reduced prices, thus erecting a barrier to entry for competitors who find small margins unattractive. Tactics must be flexible; strategy does not change fast.
Strategic decisions must be integrated with operational management. In other words, strategic advantages when combined with operational efficiencies will create competitive advantage.

1. Core Ideology and Organizational Orientation

Every company needs a distinguishable core ideology that guides and inspires its people, one that will withstand the twists and turns of the business landscape. It is supported by a paper trail that leads to core beliefs and philosophy. An organization that lacks a core ideology, even if run by a charismatic leader cannot be sustained over the long haul. While visible business executives who drive their business expansion head many high achieving companies, peerless core ideology is one of the long lasting linchpins that define the company's strength and relevance. It is the glue that keeps a vast operation together. As James C. Collins and Jerry I. Porras stated in Build to Last: "A company must be well designed as an organization to preserve the core and stimulate progress with all the key pieces working in alignment." Core ideology should not consist of words meant merely to pacify and manipulate, conjuring a false ideological nirvana. Instead, steps must be taken to identify or leverage core competency with a set of strategic toolkit. Such steps should make corporate ideology pervasive throughout the organization, and promote discretion, loyalty and camaraderie. For example, a core ideology that places upon every employee the responsibility to move the company forward; emphasizes proactive rather than reactive skills. In order to accomplish this you must embody the alloy of greatness anchored with system, passion and commitment to expand existing competency base.

James C. Collins and Jerry I. Porras further stated: "Luck favors the persistent. This simple truth is a fundamental cornerstone of successful company builders. Be prepared to kill, revise or evolve an idea, but never give up on the company." Locate where knowledge resides in an organization. Companies must continually reinvent themselves and recapture the excitement, not only in times of crisis. We need people with vigor, with clear and shared goals that create engines that fire on all cylinders. We need visionaries who will improve outmoded processes by ploughing new ground, and organizations that will support them and their dynamism.

As Bill George in Authentic Leadership: "The best path to long-term growth in shareholder value comes from well articulated mission that inspires employee commitment. Companies that pursue their mission and clear strategy in a consistent and unrelenting manner will create greater shareholder value than anyone believes possible."

2. Cultural Renovation

Many companies suffer from inbred cultural system. In order to optimize business potential during these pressing times, corporations must adopt renewed wide-scale rethinking and embrace cultural change with regard to interactions among employees, customers and suppliers. This requires a corporate-wide transition of immense proportion, even under the best of circumstances. The challenge is to change a successful culture to make it even better without diminishing its traditional repertoire of positive attributes. Transforming a successful culture is more difficult than changing an unhealthy one. Organizations must be aligned with corporate direction, one that is muscular, energetic and cohesive. Social and cultural bonds can be hard to forge and loyalty is similarly difficult to give or obtained. As H. James Harrington, Darryl R. Conner and Nicholas L. Horney (2000) stated: "A high degree of synergy allows the team to leverage its strengths and guard against its weaknesses. Before synergy can be achieved, two prerequisites must be in place: willingness and ability." Remove barriers and reduce corporate obesity among all functions: marketing, sales, engineering, manufacturing, quality, customer service, etc. Sack politicians. For people to work at high levels, they must be self-propelled yet with network connections, purposeful and committed. When we make an investment, our commitment to that investment is only as strong as the returns we are receiving. Develop mechanisms and flexible structure to ensure that the core values, change agencies and supporting behaviors are practiced on a daily basis. Inculcate an organization that is value-centered, individualistic and yet team performance-driven. Establish an organizational environment that promotes cross-fertilization of knowledge and talents without polluting an already healthy culture.

It is also important to note that corporations must learn to balance conflicting demands for short-term and long-term results as well as balancing various constituencies: shareholders, customer, employees and communities. If organizational behavior becomes entrenched over time, mediocre performance is eventually tolerated in the form of congeniality in a so-called family-like culture. This means that the system must be ventilated.

3. Corporate and Business Ecosystem

Business is a difficult system to construct and sustain. Organizations come with vastly different characteristics, just as no two people are the same. Some structures favor companies that operate on a large scale while others favor companies operating at a small scale. Operational excellence can be firmly rooted through a systematic and comprehensive understanding of a corporate ecosystem that links internal capabilities with their external environment. An excellent organization has a bare minimum of deadwood. It provides healthy conduits for creativity and innovation without the exclusion of other priorities. Efficiency is enhanced with the maximization of complementary activities of anyone, anytime and anywhere. Where the company locates its businesses is of strategic importance.

To achieve resounding success, companies must understand the business ecosystems in which they dwell and recognize the significance of their participants who mutually support each other by forming symbiotic relationships to exploit various business opportunities. Companies as powerful as GE, Microsoft, Intel, Boeing and Airbus, to name a few, can no longer achieve enduring success without being leaders in cultivating networks of suppliers, customers and others in the food chain. It also includes interrelated companies, government institutions, bankers, universities and lawyers. Unlike biological ecosystems that take thousands of years to evolve, however, high-tech business ecosystems are more dynamic. As such, high-tech business ecosystems are far more sensitive to changing business conditions. For example, new technologies are invading and upsetting the balance of traditional businesses. In order to thrive, companies need to understand their positions in the business ecosystem and be quick to adapt to changing market conditions. Theodore Levitt of the Harvard Business School suggests in his classic "Marketing Myopia" that the reason companies eventually declined is because they identify themselves too closely with a particular product instead of meeting underlying customer needs.

To detail an example, Intel mainly drives the personal computer hardware business while Microsoft leads in software side, whilst Samsung contributes in low cost DRAM, a vital component. Actions taken by these three companies affect other companies related to the computer business: suppliers of raw materials, manufacturers of systems and components, distributors, resellers, venture capitalists, etc. Intel's constant hardware upgrades, Microsoft's software upgrades and Samsung's pricing power severely impact the strategic and operational developments of companies in the food chain. Thus, companies that fail or delay in transitioning their products to Intel and Microsoft platforms and DRAM cost structure will lag behind in terms of technology and business opportunities.

Note: The industry that Microsoft and Intel currently dominate is characterized by single-user productivity computing. The most critical issue in this model is compatibility. Standards become important as users have an enormous stake in their investments. By controlling the standards, Microsoft and Intel have been able to lead the industry for more than a decade. Customer, competitors, entrepreneurs and investors have benefited handsomely from their leadership. However, several companies such as Google and Yahoo are challenging Redmond-based Microsoft in the Internet scene.

4. Strategic Resources, Barriers to Entry & Leveling the Playing Field

Companies must be acquainted with their strategic resources and utilize them to create barriers to entry by competitors. These are time-honored strategies that go hand-in-hand with corporate core competencies in order to maintain a company's staying power. Strategic resources are valuable elements that include financial and physical assets (e.g. cash, location, buildings, and assets purchased at pre-inflation prices). Resources such as economies of scale, high fixed cost and capital requirements can form formidable barriers for competitors to penetrate. Firms with economies of scale create barriers through pricing power by reducing prices to deter new competitors. A company's information and intellectual capital such as patents, trademark, proprietary information, brands equity and experience curve can be parlayed into competitive advantage by raising the barrier to entry. People like working within established and respected brands. Some companies enjoy competitive advantage because they are secured suppliers of scarce raw materials. This, combined with scarcity, switching cost, long learning curve, tariffs and government regulation constitute formidable barriers for many new entrants. Strategic resources, when addressed adroitly against competitive threats and shifting market environment become a significant advantage. If you pick an industry where the barrier to entry is low, where capacity can be added quickly, it will be difficult to attain stable pricing. A dependable competitive advantage will be something that cannot be duplicated overnight, for it has a long learning curve. However, over the longer term, competencies of even the best companies can be duplicated – talents can be hired away and processes can be replicated. Companies must then create new barriers or reposition when the existing wall is breached. Other barriers can be played out in the political, diplomatic, commercial and local fronts. It is essential for barriers to be thick, deep and constantly being reinforced in order to be resistant to destruction.

It is difficult for new entrants to penetrate established businesses where competitors have well developed infrastructure and long experience curve. Such barriers are common in communication, defense, aircraft and other industries. In the case of telecommunication, in order to overcome these barriers, Chinese, Indian and other companies are able to level the playing field with wireless technology by leapfrogging companies with decades of experience and infrastructure in land-lines telephony. The same strategy is being played out by BYD (Build Your Dream) of China. In the words of Wang Chuanfu, Founder/Chairman of BYD, China's recent entrant to the automobile industry; "It's almost hopeless for a latecomer like us to compete with GM and other established car makers with a century of experience in gasoline engines. With electric vehicles, we are all at eh same starting line."

5. Acquisition, Merger, Alliance and Joint Venture

In a new era of partnership, companies are forging more links, though some are successful while others are not. In association with organic growth, acquisitions, alliances, joint ventures and coalitions are increasingly employed as essential strategies that bolster growth by adding geographical and technological scope. The rationale behind decisions to build or acquire is that to build and grow organically takes a long time. A shorter route to success is to acquire or gain access to assets, new markets and new technologies. In fact, few companies grow without merger and acquisition. However, there must be clear and compelling reasons behind a combination. There must be synergy in cultures behind the combination to avoid culture wars and out-of-control political partisanship. Integration is crucial to the success of acquisition. Accurately choose investments that offer the highest payoffs and provide a broader portfolio of capabilities. Though many mergers from AOL Time Warner to Daimler Chrysler failed, mergers can provide access to more customers and talents. Cost synergy may also be achieved from the combination. Leaders with marketing clout need to ally themselves with new technology firms to avoid inevitable slide in profit margins as their existing products mature. Companies such as Cisco Systems, Oracle and Nokia, for example have made small target acquisitions of varying technology upstarts or strategic alliances to grow at a respectable pace. Acquisitions not only allow a business to grow but also to refresh and maintain their technological edge by exploiting brainpower over wider areas. In order to reap ample harvest in the future, corporate merger, acquisition and alliance require sound business and integration plan. To mine the value of a merger or acquisition you should successfully integrate the product lines and services. Always leave some goodwill when the seller's involvement is important for a merger's success.

It is not uncommon for a startup with a flexible, entrepreneurial culture to be damaged when investors bring in "seasoned" management. These seasoned managers are more often refugees from larger companies who immediately attempt to control the creative chaos that are keys to the company's innovation. Often, when rules and regulations appear, the startup's creative talents disappear to look for more enlightened pastures. Then the company soon develops the same dysfunctional and bureaucratic behaviors that characterized Industrial Age companies. However, the reasoning that companies must be conservative, as they grow larger is actually a myth. Thus, entrepreneurial companies may suffer by being bought out by larger companies due to culture clashes. Typically, larger companies are intolerant of alternative ways of doing things and cannot resist meddling in the creative processes of a subsidiary, ultimately creating their own lifeless clone.

On the other hand, strategic and cross-industry alliances, if handled adroitly can achieve competitive advantage using less capital. Even though there are drawbacks against alliances, alliances can be invigorated to fortify the company's staying power. Shorter product life cycle and more expensive research and development have resulted in firms seeking strategic partners with emerging technology companies. While alliances are much more complex and nuanced to deal with, such a move is another way of spreading risks. Organizations with a flexible management culture can more easily create strategic alliances with other organizations. Alliances are formed with different agents with varying core competencies and resources. Organizations can join forces to cause changes in industry power relationships that often prove advantageous to participating corporations. At the same time, however, the organizations must anticipate strategic alliances that might be detrimental to the enterprises by weighing the tradeoffs and strategic implications: benefits and exposures. For alliances to work effectively there must be realistic expectations about the relationship. It is important to remember that the alliance partners will consider what they will get out of this arrangement.

A company can join with other like-minded companies in a coalition and share both risks and rewards. Consultation is the lifeblood of coalition. Coalition occurs when the risks, financial and technical hurdles are high.

For companies that are expanding globally, it is advantageous to form joint ventures with local companies who understand local and regional markets. Joint ventures are a suitable launching pad for companies without financial and managerial wherewithal to make independent and profitable impact. Some companies accept equity position in suppliers, advance capital, provide technology and commit to long-term purchase contracts.

6. Spotting, Timing and Seizing Opportunities

Organizations must learn to quickly identify and capitalize upon the spectacular opportunities available in the planet now and in the future. We have found that companies can profit by spotting the next hot industry or riding the waves of natural market cycles through skillful and timely exploitation of relevant government economic policies. Though these opportunities are more nebulous and its contributions are harder to grasp, companies must learn to spot these opportunities before they become fashionable though admittedly, being at the right place at the right time helps. Many ventures such as the personal computer business are successful and comprehensible today but rejected previously as commodity and of low profit margins. Today, we witness the success of HP, Dell, Acer and Lenovo in this cutthroat business. The future is as full of promise as it is fraught with uncertainty. In most cases, we do not achieve success under the circumstances of our own choosing. There are risks, difficulties and compromises in business and we can be certain that there will be more in the future. Most companies naturally hesitate to venture into the unknown, which can result in squandered opportunities. It is also important to remember that that one cannot use an old map to discover new land. Companies must learn to spot trends, be ready and seize the opportunities before their competitors do. However, companies must also be ready at all times to jump into the bandwagon whenever opportunities arise, including beneficial chance events. Companies must see beyond their blind spots, expand their views, sense change early and make quick adjustments to open up the windows of opportunity. Gather yee buds come yee spring and gather hay while the sun shines. Timing makes an enormous difference in corporate success.

As Fred Wiersema (2001) stated; "when your largest customers dominate its industry, you can expect to share it its good fortune."

7. Build systems that are both Inward and Outward Looking

Against the backdrop of this new business setting, companies must build systems that are both inward and outward looking based on the collective wisdom. It means building competencies we already have and developing others we do not already have, constantly improved and refined. This requires long-term commitments. Synergy and balance are keys. Companies that are too inward or static thinking suffer from inertia, often finding it difficult to fully embrace new ideas. Ideas are door openers. As Will Rogers said: "It ain't what you don't know which gets you; it's the things that you know which ain't so." Unfortunately, front-line people who are closely in tune with customers and have intimate information regarding customer complaints, reasons for lost sales, special customer service requirements and so on, are seldom motivated to inform management. They fear that by informing management, their job load may increase or that the information they provide may not be used. As a result, their enthusiasm for the job and company are diminished. We must break out from this conundrum if we want to thrive. Management must recognize the value of this information, promote attitudinal change and unblock information from a valuable upward flow. Responsiveness to the attitudes and aspirations of external constituencies (examples: customer and shareholder) and internal (employee and managerial) issues are fundamental to business success and must be embroidered in many places within an organization. Undoubtedly, there will be tensions during these interactions. At times, things can be overwhelming, with occasional triumph of ego over reason. There need to be growing civility to which growing business depends. This will illuminate people to the organization's perspective, one that is up-to-date and high definition.

8. Focus and Reassessment of Organizational Goals, Tactics and Strategies

⌘ The secret of success is constancy of purpose.
- Benjamin Disraeli ⌘

The most important issue facing managers is how to grow and sustain their business profitably. This is done to assure consistency in delivering good short term results within the long-term strategy. There must be periodic reconsiderations of all the underlying premises in organizational goals, tactics and strategies. Management judgment must be exercised. Set goals that are high, clear, concise and cohesive. Goals that are low and haphazardly set only, become self-fulfilling prophesy. We need to market our goals to our people and thus, importance of on-going internal marketing should not be underestimated. Companies must continuously question their business formulae and assumptions. Avoid drifting with the tide. There may be a need to forge a new framework and decide which functions should be integrated and which should be left none-integrated in order to increase effectiveness and efficiency. Remember to correct misalignments in the frameworks and functions.

Invariably, concerns that should be addressed are missed or forgotten. Keep a daily list of things to do in order to keep you aligned with your organization's goals and objectives. As John Perace II and Richard Robinson, Jr. (Strategic Management: Formulation, Implementation and Control, 2000) noted: "Seven criteria should be used in preparing goals and objectives: acceptable, flexible, measurable over time, motivating, suitable, understandable and achievable."

It would be a folly to make lasting pronouncements of success for there exist no ironclad rule. Because the business environment is constantly changing, businesses must continually reassess lukewarm and fickle commitments and determine the causes of such problems. There should not be a lethargic continuation of business as usual, or, on the other hand, a devout following of fads and provincialism. New wine needs new wineskin. Redirect management effort and attention to remedy the situation. Get to the essence of the situation. An organization must constantly challenge its own concept, even if it is proud of what it has created. We are bound to make mistakes and each failure must be felt and worked through. Go back-to-basics and reassess its relevancy under current settings.

9.2 Skillful Deployment of Resources: People, Dollars, Time and Information

A. People

⌘ If you want one year of prosperity, grow rice. If you want 10 years of prosperity, grow trees. If you want 100 years of prosperity, grow people.

- Chinese Proverb ⌘

On a grander scale, the manager's role and responsibilities are becoming more challenging as the economy continues to globalize and technologies continue to advance rapidly. People, equipment and systems must quickly react to the opportunities that arise from globalization and increased market access. Put resources where the opportunities are and be ready to mobilize whenever opportunities arise, even on short notice. Grow your talents from within and hire talents from outside. Do not make the grave error of treating people as expenses and machines as assets.

In his book "*Good to Great*, (2001," Jim Collins noted that those who build great companies understand that the ultimate throttle on growth for any great company is not markets, technology, competition, or products. It is one thing above all others: the ability to acquire and retain enough of the right people. The "right people" is the most important asset. This is no longer an option, but a requirement. Unlike times in bygone eras, none of us can get very far by doing things ourselves. We need people with deep conviction, self-motivation and enthusiasm high achievers. We need people who are problem solvers, brilliant thinkers who take initiatives. Such employees are driven, intelligent, and often highly educated, though it is important to remember that education is not a substitute for experience. The challenge, however, is for a company to attract, optimize and retain good people based on a long horizon. People are the most valuable and the most volatile of all the resources we use to accomplish the work of the organization. Most businesses fail, do so because they ignore the human capital - their workforce - a critical component to winning. Drive and incredible hard work alone are not enough. These qualities must be allied with skills and built on the bedrock of achievement. Do not hire if you cannot get the right person – keep looking. A great plan without the right people will not succeed.

A company's optimal team of people will have the knowledge, skills, driving force, esprit de corp, aptitudes and attitudes to perform at the utmost level to accomplish the organization's goals with magnified effect. Every member of the team must play an important role in the success of the organization or he/she should not be a member of the team. Make rank-and-file employees feel that they are part of the company's strategy. Every member has a different role and contributes differently; each is important. Give people a voice, be genuinely respectful and tap into the often-underutilized human capacity. Managers must reconsider how rewards are doled out. The organization's future is molded by the decisions and actions we undertake today. Continuously develop talents at all levels, reshape jobs and responsibilities to match changing business requirements.

The legal side of human resource management is based on the basic principle of fairness, sound justification in making decisions, consistency in actions and keeping promises. However, it is important to note that different groups of workers have to be managed differently.

1. Total Available Talent

⌘ There is no shortage of talent. There is only a shortage o talent that can recognize talents.

- Jerry Wald ⌘

Talent is at the heart of today's business. As the business environment grows ever more competitive, companies are gearing to meet escalating global clamor for managerial and skilled talents. However, instead of immediately looking outward to extend their talent pool, organizations should take note of an existing reservoir of talents, their internal talent pool. It is not uncommon for top executives to be far removed from the realities of their existing talent pool. There may be gold and diamond mines of available talents within the companies waiting to be mined. There are rough diamonds each waiting to be cut and polished.

Companies must exhibit dedication to employees they have already hired, for to maximize the strength of an organization's workers is to maximize the strength of the company. Moreover, identifying talent is a pre-existing pool is far more cost-effective method of acquiring talent than hiring from outside. Thus, a company should consistently assess its internal pool and cultivate already present fountainhead of talent: people with finely tuned business acumen, good administrators, and doers as well as people with depth of thinking. This can be done through a wide array of personal experience, interactions and observations. Assessment of internal talent pool enables one to see and utilize internal resources in a new and different light. Though there will undoubtedly be times when an organization must hire new talent, a company's first step should be an inward one. Pick managers who have sound ethics, skills, intellect, clear thinking and who have learned tough lessons about life through experience. Spawn or promote likely stars. Fortify the company by enhancing loyalty through well crafted promotion of the right talents within.

2. Instilling Confidence, Conviction and Vitality

⌘ We can manage better by managing less. ⌘

You cannot talk about customer satisfaction and productivity if you neglect your employees. Instill pride and ownership into the fabric of the company by celebrating success while accepting and learning from mistakes. Fight the pull of negativism. Fire the imagination of rank and file employees. Articulate messages with confidence and enthusiasm. I have personally witnessed how a leader with passion ignited the passions of others, harnessing his personal power and energy to contribute to his company's soaring productivity. Even optimists have bad days. Pessimists have good thoughts now and then. An employee at work in body but not in mind should not be working in the company, for it will have a corrosive effect on the team. There should be continual monitoring of employee satisfaction and behavior. Assure fairness and equitable distribution of rewards. Only an organization that is fertile, purposeful and rich in confidence will perform at extraordinary levels, even achieving a seemingly unreachable pinnacle.

However, there must in existence a convergence of goals and interest to produce the desired results. The company must constantly communicate who the company is, what the company stands for and where the company is headed. It is a non-stop process. Mobilize and rally all employees into a force to be reckoned with via sound, just and caring leadership. People are not commodities. Treat employees with humanity and compassion. Why would employees work hard for uncaring bosses and an uncaring organization? It takes more muscles to frown than to smile. Create an exciting work environment that bonds workers together and nurture their creative capacity. Confident, engaged employees are not afraid of having their views challenged, and welcome productive discussion. They are like yeast that transforms a company, allowing it to rise. Develop employees like these by giving them responsibilities. Nurturing and giving support to employees will bring life to the organization as a whole. Actively solicit employee recommendations for improving sales, marketing, engineering, products, manufacturing, service, etc. No plan can be achieved to its fullest unless the staff understands and is fully committed to it. You cannot accomplish your goals if your employees interpret your words as yet another corporate lie. Rouse your employees into excitement, not lethargy; administer expression rather than repression. Maintain statistics as a measure of employee morale. Combine idealism and pragmatism, values and numbers and conviction grounded with reality. Create corporate culture that allows for such vital energy and joie de vive. Employees will not have that essential confidence and a bounce in their steps unless they work for a company that is competitive, winning and moral.

3. Hire Right and Place the Right People in the Right Job

> ⌘ If you pick the right people and give them the opportunity to spread their wings and put compensation as a carrier behind it you almost don't have to manage them.
>
> - Jack Welch ⌘

Companies must grow and be profitable if they desire to attract dedicated talents, satisfy their stakeholders and be more competitive. A growing company signals opportunity and success stories attract talents. Entrepreneurs and people with relevant skills will take notice. Your capacity to attract the best is an indication of their faith in your future. Similarly, the wealth of talents the company recruits will help the company grow and prosper.

High performing companies need similarly high-performing employees at every level of the organization and in every location worldwide. Hire good people and know how to get the best out of them. Hire the people you like and with relevant experience. It is essential to appoint people who look good not only on paper, but who can also manage well under various situations. Everyone is passionate and gifted about something. Leaders must be on the lookout for passion that is waiting to be motivated, equipped, energized, directed and fulfilled. As Jack Welch (Winning, 2005) frankly noted: "I would encourage you not to hire any team member – manager or not – without a good dose of positive energy. People without it just enervate an organization." Thus, hire employees with relevant qualifications, high capacities, positive attitudes and good behavior. Assess what contributions that person can bring to the party. There should be no excuse to say that you don't have the time to choose the right people. Companies must hire competent and educated managers in order to successfully face complex business environments. Hiring criteria should focus more on personal traits and technical competence in achieving job relevant requirements. It is crucial that we find out what the person is passionate about before hiring, promoting or power sharing. It is fundamentally important to appropriately match applicants with jobs, candidates with promotions, people with project teams and candidates with power sharing. The candidate must demonstrate competence in his field, i.e. exhibit the relevant skills and experience developed through education, training and common sense. One should also consider the correct fit for different positions based on candidates' differences in temperament, training and tradition in addition to industry relevant maturity and work related experience. Provide employees with adequate resources to do the job. Deploy the right people for the right mission and you will soon watch them move passionately in directions you could not have imagined. Although most people and most organizations already know this theoretically, their practices do not reflect this knowledge. While track record is extremely important, time, combined with questions will tell where the fire is.

Hiring mistakes inevitably occur. People have talents and skills that cannot be fully ascertain during the time of hiring. While it is important to hire to fulfill short-term needs, one must seriously consider whether the person is suitable long-term. Keep turnover of high performers as low as possible and turnover of low performers as high as possible. Companies must also learn to manage talented but difficult people by placing them in the right jobs with the right team.

4. Retention of High Performing Employees

⌘ **We never know the worth of water until the well is dry.** ⌘

The philosophical basis of Adam Smith's legacy (Wealth of Nations):

- ➤ All men have the natural right to obtain and protect his property.
- ➤ All men are by nature materialistic.
- ➤ All men are rational, and will seek by their own reason to maximize their material well-being.

Employers are constantly looking for people who can infuse the company with better ideas and practices. A key part of keeping good people is to attract and hire the right ones in the first place. As Alfred Sloan, General Motor's legendary Chairman once stated, "Decisions on people were the most important an executive could make." Most corporate assets can be bought or replicated with a key exception: a well-motivated, high energy and well-trained workforce that took years to develop. We need people who are able and resourceful, who can get things done. We need people who care about their work, who have the inbred will to excel and get the company's juices flowing. Every employee brings different strengths to the group. Pacesetters inspire and motivate others in the group through their examples and overwhelming enthusiasm. Find smart people who know the business and its technology. Promote managers who are adaptable and capable of making behavioral or value-based transitions while moving from one position to another. Assure that good people are adequately recompensed for the rigors of their jobs. Find employees who want to and can win: when they win, you win.

The world is more connected and people are faced with more choices now than ever before. There is employee mobility in the workforce today and there will continue to be. Turn-over in organizations is inevitable as people move through their lives and careers. There is a shortage of good and skillful employees. If you already have them, try to keep them. Stop losing managerial and technical assets. Many companies suffer from rigid promotion regulation. If promotion takes too long able men often depart. But when an employee wants to leave, offering an employee a counter offer is simply postponing the inevitable. People leave their jobs for a number of reasons: to improve their position in life, lack of personal fulfillment or unsuitable working condition. They want wide latitude to achieve objectives. Create an environment that enables employees to develop professionally and intellectually. As Adam Smith pointed out in The Wealth of Nations; "It is not from the benevolence of the butcher, the brewer or the baker, that we expect our dinner, but from their regards to their own interest. We address ourselves not to their humanity but to their self-love, but never talk to them about our necessities but of their advantages. Nobody but a beggar chooses to depend upon the benevolence of his fellow citizens."

Most employees generally do not leave the uncertainty of the environment they know to the one they don't, unless there are compelling negative reasons. Employees have considerably more to offer to organizations than what is presently tapped. Other reason people leave an employer is to escape an intolerable level of frustration. Frustrations involve both real and imaginary barriers to high performance and to a productive career. Examples include indecision, not caring, not listening, etc on the part of the bosses. Good people cannot be retained if they do not have the resources to do what must be done and moreover, secrets travel with people when they leave. One way to retain good employees is to remove the barriers that inhibit them from completing their tasks. Managers must know when to get involved and when to stay out of the way. Provide employees support and condition in which they can flourish. As business author Tom Peters stated: "the organizations will be amazed at the capabilities of their employees if they could see all the things they achieve outside their working lives." The best managers are those who understand and tolerate the foibles of their staffs. They are clear and pragmatic in the way they act. Do not take for granted that high performers will stay with you. You must continually reinforce their value, their opportunities and their long-term relationship with you. Make work challenging and fun. As Fred Smith, founder/CEO of Federal Express aptly put it: It's People, Service and Profit, not Profit, Service, People. Create a positive climate by reinforcing attitudes and practices that empower and support the individual. The path to success will not be attained if there is no strong conviction about one's work. Encourage employees to look to a higher purpose, one beyond mission and objectives, one of values, and that make them want to come to work. Liberate the talents of employees with a performance packed agenda via coaching, mentoring and being a role modeling responsibility and accountability. Once you give an individual such tools, allow him/her to do his/her work. It will be done well.

5. How to Manage High Employee Turnover in Hot Economic Environment?

⌘ Insecurity is part of the American System. Wages are high, but so is the probability of being fired. Insecurity is part of technological leadership.
- **Lester Thurow** ⌘

When unemployment is high, it is easier to find prospective employees. When unemployment is low, it is harder to find good people. In an increasingly competitive business climate, companies must develop more sophisticated approaches to talent management, a vital asset. It is increasingly costly to attract and retain high performance employees. Unlike machines, people cannot be owned and exceptional employees are not easily replaced and thus they should not be treated like a cog in the wheel of a machine. Attitudes and expectations have changed. Nowadays, people are willing to change jobs often. While you are interviewing potential employees, the persons are also interviewing you. Many companies are facing defections from their best talents, more so during booming economic cycles with high employee mobility. Talented employees leave a company where there is dissatisfaction and lack of friendship. Today's business environment is complex and employees are fast moving to be subject to old-fashioned supervision.

People may leave jobs for reason(s) unrelated to the job itself. Assign employees to positions and projects that are in tune with their interests and needs – allow each employee his/her optimal job fit. Moreover, be sure that the work is interesting and challenging instead of one that is routine and unremarkable. Nowadays workers are demanding increased participation and responsibility. It is essential to understand what the employee value. Let valuable employees know they are more than a cog in the machine. Find out when they need help to overcome obstacles or when they need to be left alone. Make career advancement viable through hard work and tangible achievement. One of the most important measures to retain employees is to maintain a relation of value to them, one that demonstrates fairness and trust. An elite group of corporations is characterized by high mobility and commitment to the workplace.

Compensation and perquisites should be structured in which rewards are earned through dedication and accomplishments, not nepotism. Pay above-market rate to attract and retain employees who have immeasurable experience, abilities, and contributions to bring to the team. This is particularly important in today's booming economy, which requires companies to keep good employees and attract talented newcomers. People who are dissatisfied are more likely to respond with negative behavior and poor performance as time goes on. Dissatisfied employee may leave or affect their own productivity or productivity of others. This requires active intervention.

6. Managing with Temporary Employees, Contractors and Fewer Workers

Today's businesses are faced with a myriad of challenges that require swift and effective responses. Investors are demanding quick return on their investments. Technological changes are rapid. Customers are more well-informed. Workers are empowered and there is pressure to reduce workforce. In a competitive business environment, it is often difficult to find and retain the right number of employees. The optimum stuffing number is constantly changing as the workplace changes, which mean that companies are always over or under hiring. Companies must maintain a balance between supply of employees and demand of customers.

Contractors and temporary employees are a fact of life for many businesses. Many companies have needs that are seasonal and cyclical. Needs change over time. Over-manning is one of the luxuries many corporations can ill afford in an increasingly competitive business environment. Excess people are baggage and cutting them reduces costs. Companies can opt for a contractor or temporary employee if they cannot foot the bill for full time employee. Another answer to cost escalation and productivity problems is to learn how to manage fewer workers efficiently and effectively, that is, how to do more with less. However, under-manning presents a predicament as well. How does a company manage to find the right balance?

Nowadays, companies are more cautious in hiring permanent employees, but still need workers. One approach is the use of both short and long-term temporary employees. Temps can compensate for this constantly changing business environment. The key, however, is to find an optimal mix of short and long-term employees. Companies must retain enough long-term employees to ensure that they have visionaries who can carry the businesses to enduring success, but should also hire the right number of temps to maintain a flexible culture.

7. About Hiring Consultants

⌘ A consultant is someone who borrows your watch and tells you what time it is.

- Anonymous ⌘

Approaches to hiring consultants have gone through a lot of changes. Sometimes, it may be worth for companies to look to outside consultants to provide extraordinary skill to make up for in-house deficiency. Look for people with track record. Though outside consultants may provide nuggets of knowledge from time to time, they must be carefully managed as there are pitfalls associated with it. Hiring consultant for a single, clear and limited purpose based on a particular skill set can minimize pitfalls. It must be in congruence with the needs and expectations of the corporation. The consultant's job will be done as soon as the purpose is accomplished.

Hiring consultants has its virtues and vices. As Jack and Suzy Welch noted with admirable succinctness (Businessweek, Sept. 18, 2006); "The problem with consultants is they are fundamentally at loggerhead with managers. Consultants want to come to a company, solve its mess and then hang around finding and solving other mess – forever. Managers want consultants to come in and fix a specific problem fast, and get out, also forever. The tension between these conflicting goals is what makes the use of consultants intractably problematical."

Cynics may have good justifications and they usually have first-hand observation on what works and what doesn't. Consultants can find plenty of reasons to stay, if they so desire. Efforts which are not home-grown often do not take root.

8. Attitude, Meritocracy, Opportunity and Respect

⌘ Success is not an entitlement. It has to be earned.
- Howard Schulz, Chairman, Starbucks ⌘

While people may not be able to control circumstances they can control how they respond to the solutions. Put stock in sincerity as an important persuasive tool.

As it was once said, "if you pay in peanuts, you must expect to get monkeys." Set up an appropriate compensation scheme tied to performance and corporate success. Remember to have in place a system that recognizes which performances are critical and who are delivering these performances. The workplace should be managed based on performance and fair distribution of bounties. Performance is the only fair test and performance measures drive behavior. Balance the exchange of rewards and contributions. Employees' satisfaction with wage is not going to be a factor when there is wage stabilization in comparable industries. Labor market forces tend to keep pay level relatively stable within occupations while allowing for regional differences or at least consistent with employees' needs (Robert Levin and Joseph Rosse, 2001).

Outstanding performers are encouraged to set galloping goals. Promotions therefore, should be based on ability, not favoritism. Employee empowerment needs to be coupled with responsibility. Make sure that there is shared understanding of job roles and performance expectations. The performance of an engineer is measured by how his performance is measured. Performance evaluation is a constant effort but should be formalized through periodic appraisals of employees. For such appraisals to bring about higher performance levels, however, it is imperative that performance expectations be clearly expressed and understood by employees. Expectations must be realistic and in proportion to the skills and abilities of the employees. Establish a system of economic incentives by linking an employee's evaluation with a series of personal development options. Change a reward system that rewards people on a transactional basis into one that rewards people for building and maintaining relationships. Different kinds of rewards attract different kinds of people and in turn encourage different kinds of behavior. For example, a candy that rewards a toddler will be an insult to a teenager. Edicts that impose a uniform pay increase, pay cut or pay freeze undermines the need to nourish the best. Money alone will not prompt people to work harder. Employees deserve genuine appreciation and rewards based on merit.

Find performance evaluation schemes that would keep people on their toes and help identify those who should be fired, particularly those who habitually rationalize poor performance with equally poor excuses. Low performers are beneficiaries of under-management. Establish a system in which you won't last if you are deadwood. Highly successful performance schemes are focused and measurable. Provide timely performance feedback. Avoid conditions in which people who should be fired stay on and those people who do real work leave. Avoid a culture in which certain employees (lemons) cannot be terminated without going through near interminable series of hearings and appeals. Mediocre work and/or habitual tardiness should lead to search for a better fit, demotion or dismissal. When a company finds that its good people leave and those who stay, are too comfortably ensconced in their daily routines, the organization is surely facing a crisis. We are creatures of habit, and have a tendency not to terminate unsuitable employees as soon as we should, and after time, leaders are faced with interpersonal and emotional obstacles confronting sub-par performers with whom they have worked with a long time. Removing people will be one of the hardest decisions a manager makes. As Jack Welch remarked; "Anyone who enjoys doing it should not be in the payroll and neither should anyone who cannot do it."

However, beware of terminating employees without just cause and one should not underestimate the human costs and hardship it entails. There should be utmost care to prevent "throwing the baby with the bathwater." Be ready to confront reality. Reward the best and weed out the ineffective. Job security must be directly linked with employee contribution to company profitability and supported by a merit based recognition and reward system.

9. Cooperation

⌘   If you want to go fast, go alone. If you want to go far, go together.

- An African Proverb ⌘

In order to achieve certain business goals, one must work with and through other people, including friends, bosses, peers and subordinates. Business is becoming more interdependent and as a result, work environments are becoming more complex. We need all the help we can get. There is an inbred need for people to interact with other people. The network of people to draw support from must be widened, crossing disciplinary boundaries. We need people who are generous in sharing their experiences in imaginative and constructive ways. We need strategic collaborators rather than unilateral superstars. Information, cooperation and help from interdependent departments are needed. Studies show over and over again that the capacity of team members to work together in an unfettered and proactive manner will contribute to a company's growth in scope, scale and speed. As Daniel D'aniello, Founder of Carlyle Corporation said; "We don't want isolationists. We also don't want crybabies. And we don't want mercenaries – people who are here to put a notch on their own gun. We want people to help us build a canon." If I may add: "we don't want prima donnas with independent power bases."

Cooperation exists when there is corporate fabric that binds. Cooperation is synergistic, for often times, more can be achieved when we work together than when we work alone. Without cooperation, the work environment can be plagued with individual distractions and negative energy, delaying a business' progress. Cooperation, however, cannot be obtained by edict but requires a collective capacity in which individuals work together toward a common goal. It requires actions that entices rather than alienates. Important differences in perspectives can stand in the way of genuine cooperation. On the other hand, a cooperative and concerted effort can allow for each individual to bring his or her unique talent and energy to the table, creating a positive tension that, in turn, generates a constructive forum in which new ideas are debated and ultimately worked through. Instill a culture in which such a forum can flourish. Team spirit and morale can go a long way in increasing productivity and yielding winning ideas.

Often, however, we need the cooperation of people who are not within the purview of our authority, and obtaining such cooperation requires the skills of persuasion and negotiation. At times, we need to be effective in cooperating with adversary. Cooperation involves the determination of precisely what is negotiable or untouchable, and combining one's own effort with those of other cooperative elements. Thus, team processes are naturally slower. Remember, therefore, to recognize team performances but also reward outstanding individuals. Do not unduly penalize failures.
There are times when we may face intransigent people who take consistently extreme position and will not compromise or back down under any circumstances. There are also die-hard obstructionists. They may be acting alone. Though certain

doggedness can be a positive attribute, a stubbornness that impedes positive cooperative efforts may be a sign of an employee's unwillingness to be part of a larger team. The recourse may be to get rid of that person.

10. True Test of Character

⌘ Of all the manifestations of power, restraint impresses men most.

- Thucidides ⌘

People make occasional errors in judgment, but an employee's character, which is longstanding, can be tested by his or her reaction to the environment. Failures, for example, test character. It is through failures that we discover who we can really trust. To a great extent, you can determine a person's true character by observing how he reacts when he cannot get what he wants or ask for. How does the employee react to failure? Does he or she give up, or try harder, despite long odds against success? Does the employee think about how to improve upon the failure, or simply blame it on extenuating circumstances, learning nothing from the hardship? Often, it is during the difficult times that one's true character is more easily discerned.

However, failure is not the only test of character. As people usually do not want to appear vulnerable, they may not show outward signs of weakness. Observing an employee's reaction to a high-pressure or crisis situation can also tell much about a person. Does he or she handle a difficult situation with grace, or falter under pressure? Does he or she say idle words or treat them as covenants to be kept? Does he or she stand firm on principles or move with the tides. Does he do well when no one is looking? Business is not constantly flying high; in fact, to be in business is to become accustomed to potentially knotty situations. An employee must have a strong constitution and sense of self to successfully weather such times.

It is also important to observe employees during favorable times. Does the employee become overconfident, or does he or she continue to make reasoned judgment? A person of character will remain steady and even-handed throughout different environments, whether of failure, stress, or success. People have the tendency to slip back to old behaviors even after facing crucible of trials, but someone of character will learn from his/her mistakes, and will incorporate what has been learned past experiences into future situations.

Power can become addicting and people can change when they get more power. Some may be intoxicated with power and cause serious grief to people while others are rendered more effective to do better things when empowered.

In short, how a person handles failure, success, power and life's challenges is a character crucible. It can reveal both the public and private side of the personality.

11. Show-horse and Workhorse

⌘ The holding of office and title should not be an end itself but a means of achieving inspiring goals. ⌘

Sometimes the exterior may be more interesting than the interior. In business, image may even be more important than reality. Companies need to step up public relations efforts to complement corporate finance, marketing and other initiatives. Modern instruments of presentation are abundantly available and many well-healed leaders luxuriate in the limelight and are capable of demonstrating great eloquence and passion. Showmanship and public displays, though seemingly superficial, are important in that they promote company exposure and relationships. In fact, showmanship puts companies in the spotlight. It is sometimes crucial for success, depending upon the situation.

However, it is important to balance showmanship with real work. In other words, style must be complemented with substance in order to gain respectability and credence. When showmanship is combined with substantive activities, the two can be mutually reinforcing. Essentially, the gap between the symbolic and substantive must be narrowed. Leadership styles and models cannot exist as empty examples, but must translate into substantive performance through tasks that may not be glamorous. Balance substance and style on a deeper level: allow the two to feed into each other.

12. Be Tight, Be Loose and Other Paradoxes of Management

A good leader's responsibility is to place the right people in the most fitting positions, clarify expectations, provide needed resources and finally, get out of the way. A high level of job satisfaction may not translate to high performance though it leads to stable relationship. The dignity of an employee must be reconciled with a coercive element in his/her work. Be loose if employees have a maturity that allows you to do so. Hold the reins loosely, allowing employees the freedom to act on their own initiatives. On the other hand, be tight if there is lack of maturity. It is important to note that it's much easier to loosen up than to tighten up. There are times when process driven actions triumph over personality driven activities. At other times, personality driven actions are more effective.

At times, situations are not clear cut. Paradoxes are seemingly contradictory statements that nonetheless may be true. Out of these paradoxical blends come remarkable results. The paradox of information openness and intellectual asset protection, for example, is a particularly important one in business. In decision-making there exist continual trade-offs, the constant weighing of risk and benefits of projected outcome with respect to expected objectives. The need is obvious to balance buoyant short term business outlook with long-term perspective and planning. Therefore, one must balance the old and new, permanence and change, tradition and innovation.

As Richard Hamermesh noted in the introduction to Fad Free Management (1996): "When Digital Equipment Corporation told people both to take risks and work in teams, it put them into a hard-to-win situation. Individual risk taking calls for

114

decisiveness and experimentation, whereas teamwork calls for due process and inclusive participation. Either might be appropriate at a given time, but emphasizing both at once is asking for trouble."

Companies work hard to keep employee turnover low. In fact there are times when keeping turnover low may hurt performance as low turnover accumulates hiring mistakes.

13. Decision, Planning and Execution

How do we translate lofty goals into concrete results? Though people are human and make mistakes, there are business executives known for making extremely wise decisions. These executives are adept at weighing and examining issues with diligence. All activities begin with thought and end in action. Think, learn and implement simultaneously. Nonetheless, there is still a widespread inability to make the right decisions at the right time in organizations today. Decisions are not always digital – simply yes or no. At times, it may be very difficult to make judgment call, especially when the outcome is unknown. Moreover, many decisions are hobbled in the mist of ambivalence. Execution is stymied as information is shrouded in fog and ambiguity. Critical decisions may be made with necessary tradeoffs. Dreams alone are not enough. The hard part is to act on these dreams by making courageous and decisive actions. Ideas and vision are important but more often; they are amorphous, easier said than done. Usually, they are simple to understand, but difficult to carry out. It is not surprising that there are often gaps between formulation and implementation of policies. Vision must be tempered by reality. Some situations require deliberations; others require teamwork.

There should be interplay between tomorrow's vision and today's execution. Disciplined execution is what differentiates a mediocre company from a great one. An organization needs doers and dreamers. A business must be decisive, creative, consistent, and execute decisions effectively, moving speedily from ideas to action. Employees are watching every decision a manager makes. Managers must have a big dose of common sense and be able to gauge the prospect of success on any undertaking. One must avoid paralysis by analysis. Use good judgment, intertwine your vision with reality, and execute those decisions faithfully.

The manager is a dynamic element in every business. Hands-on management is normal and desirable. Delegation without control is essentially resignation. A manager helps and makes decisions from an array of choices, translating intentions into reality. In order to make important business decisions, the manager must acknowledge that the risks are manageable and acceptable. He/she must have clarity and specificity in understanding the issues surrounding the decisions and must have access to resources in order to achieve winning results. Provide a forum to air issues and make decisions. Debates and study lead to decisive and coherent actions; thus it can take a while for decision to get traction. In decision-making, one must choose a best course of action or the next best alternatives. In a sense, decision by the heart and by the head is admirable.

Vision, decisions, strategies, planning and execution cannot be substitutes for one another as they serve different purposes.

Good planning is important due to the complexity and interdependency of various groups. Without planning commitments to customers, employees and other stakeholders will often go unmet. Go right to the heart of the issues, drawing from the executive toolbox. Planning is but a piece of paper until you put it into action. Test and re-affirm key decisions by analyzing their results. The key to achieving total success in business is crucially dependent upon the skills involved in executing these strategic and operational actions. It involves equal parts patience, persistence and persuasion. Manage the chaotic flow of information and deliver on commitments. Good thinking and good actions create foundation for sound results.

Once that decision is made, a business must successfully implement it, which often involves building coalitions. This is where the manager becomes a particularly key figure. Important functions of most managers are planning, organizing, reviewing, communicating, controlling, delegating, coordinating, listening, deliberating, problem solving, advising, decision-making, executing and improving. Mistakes are far more forgivable if the decisions are effectively communicated and accepted by people who are responsible for its execution and success. Managers often wrestle with the question of whether to compromise company standards for the sake of expediency. They are also faced with a plethora of decisions ranging from hiring, firing, choosing the right target markets, developing optimal product features, making effective pricing decisions, budgeting, capital acquisition, facilities improvement, etc. It is not uncommon that these decisions are often made in a fast-paced environment, in a haphazard way, often without complete information. Ambiguous situations can contribute to delay and indecision and often lead to perpetual pas-de-deux.

14. Follow-through

A manager's job is to prepare, negotiate and implement. If you are a manager it is your responsibility to make sure that everything goes well. There should be frequent invocation of this imperative. There are plentiful of ideas but implementation is difficult. Actions may be piecemeal and disorganized. A key part of a winning formula is to establish a system to accelerate the process whenever progress is glacial. This system must be reinforced with pillars of support and encouragement, manned by people with good process skills. Under-management appears to be the norm for quite some time. Communicate the views forcefully and effectively. Keep a clean record and follow through with agreements. Though business is often portrayed as "making the deal," following through afterwards is equally as important, especially in a business environment that are moving at a blistering pace. Remember your responsibilities, and carry them out assiduously. Ideas and plans may be largely forgotten. Follow through with ideas and give them shape and substance. To do otherwise will lead people nowhere.

People are often easily distracted by the humdrum day-to-day activity. Some are simply unaccustomed to following through – these are the folks that forget to return e-mails, are frequently late to meetings, etc. Such employees need further training and reminders. On the other hand, acknowledge and reward those who demonstrate a commitment to responsibility.

15. Fire Politicians

⌘ The great enemy of the truth is very often the lie –
deliberate, continual and dishonest – but the myth –
persistent, persuasive and unrealistic.

- John F. Kennedy ⌘

In every company, there exist a mix of doers, advisors and
courtiers. Doers are professional types, constantly translating
ideas into action; advisors give impartial advice and courtiers
flow with the wind, telling the boss simply what they want to
hear. And there are those who only seek to criticize but never
to act. If not well managed, such people can break an
initiative. As Billy Graham, world re-known evangelist said:
"Politics has always been ugly to me, and yet I accept that as a
fact of life." Politic, however is rarely simple. Political power is
ephemeral. We need pathfinders as well as people of
compromise.

Some executives view politicking as a way to compel managers
to lobby one another to get things done. They reason that the
test of the political arts can be combined with professionalism
in the pursuit of a company's interest and be intertwined with
personal interest. This could not be farther from the truth.
These executives are usually the end products of the process of
elimination, not the process of cultivation. There are many
who maintain a healthy strain of skepticism about the pitfalls
of involvement in politics. Do not be caught up in the politics
of the organization with its competing wings and opaque
backroom politics. Business organizations should not become
a debating society; you do not want business organizations to

be like US Congress or US Senate. Such environment often ends up in cauldron of arguments that undermine companies, not help them. Politics suffers from difficulties in reaching collective decisions and causes various subordinate manifestations. It polarizes, enervates and blunts the effectiveness for organizations to solve problems. In some worse situations, things can get careened out of control. Effective leaders take a less charitable view of politicking as political activities encourage rivalries and distrust among the various organizations thus wasting valuable time. They possess the discipline to transcend petty politics and adversarial relationship. They understand the role of politics but yet would not get dirty themselves. Politics tends to degenerate into competition, tribalism, turf protection and corporate bloodletting among ambitious managers resulting in adverse repercussions. Politics can be downright nasty and dirty. When stakes are high, infighting can be vicious and politicians tend to spread their influence in self-serving ways. Stop bickering and start producing. Do not be caught up in political crosscurrents. There should be no room for territorial squabbling, feudalism, conspiratorial activities or making egregious mistakes. Kick the bad guys out of the game.

It is fair and indeed necessary to fire politicians and employees who commit improprieties. It is tantamount to surgical removal of cancerous cells before they become malignant. Having to fire people is not an unenviable task. One has to be extremely careful to fire those who need to be fired. It is not a good position to be in for a company to fire the wrong person. Provide an equitable severance package that will soften the blow. Gossip and intrigue do not belong in the workplace. Politically oriented managers engage in personal survival tactics instead of nurturing the business. More often they produce more heat than light. These executives are promoted not because of their talents but because they know how to play the system through calculation and careerism. Some jockey for position and engage in political infighting and back stabbing while others snipe at each other instead of working together toward a common goal. Often, politicking involves managers withholding or using information to their advantage, thus skewing the information base. Unfortunately, such managers have learned that power stems from hoarding information, keeping key items under a cloak of secrecy rather than sharing it. Do not allow your company to foster a culture in which such counter-intuitive thinking becomes the norm.

One way of diffusing politics in the workplace is by instilling common goals and shared values. Form teams instead of committees. Teams focus on a common goal. Committees represent their own interest or the interest of certain functions. Also, a balanced power structure with clear lines of responsibility provides managers a sense of security, thus minimizing the need to play politics. Employees should be judged by their deeds, not by empty words.

16. Managing Diversity

⌘ A great many people think they are thinking when they are really rearranging their prejudices.
- William James ⌘

We do not live in a society with monolithic beliefs and practices. Businesses are experiencing the unstoppable force of increasing diversity and globalization. Diversity, the result of demographic and other realities describes the variety of people, information, markets and technologies that businesses must deal with today. These issues are by no means confined to the United States. This is part of growing and international trend. Diversity is created by history, culture, geography and life experience and can only be bridged by direct relationships. Businesses must be prepared to face the challenges presented by the increasing diversity and richness of today's workplace, multi-chromatic demographics and the internationalization of the marketplace and sources of supply. This entails the embrace of interdependence, pluralism and ensuing change including managing groups of people with diverse personalities. In order to avoid potential cultural clashes, one must be willing to make the effort to understand substantial differences in values, culture, sensibilities and vocabularies and between cultures and industries. It is essential to replace ideology and exclusivity with pragmatism and inclusiveness. While this was important before, it is more important now. It is important to be aware, understand and respect the cultural values and differences of others. Globalization has not homogenized cultures and the ability to adjust to a work force of mosaic cultures is essential and will be for some time to come. Leaders must bring cultural insights into decision-making, rid themselves of outdated prejudices, have access to a wider pool of talents and understand culture and diversity in order not to overlook entire groups of people. Such leadership requires skill in managing diversity of talents, personalities and creative forces. Moreover, diversity in the workplace often does good not only for the business, but for the leaders and people themselves. As Vernon Jordan, Jr., the eminent former CEO of the Urban League eloquently noted on the benefits of

122

diversity (Vernon Can Read, 2001): "Blacks in general were unaffected by the fact that a handful of black people were becoming corporate directors. The primary beneficiaries of this phenomenon were the white corporate directors themselves. Having a black presence in the boardroom was quite simply, an education for them. Many of the men had never in their lives come into any serious contact with black people, other than the ones who cleaned their houses."

As Nicholas Imparato and Oren Harari (Jumping the Curve, 1994) pointed out, "Diversity of ideas provokes creative conflict and innovative decision-making – both aimed at fulfilling a common goal." When diverse groups and individuals bring broader perspective into the picture, hold shared vision and values; there will be cohesion and control. The fault line that separate people on race and color is anathema to these values. Companies that lack diversity may become inbred, parochial and insular. Cognizance of cultural differences facilitates coalitions instead of collisions. On the other hand when an organization consists of people with different philosophies and conflicting agendas, diversity could lead to divisiveness.

People will always be motivated to give and return personal favors and allow friendship to influence decisions. We can change people's behavior but not the ingrained structures of their personalities. These grow out of inborn profiles of temperament, cultural traits and social gel. Nevertheless, here is a need for moral, legal and business rules that are accepted and governed all over the multinational economy. These include management of negative cultural forces. Contrast in motivation and performance appraisal exists in diverse cultures, both at home and abroad.

17. Managing Globalization

✻ Personally, I'm fond of strawberries. For some reason fish is fond of worms. So to catch fish I feed it worms instead of strawberries.

- Dale Carnegie ✻

US companies can no longer rely solely on the safe haven of the American domestic market. Instead, they must establish a global presence in order to demonstrate America's ability to compete in a global setting. The question is how can a company survive and prosper on the global stage? Global competitiveness should be a strategic goal. In order to enjoy co-prosperity global business participants must do more to contribute to financial, economic and political stability. This may require taking a new approach to deal with issues in consonant with current wave of global thinking. The pace of globalization today is faster and more sweeping than at any time in world history. This is a fact of international business, though it may seem clichéd. Business management and markets are no longer an American phenomenon. The wave of global integration is different from what the world has seen before. Globalization nullifies traditional comparative advantages and exposes US companies to rivals from around the world. These companies must deal effectively with global forces exerted by these global phenomena and find new ways to meet the challenge. Companies can benefit from various economic dimensions of globalization if they move aggressively to expand overseas operations and manage well in widely dispersed worldwide locations. Managers who are uninformed about global business will be at a great disadvantage.

Remember to periodically review the role of each subsidiary and plant in the global network and compare it with the evolving global strategy.

These are exciting times. The globalization of the economy is changing the rules of doing business, spawning numerous geographic and social challenges. Companies have different and often unique ways of doing things. Companies face fierce competition at home and abroad. Thus, globalization presents opportunities and threats. To a significant degree, even such progress has not kept pace with expanding globalization. There is growing entrepreneurism in foreign countries, contributing to increasing business complexity and diversity. Foreign competitions have made successful inroads into US markets as many foreign companies are becoming well versed in the capitalistic arts. Companies will be increasingly drawn to countries with large populations, stable governments and good purchasing power. Globalization subjects a company to varied set of opportunities and risks. It provides the opportunity to expand its horizon beyond the geographical boundaries within which it is currently operating. Technological advances during the past two decades have driven globalization to new dimensions with the increasing global influence of multinational corporations. An increasing number of companies are establishing R & D centers in various global locales. Many companies set up R & D centers overseas to take advantage of access to new knowledge and talents from foreign universities. This facilitates the grafting of best foreign systems and ideas. Companies can take advantage of national growth policies and entrepreneurship. The trend toward globalization has been accompanied by a trend toward regionalization. Such companies stay global in scope but regional in focus.

US global corporations with subsidiaries worldwide experience difficulties associated with operating in different cultures and competitive arenas. There are language barriers when venturing into foreign turf, even though English is recognized as an international language of business. We need people who can quickly grasp and adapt to different business environments in foreign lands and managers who can master opportunities on a wider scale are in demand. An understanding of nuances in operating and competing in the global marketplace, as well as knowledge of business and social norms in specific locales is becoming required competencies. To increase corporate wealth, companies must reduce friction between corporate centers and foreign subsidiary units by striking a delicate balance between local and global issues.

18. Improvement of Problem Solving, Decision Making and Persuasive Skills

⌘ As iron sharpens iron, so one man sharpens another.
- Proverbs 27:17 ⌘

Work as well as life itself is wrought with difficulties. Problems are becoming increasingly complex. Things happen every day that may put obstacles on the path to achieve success. As Peter Drucker asserted; Companies have to starve problems and feed opportunities. It is rare to have unanimity on many issues. People will disagree or have dissenting opinions but we must minimize negative energy. It is impossible to prevent mistakes but possible to fix mistakes.

Learn where to look for answers through critical thinking and gap analysis. When the problem is new we must think anew and act anew. Managers today have large amount of information available to them or situations may appear to be murky. There always exist potential hazard in drawing conclusion from superficial or insufficient data. It is easily tempted to dump diverse problems under oversimplified formula. An argument can appear to be compelling but still be wrong. Incorrect assumptions and distorted view of reality will eventually lead to wrong conclusions. Do not to view things as simply black-and-white; do not ignore the shades of gray that defines so many business problems. The world is replete with paradoxes and contradictions that we must face in our business decisions. It is critical to manage emotions that can muddy detail of an issue. Look at the facts objectively and understanding the context from which the problem arises. Vagueness may be useful in diplomacy but it is disastrous when trying to solve problems. A large proportion of time spent in problem solving should be devoted to identify and describe the problem with accuracy, clarity and with a broad perspective. The approach should be fact-based and analytical. It is essential to be able to pick out significant sound from background noise. While it is important to confront issues head-on and take the sting out of it, deferring judgment is an important guideline in generating ideas for problem solution. When you defer judgment, you create space for other people around you to voice their ideas. You also will be able to open up to ideas that you were not able to see before. An idea is not an action but a potential action to be taken later after the situation has been fully assessed. It is essential for leaders to develop the skill to handle difficult and seemingly impossible situation.

The obvious may often be overlooked. Listen to what is said and what is not said. Watch what is done and what is not done. Use textbook and gut solutions whenever appropriate. See things from different angles and with different lens. Acknowledge the negatives, but accentuate the positives. Inculcate problem solving with creative and rational approaches based on facts and information you can find including the practical aspect of data collection and interpretation. When you run into roadblocks, shine a light on them, making them clear and discernable; then knock down the roadblocks one by one. Also, remember to question the problems. New data may be uncovered that contain enough truth to require reconsideration of decisions already made. What we think is the problem might not actually be the problem at all. Always examine problems using varying perspectives. Avoid distractions; focus on concrete measurable facts. The more we understand about a problem, the better we are equipped to deal with it. One technique is to redefine a problem so that it can be solved. Better yet. Present the problem and make it interesting. Solutions that worked before may not work anymore. In order to solve complex problems one must exhibit humility, openness to new thoughts and a willingness to ask questions and accept the right answers, even if they are unfamiliar. Start by probing, asking tough questions and targeting trouble spots. Examine the cause(s) of the problems before dealing with its effects. Take all the information, deliberate, analyze, distill it into a coherent thought, make recommendations and finally fix the problem. All analysis is based on personal knowledge, experience, values and beliefs. Some people may already know what works and what doesn't. Consult them. There are things that you might have to judge now, things that can be deferred for later judgment and things that you need not judge at all. Sort out company problems based on their urgency and then work to fix them. Remember that coming up with a solution is not enough. You have to convince yourself before you try to convince others, that is, be sold on your own idea. You must also refine, sort and implement your ideas.

When confronting problems, some friction is inevitable, but not necessarily bad. Critics can sharpen the minds. People bicker but keep on coming back to the dinner table. At times, it is beneficial to stoke debates. A persuasive skill involves the ability to assure others that you have a good grasp of the issues, what could go wrong and are prepared to minimize the risks involved when taking a particular course of actions. Be prepared to find common ground or concede some points when diplomacy demands.

19. Managing Differences, Obstacles and Conflicts

⌘ You have not converted a man because you have silenced him.

- Lord John Morley ⌘

Barriers and competition between departments frequently lead to a lack of cooperation and distress. They contribute to an enormous drain on productivity and competitiveness. Make various departments collaborate and work harmoniously by lifting the steel curtain that has contributed to the compartmentalization of organizations. Cultivate a working environment where there is room for honest disagreement in which people can disagree agreeably. Though it is hard to do practice in actuality, critical comments should be taken in a friendly spirit. Disagreements arise when there are opposing perspectives and lack of well reasoned answers. Calmly till your own field than attack others. Avoid internal division, correct longstanding deficiencies and work for the good of the company by rebalancing the elements that are sources of discord. In his book – *The Passionate Organization*, 1999, James Lucas clearly noted: "Problems and opportunities can be viewed through the grid of the specialty. It is natural for a finance manager to essentially concentrate on financial activities. A financial perspective might lead to too much caution, while a marketing perspective might lead to too much risk." You will inevitably work with people you fundamentally disagree with. It's easier to say what went wrong than to prescribe solutions to the problems. Manage conflicts by better understanding interweaving human experiences, biases and values. During meeting, it is essential to take the lead in shaping the direction and contents of discussions positively. Shift the focus from personality and blame game to finding the real cause of the problems and provide solution. When emotions kick in, reasons exit. You can prevent trivial objections by coming straight to the point. Do not tie yourself in knots. It is essential to lay out the difficulties openly, provide lucid accounts of the issues and strive towards conciliatory solutions. Make it appropriate and easy for colleagues to understand. Anyone has the power to implement, delay or block a strategy. It is essential to include them in the process and obtain their acceptance. Facts make persuasive arguments. Address people's concerns and viewpoints by considering workable alternatives. Have an open but not empty mind. However, persisting in a course that defies reality will lead nowhere. It will only incur opposition and resistance by others. However discomforting, keep politics in the open where they can be seen and managed. A person's behavioral styles are strong determinants as to how that person will function, respond to motivation and fit in with the rest of the team. Act promptly to reestablish the equilibrium in response to developing conflicts before the problem becomes serious.

Obstacles are either internal or external or they may be interconnected. Internal obstacles include lack of cash, laziness, poor attitude, provocations and other emotional obstacles. External obstacles consist of lack of opportunities or luck.

Managers have an interventionist role to play by bridging the gulf whenever conflicts arise. This includes effective management of smart and strong-willed people. Be sensitive to the issues at a deeper level and recognize the undercurrent of disharmony. An important job of management is to recognize the interdependence of various components of a firm. The greater the interdependence between components, the greater will be the need for cooperation and communication between them. A manager must understand that all people are different, and thus, cannot be systematically ranked. Understand the significance of generational shifts and its impact on attitude and motivation. Three generations are working in today's organizations. They have experienced certain historical events unique to their specific generations.

Unify fiefdoms, curtail narrow-minded antiquated tendencies and encourage people to participate even if it is not in their personal interest. Recognize the constant undercurrents of disharmony and take remedial steps to address them. Employee indifference, lack of civility and disrespect are sources of conflict. Break gridlock whenever it occurs. Set objectives, communicate them swiftly to all employees and set out to achieve them. Enable constant high level of communication and coordination while allowing room for creativity. Create an environment that is not stifled with fear or poisoned with animosity. One's level of performance is largely governed by the system one works in; create a system that produces only the best.

B. Dollars

Please refer to Section 9.4 - Maintaining Superior Financial Management.

C. Time

1. Sense of Urgency and Propensity for Action

People who are astute at navigating in the fast lane staff highly successful enterprises. Such prolific people are wary of meandering academic analysis and possess an energy that produces results. They are driven by compulsion to strive for something worthy and to bolster the business. They have the tenacity and intensity that do not fade even with a long tenure. They are incisive and good at making progress within a much shorter timeframes, moving like a hare on adrenaline. There is self assurance and preponderance to continuously raise the bar to compete and to move with speed, if needed. There is fire in the belly.

At times, an organization may need a jolt. Swift actions may appear disruptive. You need to be nice and pleasant but also a sense of urgency to get the job done. People are bounded by time and feelings. Do not over analyze though it is important to correlate assumptions with factual evidence. Find a balance between speed and deliberation. Once you have carefully thought through a decision, stick to it, or up the ante. The business catchphrase "paralysis by analysis" exists for a reason: in order to remain competitive in a business environment that is constantly in flux, leaders must think and act quickly and decisively. They must multitask, using their time effectively and efficiently to achieve seemingly un-scalable heights in little time. Good leaders are a real force who is oriented for action. They understand that time is money and can provide real impact. Faster is not only better, but necessary to be ascendant. If problems are allowed to fester, they will become more pressing and more difficult to manage.

2. Cycle Time Compression

In order to maintain continuous leadership and corporate longevity, companies must mobilize employees to reduce the time it takes them to fully complete tasks. Otherwise, they will fall behind nimble and fast competitors. In a fast-moving business environment, quicker is invariably better. Indeed, this is a global trend. Therefore companies need fast learners. It increases corporate agility to do things that will have multiplier effect in achieving positive benefits for the company. Many companies are plagued by inefficiencies as they grow. Businesses must examine the total cycle time for every stage of any given operation, from top to bottom: marketing, design, manufacturing, quality, logistics, customer service, etc. To make this theory a reality requires availability of a banquet of data and understanding a plethora of detail. It includes not allowing unnecessary employees do unnecessary work and eliminate misalignment and congestion among various operations. Find out how you can markedly compress the cycle time while keeping the quality of the operation high and not sacrificing accuracy for brevity. Look at what can be shrunk or rearranged and make the appropriate changes, be it on the shop floor, in the offices and in the field. Long lead time required to produce goods necessitates skilled planning. Moving fast and moving smart should be of high prominence in every company. It is part of a winning formula. This is will be ever more serious, particularly for existing and emerging technology companies such as Google, Apple Computer, Intel, Dell and Tesla Motor, to name a few. Such companies must be quick to adapt to quick-changing technologies and markets. There may be no choice if companies want to be in business. As they say: "Early birds get the worms."

3. Time and Managing Time

⌘ I recommend that you take care of the minutes, for hours will take care of themselves.
- Lord Chesterfield ⌘

Time is a valuable asset. There are more work to do and less time to do it. In today's working environment of two working spouses and more demanding jobs, time is a scarce and irreplaceable commodity. Time will be a key factor in measurement of an organization's success. It becomes necessary to manage your time by balancing your life or for that matter managing your life by balancing your time. How well it is being used affects performance. Exploit time through the lens of business foresight to create strategic advantage. How we prioritize depends on urgency and importance of the matter. Know when and how to act. The key to time management is to accurately know how you or your employees are spending company asset. Determine pressing needs and activities that consume much of the time. Seek improvement for tasks that could be delegated or eliminated all together. Follow proven ways if they make sense. Set priorities for task assignments, as you cannot handle them all at once. We have to give an idea a significant amount of time to be nurtured and developed. Not enough time leads to impatience and corner cutting. Determine how performance of the tasks can be improved either by reducing amount of data required or improving efficiency of data gathering via utilization of information technology. Interruptions will always be part of a manager's life. Some interruptions are direct result of management style. An "open door" manager allows free access for interruptions. Poor communication is fundamentally a time waster. To save time, arrive at meetings well prepared. Long period of idle time, such as when traveling and waiting for appointment; are wasteful. Use this time to read or plan.

D. Knowledge and Information

In order to prosper, companies and employees must develop unquenchable thirst for knowledge and information. The economy is changing and a new workforce is needed to operate it. The financial market reflecting a broader trend, now value knowledge and information more than hard assets. This trend is already visibly underway, more so; as the time progressed. It represents the triumphs of increasing human interactions around the globe, due in large part to ever-improving information technology and communication. In the internet era, there is no shortage of knowledge, data and information. Access to information is unparalleled in history, boosted by a drop in the cost of information. It is critical for companies to find and manage new knowledge and info-nuggets and to extend knowledge range and capacity. Information empowers and energizes. Information is necessary to achieve a multidimensional view of business. It unlocks employee capabilities by broadening their awareness through access to knowledge and information. This may create a positive chain reaction to satisfy the insatiable curiosity of employees, resulting in the betterment of the company. It is important to access, interpret, translate and connect information to achieve useful purpose. It entails highly interactive communication at all levels, internally and externally, tying the parts with the future. To a great extent, companies of wide acclaim generally operate with openness, consistency and continuity. Employees who are knowledge and information deprived will not function with efficiency and effectiveness. Those who reflect ignorance or are trapped in gilded cages will not be respected by customers and colleagues.

1. Develop a Repository of Resources and a Clearing House of Information

For growth and prosperity to be sustained, a company should be at the forefront to develop and amass a repository of expertise that can be tapped as needed. This is vanguard thinking and practice for dynamic and progressive companies. Information is the mighty river of resources resulting from many tiny streams across the organizations that finally merge. Companies can take advantage of these resources by drawing from the same well, rather than learning the lessons the hard way. Companies must find ways to acquire and replenish their resources, in terms of volume and value, in order to further future advancement. Larger companies can grow talents by setting up "university" where employees learn business, technical and interpersonal skills that are important. The "university" can also be a magnet for talents.

For example, businesses should keep their network of contacts updated, business and technical literatures available, adding to them whenever possible. Similarly, they should keep their equipment in good shape and up-to-date, and their employees well trained and subject to periodic evaluation. By cultivating and building these resources and in enabling worldwide accessibility, companies will inevitably expand their capabilities to confidently face the challenges ahead. Employees can do well by being able to search for every piece of silk and satin in the shop. Over the long haul, these efforts will create gems, paying rich dividends.

2. Collaboration with Universities

The challenges companies face today require multilateral answers. Companies must be creative in utilizing resources from all quarters. Studies and research from academia when combined with practical experience broaden the spectrum of knowledge to a far greater degree and be powerful. This interaction is one of the most important springboard but least heralded, though it has assumed greater validity in recent times. Though it may represent a small fraction of a company's activities, partnering with universities creates a symbiotic relationship in which both parties will benefit immeasurably, in tangible and intangible ways. This can be done through well planted seeds via internship, apprenticeships, curriculum development and networking with researchers around the world. Collaboration with universities provides companies visibility and in-depth knowledge for rich sources of employees and materials. It is low cost with broad appeal. Moreover, it creates an additional platform to drive the research agenda. Universities in the San Francisco Bay area such as Stanford, UC Berkeley and others are credited with influencing the growth of Silicon Valley. The collaborations are fed by a confluence of economic opportunities and benefits. For universities, collaboration with companies allows their students to stay ahead of the learning curve by first-hand experience and adaptation to the changing needs of industries. Also, curricula can be updated with a suite of educational courses to reflect actual practices in the industry.

3. Knowledge and Information Management

Knowledge is an economic resource and its value must be recognized. Therefore, companies must devote a considerable amount of attention to identifying, evaluating, building, managing and leveraging their knowledge base. More and more companies are utilizing feed from various sources of information to gain better understanding of the business and competitors. Knowledge that was important for one generation may cease to be important for another generation. Knowledge needs to be utilized for beneficial purpose, lest it becomes obsolete over time.

Because there exists a new social mobility in the workforce, upward mobility is potentially unlimited for knowledgeable workers. Competitive bidding for knowledge workers is not uncommon. People change careers, homes, etc. with increasing frequency. Old employee retention systems and the ways of old guard managers can no longer be relied on. Employees, especially executive, knowledge workers expect an expanded role in which they share financially in the fruits of their labor. Reengineering and downsizing has eroded worker's loyalty. They are taught to look out for themselves. Nowadays, companies sack people without serious consideration of core knowledge exiting the company. Restructuring, employee departure or retirement usually result in loss of a pool of knowledge in some functional areas, resulting in information deficit. Companies need thick layers of talented managers who are unshackled to respond effectively to these challenges.

Successful companies are replete with useful information and knowledge. Information and knowledge will have powerful impact when used with wisdom and passion. These are the operating norm for these companies. However, one has to be mindful of the fact that there is a significant degree of uncertainty about the validity of information. Managers need to learn to manage a barrage of information and make it useful instead of being dictated by it. It is essential to know how to handle confidential and sensitive information with discretion.

4. Open Communication, Network and Access to Information

Good managers are, first and foremost, good communicators. They must astutely manage a gold mine of information so that employees in the organization have the necessary data to perform their jobs well. Manager must also filter out clutter and prevent it from stultifying the flow of useful information. Without accurate and necessary information companies will be at the risk of being blind-sided by unpleasant surprises. Knowledge should move horizontally instead of hierarchically so that the right people have deep and immediate access to the right information. Long distance communications do not replace face-to-face relationships.

Knowledge is power, and today, we have more of it than ever before. Technology has connected people into an electronic global village. Assure that knowledge flows freely, for purposeful, organized and systematic information must be diffused as swiftly as possible if the company is to make the right and timely decision. Leverage the power of knowledge by spreading it across the company, taking care to avoid misinformation. Be sure that available information is a current as possible. Assure that appropriate managerial and technical jargons are used so as not to undermine clarity in communication. The desire to inform must be sincere. Instill values of sharing so that valuable ideas and experiences become a collective base of information. Teach employees how to read their balance sheets and income statements to demonstrate how they are connected with their performance.

Develop open and on-going communication with customers, employees and the investment community. Communication fails when the lines of communication are slow, too long or too fuzzy. Cultural issues associated with sub-par implementation must be overcome. In international business, solutions from distant bureaucracies must be minimized. Localize solutions. As channels of communication are globe-spanning and instantly interactive, people must be sensitive and use good judgment when communicating. Apply alternative avenues of communication, where appropriate. For example, most people hate negative feedback and do not like to give it, but employees may end up receiving the information extrinsically rather than directly from the organization. Do not just give lip service but act on what you say. Let employees know that you value their ideas. Reaffirm through words and actions, the company's commitment for open communication at all levels. Promote an open and dynamic organization where employees learn from the past and focus on the promise of the future. Encourage diversity of thought and support anyone who has a good idea to speak up, anyone who has a question to ask it without fear of retribution. Instill a work culture in which information is shared rather than hoarded. Many bosses are so busy playing golf and so involved in long range planning that they are out of touch with their people and customers. Reach out to obtain the unvarnished truth about what is going on at every level of the organization. Every time information passes a person, it morphs a little. Actively listen to employees while giving them the guidance and direction to do their jobs well. Facilitate, teach and reinforce values. Keep in touch with customers and suppliers. Quality communication between and among people can be the lasting glue that holds an organization together. Assure that the right message is conveyed and that those who receive it are receptive to its content. A large part of a manager's work is to provide information, know-how and guidance to the group under his influence. Developing and encouraging team members require lack of prejudice and sophistication in communication and listening skills.

The work environment should be conducive to teamwork and multilaterally-reinforcing. This is encouraged by candid and comprehensive useful information sharing.

5. Information Filtration, Information Access

A business is nothing without vital information, which, when channeled correctly and efficiently, can translate into productive actions. Unfortunately, many companies are obstructed by faulty information filtration. Sometimes substantive and illuminating information is filtered out or not forthcoming. Some leaders are ill informed, receive incomplete information or are shielded from the truth. The information may be unreliable or the misinformation is deliberate. Often times, information must go through numerous tiers before reaching the right person. This can be both intentional and unintentional. A self-serving and ambitious employee may want to retain valuable information for him or herself, thereby hindering information flow, or bureaucratic layers might prevent information from traveling directly to the right people. There may be other motives and personal agendas. There need to be established and enforced, behaviors that are acceptable and those that are not. Poor information flow would not produce the kinds of decisions on where to focus and shift resources to areas of greatest need. This will inflict grievous damage to a company. It is essential to distinguish noise from information, truth from fiction. Get people to open up. We need advocates to foster candid discussions and bring information to the forefront. People can learn from criticism even when they are not persuaded by them.

When you cannot obtain the information you need from your employees, you need to turn to outside sources for help. In any case, layers must be reduced so that the right people have access to potentially balance and high quality information. Counter information filtration or blockage through redundancy – ensure that important information travels through channels repeatedly. Moreover, establish a business culture in which information is openly shared and accessible, where candor is the norm. It is a monumental task to determine how well knowledge is producing value in the corporate process.

9.3 System, Accountability, Commitment and Responsiveness

The goal is to have a better control of the future of the company and to respond effectively to the ebb and flow of business cycles but not budging on fundamentals. Realign functions to assure people are made accountable for both failures and successes. Managers must be responsible for all final decisions: talented ones will deftly balance conflicting demands.

There must also be whole-hearted commitment to make deep-seated changes, whenever necessary. Commitment should be considered as essential virtue and indicates the seriousness of the agent. If the entire company demonstrates real commitment to a common goal, it will be united in a powerful way – it will be able to move mountains. On the other hand, without commitment from its employees, a business will flounder, never accomplishing its big-idea goals. Remember that people who lack confidence or motivation will likely show low commitment. Ensure that employees feel they are part of a team working for a larger goal. Higher job satisfaction will lead to correspondingly higher levels of commitment. Commitment both values the valuable and makes the committed invaluable.

The corporate office should act as an enabler rather than obstructionist by cultivating and maintaining the entrepreneurial fervor among its managers. It should initiate programs, play a clear role in overcoming problems, remove roadblocks, effectively execute its goals and accelerate the payoff. In many corporations, the majority of people are not speaking because they feel that they cannot or have not been asked. Increase your employees' awareness of the need for responsiveness.

A. System

1. Superior Organizational Processes and Capabilities

The business environment is rough. Without sound management, organization becomes chaotic. An organization consists of a collection of linked processes that are multifaceted and subtle. These linked processes begin from product concept and proceed to market launch, receipt of order, order fulfillment and payment. Most processes encompass integration of multiple technologies ranging from microprocessors, communication, wafer, packaging, power, etc. These processes are getting more and more complicated, especially when organizations grow in size, strength and tradition. In coordinating the activities of a complex process, jurisdiction boundaries may have to be crossed. Competitive survival demands that projects and studies be viewed from every angle and hard questions be asked. It involves judicious combination of the tested and the untested and the exercise of flexibility and control. The power of superior organizational processes and consistent practices are recognized to deliver value to the customers year after year. It is a logical outgrowth of processes that are capable of learning and continuous improvement, free from the limits of preconceptions. There is an importance in the interplay of ideas in an environment fostered with energizing systems and structures. Review all practices at every level and identify activities that do not add value to the process. There should be no sacred cow, no activity that does not add value.

Managers must grapple with the critical question of aligning the department's activities to the organization's direction. Eliminate redundant paperwork and excessive expediting. Make work and processes useful instead of mere pointless tasks. In his book, *Firing Back* (Harvard Business Review Press, 2007), Jeffrey Sonnenfeld and Andrew Ward noted on the Greek mythology on the extreme form of punishment inflicted by the gods upon the character Sisyphus was the condemnation to a daily shear pointless task of rolling a boulder to the top of the mountain, only to see it roll back down again. He further asserted that it was thought there would be no worse human torture than futile, hopeless labor.

The organization would not be able to implement effective business strategies without the process and capabilities to do so. Effectiveness is the foundation for success; efficiency is a minimum condition for survival after success is achieved. Capabilities are the glue that brings corporate assets together and deploy them advantageously to accomplish desired results. Capabilities take time to build and cannot be readily imitated. Organizations must provide fertile ground for ideas. Fountain of ideas propels a firm ahead of the curve.

Business processes need to integrate and improve the supply chain from supplier management, incoming logistics, work-in-process, outbound logistics and customer fulfillment. Identify processes that are moving at glacial pace, find out why and accelerate the processes. Doing so will minimize the time between an order and delivery.

2. Superior Situation Management

❦ You'll never understand the true meaning of a businessman's statements unless you have a firm grasp of the events of the period and see exactly what kind of situation his company was facing. Fragments taken out of context can come to mean something completely different from what was intended.

- Takeo Fujisawa ❦

Organizations are shaped differently for different kinds of business, different people and different cultures. Leaders and managers must differentiate between the changeable and the unchangeable. A general prescription cannot be applied, as each firm's circumstances are different. It requires a virtuoso demonstration of the ability to apply varying managerial prescriptions to different sets of problems. The passion that builds value has to be based on reality and is able to withstand the test of time. Solutions differ by industry and enterprise. Steven Covey (The 8th Discipline, 2004 puts it this way; "We live in a knowledge worker age but operates our organizations in a controlling Industrial Age model that absolutely suppresses the release of human potential." Adapt leadership style to the situation. Solutions must be modified to fit various real-world situations rather than black and white rigidities. One should not be overly focused on process over substance. Instill a fresh perspective to challenge the norm and develop a new and better approach to turn opportunities into successes. In business, planning, experimenting, testing and adjusting should be a routine. Circumstances change; you must constantly learn and improve, change accordingly, and challenge prevailing beliefs. Look through a prism and see things in new ways under varying scenarios. Give ideas time to simmer. Decisions can be improved by better understanding of apparent paradox and contradictions. Some situations, for example, call for transformational leaders rather than power-based or charismatic leaders. Determine what kind of situation your business is in, and respond appropriately. You have seen the same situations so many times in your life or career that you know what is going on without the data or deep thinking. There are times when one may not resolved the difficulties at hand but can regain the initiatives at later stage.

3. Adapt, Do Not Adopt

How do we replicate excellent practices of successful organizations into our own? Information and knowledge come in all shapes, sizes and styles. Circumstances vary widely. Sort out the successful from the unsuccessful. Look at what is working and move fast to emulate the best, adjusting and adapting new organizational features to local conditions, making them uniquely effective.

Change should be made before a desperate situation occurs; continually look for ways to improve your business instead of waiting until the environment demands it. If you see a good idea, adapt it to your own needs. With an abiding commitment to excellence; institute diligent and relentless concentration on the mastery of technology, marketing and production. Learning the success and failures of others drives the process of benchmarking.

However, one must be aware that what worked at one place may not entirely work at another. Blindly mimicking the practices of others without adaptation makes no sense. Learn from others and fit their practices into your situation, making any necessary changes for a better fit. As part of continuous improvement, institute ongoing comparative analysis. Borrow a lot of ideas and to further improve upon them.

4. Gratitude and Loyalty

⌘ **If you expect the employee to take care of your company, you must take care of your employee.** ⌘

Though loyalty remains a prized attribute, it can be fleeting, especially in today's business environment. Work has become unstable. Employees are often treated as costs rather than assets. The spate of corporate downsizing and reengineering has stripped away much of the vestiges of employment security. It is like Kings and Queens of old, blithely discarding unwanted retainers whose past achievements and contributions have been forgotten. It has diminished capability and the willingness to work in harmony. Cynical employees quickly lose their sense of loyalty.

A leader has to know who his true friends are. Know your true friends watch your adversaries. Companies need to institute programs that encourage ties that bind, rewarding loyalty and performance. Loyalty must be earned and some leaders are good at doing that. Take care of your people. Strengthen loyal and endearing part of the team while there should be a realization that loyalty is different from fealty. You owe it to your loyal employees to provide them training to upgrade their skills to keep up with technological advances. There will be strong work ethic and loyalty among employees when leaders are caring. Loyalty is a two-ways street and is often misunderstood. There may be one-sided notion of loyalty. Celebrate hard work and steadfast loyalty while recognizing the importance of differentiating the positive against the negative aspect, for example, loyalty among thieves.

Like all things in life, however, there must be a balance. Lifetime employment is one extreme end of loyalty, while constant turnover represents the other. Layoffs are more likely to occur in a slowing economy. Layoffs should be a last resort when all remedial measures failed. Workers must be flexible, while knowing the company and its long-term vision. Clearly, there will be exceptions: for example, every company has at least one uniquely talented employee who continually reinvents himself, bringing both seasoned knowledge and fresh ideas to the table. When you find such exceptions, make sure to keep him/her. Remember that a positive work environment, challenging and satisfying work and fair compensation go a long way toward cementing an employee's loyalty.

5. Balance and Moderation

There are times that call for a command and control mentality and even taking draconian measure. But other situations may require openness, self consciousness and moderation. Use the right leadership style at the right time – allow for the right fit. In times of high pressure or stress, for example, try to lessen negative energy by reestablishing basic values. At other times, balance speed of actions with broader based acceptance of decision based on information that is rich in texture and detail. On the other hand, when business seems to be running smoothly, do not allow employees to rest on their laurels, taking good fortune for granted. Success can be intoxicating and seductive. One needs to balance decision from the heart with decision from the head. Reformulate, recalibrate and make reality check to value assessment.

The tenet of balance and moderation applies not only to leadership style, but to other areas of business management as well. Remember to strike a similar balance in terms of compensation, cultural standpoints, interactions with others and customer service. Balance judiciously the pull between the forces of tradition and transformation. In essence, adjust the current style and tempo of any business situation or issue to properly fit the occasion.

6. Celebration

⌘ I can live for two months on a good compliment.
- Mark Twain ⌘

There are endless possibilities and ways to inspire customers and staff. There are also ways to breathe life into the moribund. In today's hectic environment, employees often feel under-appreciated. Work environment can reach a point of being dull and uninspiring. Employees must be treated exactly as you would like to treat your customers. Find joy in working toward endeavors; be proud of your successes and share ideas about business success with others. Inspire people with new energy. A leader's mood and actions impacts the people he leads. Bring out confidence by celebrating success with aplomb and grace. People crave to know about extraordinary achievers and what they have achieved. Use a variety of methods to celebrate success such as having meals together, recognition during meetings, public endorsement, congratulations and notes, passing out coffee cups with company logo and text, etc. The team that fields the best players wins. Winning is a cause and provides a wonderful opportunity for celebrating. The audience applauds after a great singer leaves the stage or when runners reach the finish line. Celebration is a great way to recognize and encourage achievement and imagination. It is important to note that winning is a process, not an event.

It is essential to avoid common problems of recognition and awards that de-motivate those who do not win them. Share credit with the team rather than taking full credit for your own. Accept and celebrate ideas by making them visible, publishing them and putting them on-line (Jeffrey Krames, 2002). Celebrations are opportunities to reinforce company goals by highlighting achievement of objectives. It can be a new impetus that helps set direction for the future. They also communicate to employees precisely what kind of accomplishments the firm is looking for.

B. Accountability

Discipline and Integration

⌘ Management is people, tasks, discipline and responsibilities.

- Peter Drucker ⌘

Corporate success requires a marriage between entrepreneurial creativity and corporate discipline. Organizational activities, particularly those of large corporations may be disjointed and at times may be at loggerheads. People who can forge collaborations across programs and departments are in high demand today. Organizations at large need employees who can integrate functions by weaving the disparate pieces together so that they are seamlessly connected. Do not allow your company to become fragmented – the left hand must know what the right is doing. It is important to note though that discipline and reason transmits, routinizes, normalize; it does not create. Thriving organizations must make concerted efforts to supplement, complement and enhance each other using interdisciplinary approach. It would be marvelous if these are done with spontaneity, sincerity and without supervision. This is possible if the goals of employees are congruent with those of the enterprise coupled with an alchemic convergence of a variety of strengths, that goals are based on solid projections rather than on wishful thinking. It is further strengthened when the reward system are aligned with stated value system of the enterprise. Organizations that are compartmentalized and not interactive will lack the staying power of success. These organizations are ill-prepared and poorly coordinated to deal with the frenetic pace of business today and tomorrow. It is an indisputable fact that dynamic achieving companies are built with sweat and discipline,

C. Commitment

Customer and Quality Orientation

> ⌘ Obviously everyone wants to be successful, but I want to be look back on as being very innovative, very trusted and ethical and ultimately making a big difference in the world.
>
> - Sergey Brin ⌘

Five key business and customer values are cost, quality, convenience, speed and innovation. According to Drucker's dictum, the purpose of business is to create customers. How high is quality and customer satisfaction in your agenda? The point is clear. Customer satisfaction should be regarded as a company's highest priority. Customers today are much more exposed to the world, well informed and knowledgeable, resulting in higher expectations for quality and service. The customers decide what is important. Generally, customers have a lot of options and therefore they rule. If your company cannot meet the needs of your customers, others will. The foundation of business is sustaining client loyalty and retention. It means managing the business for zero defection, staying connected with customers and providing excellent customer service across all channels. It means making it

154

easier for customers to do business with you, ensuring high quality, demonstrating genuine respect and sensitivity to the needs and frustrations of customers. It means moving from lip service to real service. Customers are more careful because major purchase decisions that turn out badly can be job threatening. Customer loyalty is becoming a precious commodity. Customers want as little hassle as possible. They want to count on receiving products or services orders within the promised time frame. Keep your word. Be sensitive to customer impatience with "stock-outs" and "backorders." Many companies spend millions of dollars on customer relational management (CRM) software that is often negated by the rudeness and impatience of their people in direct contact with customers. Do not view customers as problems to be manipulated, serve them with kindness and respect. If customers talk to you more, they will be talking to your competitors less.

Think globally, but act locally. Learn to see your company the way your customers do. Exceptional customer service comes not only from superior products and services, but also from the skills and attitudes of personnel who interact with customers. Treat your employees well and fairly. You can't treat your employees poorly and expect them to treat your customers well.

Customer behavior is complex. Customers prefer simple and easy decision-making and interactions. Communication is inextricably linked to the quality of its process. Some customers like to use email, others would rather use the phone and still others prefer the web. Some prefer a person to call on them and others prefer in-store purchase or browsing catalogs. Customers may not provide clear information about their needs especially their needs in the future.

Actively study customers and put your customers' interest at the forefront. Remember that employees win only if the company and customers win. If the company and customers lose, we lose. Customers often influence other customers. Winning requires customer respect and intimacy. Whenever there are defections, find out not only where defectors go, but also why they defect. In order to prevent such defection, your business must offer something that the customer perceives to be of value including but not limited to customer expectation of flawless experiences. It takes stellar customer service to hold market share. Go above and beyond in assistance to clients. A service that is efficient but lacking in warmth is not good enough. The importance of follow-through must be emphasized. To win business loyalty, businesses must satisfy the customer repeatedly, just as loyal fans are the key in a sports team's enduring success. It is reinforced by a reward system that rewards employees that go the extra mile for customers. Customers are the real reason any business exists. Teaming up with customers is good business. Take exceptional care of your customers through superior customer service, superior quality and speedy responses. Remember that in this day and age, speed is highly valued, and is often equated with quality service. Companies must also learn to manage customer lifetime value, instead of attempting to make a profit on each and every transaction. As it was once said: Do not treat customers like dogs, giving them what you want them to eat. Do not sell customers just on your own solution but assist customers in selecting solutions that fit customer needs. Customers are primarily interested in the value we deliver. Be courteous and listen to them.

As Barbara Bund (The Outside-In Corporation, 2006) noted; "The discipline calls for customer pictures, not lists. Lists don't make clear which aspects of customer needs and behaviors are especially important. They don't make customers come alive." Customer service personnel need to do more to demonstrate more than mere ability to take orders. There should be no room for arrogance, any behavior that might alienate customers. The first goal is to prevent problems and the next is to quickly resolve problems whenever they occur. Customers expect quick response when there are mistakes or lapses in service. Quick response and follow-through are possible when people are empowered to make decisions and are motivated to solve problems. High employee satisfaction will lead to high quality service. Contempt for customers for whatever reason is one of the biggest barriers to superior performance. Exhibit genuine interest in people and always be friendly. However, at times, courtesy alone is not enough if there is no solution to customer problems. Courtesy must be paired with high level of product knowledge and the ability to accomplish what the customer expects in a single call is essential. Build an integrated approach with attention to detail, incorporating competitive benchmarking evaluation in an interactive process with team members and customers.

In his book "Solid Gold Success Strategies for your Business," sales executive and author Don Taylor listed ten good questions for self-query prior to positioning or reposition one's business:

1. Who are your customers? How can you describe them? Can you divide them into groups or classes?

2. How much do you know about them? Do you know where they live, their lifestyles, their buying habits and their personal tastes?
3. Do you know your customer batting average? You can calculate it by dividing the number of customers who make purchases from you by the total number of customers who come into your business.
4. Do you know what your customers think about your business? If you don't know, ask them.
5. What do your customers think about your competitors? How can you find out? All you have to do is ask them.
6. Do you know who your ten best customers are? How about the top twenty-five? The top one hundred?
7. Have you personally had contact with your top ten or twenty customers in the past month? In the past three months?
8. Do you make it easy for your customers to complain to you?
9. Do you have a follow-up program for ex-customers?
10. Do you know what is going on in your industry?

The plain fact remains that consumer perception about affordable quality and reliability does influence sales. It is essential to know what the terms quality and service mean to different customers in specific situations. Poor quality is bad for business. Customers who have experienced bad quality will not return and will bad-mouth the company. The bitterness of a lack of quality remains long after the sweetness of quality is gone. As Carl Sewell and Paul Brown (Customer for Life, 1998) said: "Yes, everybody wants a good deal. But price is rarely the sole reason customers decide to buy. After you have been to a restaurant, you don't remember exactly what a hamburger costs. You only remember whether you like it or not. Quality is essential in all functions of a business, not just manufacturing. It involves inculcating a quality culture and value system throughout the organization that includes providing quality output to internal and external customers. Claims of quality, without definition are meaningless. Quality is determined by top management and cannot be delegated. Quality personnel should not be regarded as policemen, but as business supporters. There should be a renewed focus on quality of product and services. Quality is dependent on what happens in sales, marketing, design, engineering, manufacturing, maintenance, supervision, operators, customer service, suppliers and so on. In Deming's word, a product or a service possesses quality if it helps somebody and enjoys a good and sustainable market. There is a direct correlation between quality and market share. Moreover, quality eliminates costly rework. According to Siemens quality motto; Quality is when our customers come back and our products don't.

It is no mystery that customer and quality-oriented powerhouses thrive.

D. Responsiveness

Quick Response to Changes

⌘ To reach the port of heaven, we must sail sometimes with the wind and sometimes against it, but we must sail, and not drift, nor lie at anchor.
- Oliver Wendell Holmes ⌘

Companies must be prepared to modify business principles in response to changes in the marketplace. The days of constant, predictable business environment is gone. The only sustainable competitive advantage lies in an ability to learn and change faster than your competitors. The ability to sense change ahead of everyone else is developed on the basis of a finely tuned antenna. It is easy to romanticize the past and demonize the present. There are times when we need to scrub away conventional wisdom and come up with new thinking. Old habits must be replaced with new habits. Nimble business can outsmart the Goliaths. Changes create new exposures and new opportunities. There has to be a sense of urgency. If you face the truth you can begin to change them. All change activities are linked to knowledge of better practices. Changes should be an outgrowth of a strategic planning process, well defined and committed. In order to perform well year after year, firms much inculcate a capacity to change and upgrade to sustain increasing scope of activities as the companies grow. Flexibility and sense of urgency enhance quick response capability. Understand the scope of transformation in business and adopt new core competencies to navigate through the twenty first century. There has to be creative movement at frequent intervals with the ability to establish a rapid action workforce to operate in the fast lane. Our corporations need to change as civilization is changing. Markets change, products become obsolete and new technologies develop. Companies need to change from the force of habit, or they disappear. This is one of the pitfalls that plague many companies. Change is a constant and opportunities that come with change must be exploited. The ability to change is a competitive advantage. However, we need to recognize that people cannot handle too many changes at once. The changes should be anticipated and designed to preempt resistance. Encourage change process as a positive experience to be understood and embraced instead of a negative experience to be avoided. Discuss how past change efforts have succeeded or failed and lessons learned. Existing managers and personnel may be set on certain approaches in their work and are immune to changes that may be necessary. In such circumstances, it may be necessary to upgrade/change managers, people and processes in order to reach the next level of excellence. Companies may purposely abandon traditional ways of doing business by starting over from scratch rather than incremental change.

There may be certain validity as to the reasons why people resist change. There is a tendency for people to be frustrated when they challenge the status quo.
This and other reasons need to be addressed.

A combination of forces may cause fundamental changes in strategy. How does a newspaper publisher cope with the velocity of change in an information age when news is freely available in the internet and the advertisers have multiple channels to disseminate their messages? How do companies compete under conditions of open trade and deregulation? Be a step ahead of change by monitoring the competitors' websites, economic trends and communicating all over the company.

Speed is critical in today's competitive global marketplace, though speed leaves little margin for error. However, one must distinguish between haste and speed. Haste characterizes spontaneous and inadequate planning whereas thorough preparation enables speed. Rules may change just as companies are becoming good at the game. We have to learn to differentiate between the 90 percent of the time that we need to move fast and the 10 percent when moving slowly is crucial and speed kills (James Lucas, 1999). In other words, there are times when things have to be placed in the back burner and let it simmer for a while. Inculcate agility, flexibility, attentiveness and rapid response to changes. Develop humming bird's agility in response to changes in business, economic and technological conditions. Revitalize the entrepreneurial spirit that governs a nimble company though one should strike a balance between un-encumbering the business and being reckless. Set up a loose structure, anti-bureaucratic and small team culture with a new twist. Customer wants, expectations and demands continually change with changes in socio-economic and market conditions. Companies that are ahead of the curve and are able to respond with lightning speed to ever-changing market conditions will reap the benefits of first movers and be a step or more ahead of competition.

Managers who remain unmoved and are ill prepared to cope with complexity of changes will be frustrated. New maps may be needed to chart the course through stormy seas of change. Once you encourage employees to embrace change, you must demonstrate that their inputs will have a real impact on the way your company does business.

9.4 <u>Maintaining Superior Financial Management</u>

⌘ No one would remember the Good Samaritan if he's only had good intentions – he had money too.
- Margaret Thatcher ⌘

The central tenet of business is sustaining profitability and growth. In order to sustain prosperity, all companies must be disciplined, strong and well funded Superior financial management is an essential cog in the wheel of commerce and provides a strong foundation for wealth building. It is the raison d'être of business enterprises. It is an unquestionable fact that sustaining on-going prosperity requires leaders who are literate with numbers, understand the intricacies of financial management and competent in their field. It is essential to be numbers-driven with accurate accounting and financial records. Yet, companies are blind-sided by financial mismanagement through errors of omission or commission. This is particularly important in an era of vast credit expansion and immense flow of risky financing. Oftentimes, limelight shone where a searchlight should have. Anyone can achieve a goal through redefinition of terms, distortion and cost overrun. Superior financial management, on the other hand, lubricates a profit-generating engine and organization qualities to power corporate growth. The most important managerial step is to exercise stringent financial control and discipline whilst unlocking the value to do great things. This means a good control of the purse string and having the ability to close the books within a week. Superior financial management has a firm grip on the rate of new production introduction, supports expansion of market share and controls advertising, selling costs and gross margin. While innovation, marketing and customer service, etc. are important, profitability is still key to a company's existence. Companies cannot sustain profit growth without revenue growth. To be continuously successful, companies must be well poised financially and achieve a previously unattained level of accuracy in financial accounting, reconciling the new arithmetic. Companies must develop budgetary strategy that will handle disappointment. Decreasing financial volatility and vulnerability greatly reduces risk.

While companies should focus on building considerable fortune, they should be mindful of the fact that stellar balance sheet makes great acquisition targets. Acquirers can leverage the targets balance sheet to finance the purchase.

1. Critical Financial Performance Factors

⌘ **It's easier to predict the actions of an institution than an individual.**

- Mike Johnston ⌘

Financial proposals must have high credibility in order to be translated into action. You need a long-term financial strategy, but you also need to make it through the next quarter successfully to survive. Watch out constantly for cash flow, cash position, cost, expense, inventory movement, payables and recovery of receivables. Revenues and profits are a good way to keep score in business. For a firm to operate in the long run, it must attain an acceptable level of profits. Sales get you in business; profits keep you there. Increased revenues lead to increased cash flow and profits that in turn drives growth. By any calculation, firms that improve productivity increase profitability. The best way to increase profitability is to eliminate unnecessary costs. However, one must be cautious when focusing on cost reduction as it may lead to downsizing without improving organizational effectiveness. Keeping an eye on cash flow also ensures long-term success. Cash flow is actual movement of cash inflows and outflows. Cash gives company flexibility in doing business. You can lie about profits but you cannot make up cash. It is essential for corporations to maintain a substantial cash level in order to sustain sound performance. During periods of growth, capital expenditures such as equipment purchases, facility constructions and increase material purchases and accounts payable become cash drainers. As demands falter, cash to finance these expenditures falls short. Watch out for clear sign of slippage. Keep balance accounts payable with accounts that are receivable. Reduce time in collecting receivables. Reduce time in collecting receivables. Remain on the alert to prevent miscalculations or errors in accounting that could lead to disastrous consequences. Punctuality in reporting indicators and operating results contribute to effective decisions.

2. Strategic Financial Performance Factors

⌘ Entrepreneurship and credit creation are the wellspring of economic growth.
- Joseph Schumpeter ⌘

Protect and expand the gross margins of your business by leveraging existing assets, infrastructure and strengths. High profit margins and earnings growth inevitably attract competition. While expanding gross margins is essential, one must also recognize that turnover is equally important as actual profit is profit margin multiplied by inventory turnover. A higher sale to assets ratio demonstrates an efficient and effective deployment of assets. Return on asset (ROA) represents the net income relative to its asset such as buildings, trucks, computers etc. It requires discipline to maintain reasonable cost of capital and debts. Efficient financial management includes unlocking and redeploying underlying corporate value for better returns. If there is no synergy in the portfolio of assets you need to split them up. It is interesting to know how companies count the number of employees. Revenues per employee can be distorted by not counting consultants and temporary staffs.

Today, the new knowledge based economy has shifted value activities from tangibles to the intangibles. Asset value, sales and market share can be increased by sound investment in product development, developing a profitable and loyal customer base or establishing an integrated supply chain activities to provide customers with faster, better quality and lower cost products and services. The average selling price of products and average cost of products provide insight to profitability trends. A traditional accounting system does not fully and accurately record intangibles such as valuation on the market side, product development output, successful and unsuccessful execution of a new strategy, etc. The value of intangible assets (e.g. market perception, goodwill) is dependent on broader external factors that are not under full management control. Accounting must provide more and complete information on intangibles. As Baruch Lev, Professor of Finance and Accounting at the New York University Stern School of Business suggests: Investment in research and development should be capitalized once the probability of success is proven to be significantly increased; e.g. by a successful beta test (hardware/software) or a successful clinical trial (biotechnology/pharmaceutical). The capitalized investment should be reviewed periodically and adjusted upward or downward, based on whether the outlook is better or worse."

3. Deciding How Much to Invest and When to Cut Losses

⌘ We cannot eat the fruits while the tree is in blossom.
- Benjamin Disraeli ⌘

In business as in life itself, there is a deep vein of opportunities waiting to be mined. In order to reap the benefits from these opportunities, companies must be willing to invest and take sizable but calculated financial risks. Some investments will make it, others will not or with mixed success. Therefore, companies must have an exit strategy and should be ready to decisively and promptly move away from investments when forecasts reveal limited short and long-term prospects. It is wise to prepare for victory and for contingencies. While high-flying companies must assume the burden of paying for high cost for investments, they must be on guard against unbridled growth, reckless investments and be ready to take prompt and decisive actions when expected results are off the mark. For investments to be viable, companies must translate inventiveness and good ideas into commercial success through adequate financial backing and planning. Prudent investors should be rewarded for their insights when their investments start to foliate. Ignorant and irrelevant research must be curtailed decisively after patient consideration. Investments, however well calculated may be fraught with potential losses or unrealized expected returns. Financial and economic projections may be reasonable but sometimes they may be just prayers and hopes. Trust the data but also trust your instinct. Lofty claims must be examined and reexamined. Investors don't like surprises. Balance safety of investments against potential returns with healthy skepticism. Challenge the original assumptions based upon which the investment was initiated. The conclusion after extensive research shows that companies may tend to spend lavishly on mistaken ventures simply because the money is there.

On the other hand, companies must be careful not to suffer from premature abandonment of investments, especially if the companies can afford to rely on steady streams of profits from other ventures. It is important to recognize that it is not to the interest of some managers who is more concerned with their next quarterly report to look deeply into strategies that yield long term results, however predictable the results may be. Companies can take advantage of the benefit of hindsight and history of the investments and retune with new approaches to improve business performance and management. However, in many cases, a combination of tried and tested may not be available. For certain business ventures only time can bring out the true prospects. Such ventures involve risks and require and an incubation period. It is a great challenge to score victories in uncharted business territories. To be sure, companies must hold spending so that it is balanced with projected revenue. Whenever possible, companies must stretch out utilization of fixed costs. This action also applies to companies flush with cash or from venture capital. Money that comes out of venture capital, not your own pocket is much easier to spend. This does not mean it should be spent thoughtlessly.

4. Lower Producer, Administrative and Service Cost Structure

⌘ Beware of little expenses; a small leak will sink a great ship.

- Benjamin Franklin ⌘

Managers must not accept or continue to accept an inflexible and unchangeable model of action. US companies are currently facing wage and price pressures from low cost foreign competitors and many companies fail because they wasted resources and are unable to control costs. It is easier to cut expenses than to increase revenue. Therefore, US companies must achieve a cost structure competitive to those from developing countries in order to be successful. This is true particularly in labor-intensive industries where wage rate is one of the major costs. Reduce or eliminate elements of the business that contribute to the most cost. Product, facility and service administrative costs as a percentage of revenue should be brought to a minimum. The significance of competitive wage differential is greater now than in the past. Technological advances and significant cost reduction in communication and transportation enable competitive advantage by utilizing low cost labor in foreign countries, particularly in manufacturing. In other words, lower communication and transportation costs do not negate the advantage of lower cost of manufacturing overseas, especially across oceans.

The cost of transportation increases as the distribution territory expands. An aggressive business and marketing strategy, low labor costs and a freight optimization system that minimizes shipping cost and maximizes response time will undoubtedly provide a formidable competitive advantage. Low cost companies can charge low prices or enjoy high profit margins though it is important to note that companies do not gain profits by just cutting costs. Low cost strategy is most effective in markets where product differentiation is difficult to achieve, where there is surfeit of products on the market making price sensitivity a major market factor. In such a situation, the key to winning is to be a low cost producer. Cost leaders are able to provide products and services below what their competitors can achieve. They are capable of producing more for less. A firm can be low cost through economies of scale, experience, inexpensive locations, efficient processes with a minimally padded workforce, superior cost control and stronger bargaining power with suppliers, subcontractors and distributors. Cost declines when more efficient methods of production are introduced. The cost advantage must be sustainable. Though cost cutting can result in immediate improvement, companies must follow up by investing in opportunities that will bear long-term results. It is important to note that inside businesses are cost centers. Profits are generated from the outside.

In times of recession, buyers purchase primarily on the basis of price. Companies must lie out plans for a low cost strategy and place them into long-term action. Too many productivity programs are short-lived. Costs eventually take its toll. Some programs worked dramatically for a brief period of time, then petered out. Get the involvement of decision makers in your cost reduction process. Cost reduction approaches will be effective when all who concerned fully accepts them.

Cost reduction efforts must be part of the ongoing growth process and must result in traceable savings. Volume sensitivity is a common concern of industrial activities.
It is impractical to produce small batches of highly customized items with dedicated equipments geared towards high volume production. Similarly, one cannot manufacture a product at high volumes with low-tech machine meant for small job shop production.

5. Outsourcing

⌘ If you deprive yourself of outsourcing and your competitors do not, you are putting yourself out of business.

- Lee Kuan Yew ⌘

More organizations are moving towards outsourcing non-core elements of the business to avoid unnecessarily substantial investment in capital equipment and supporting personnel. More and more companies are manufacturing products in whatever nations that offers good purchasing power, manufacturing advantages and open markets. If a company does not find the cheapest place to manufacture its products

171

and the most profitable place to sell its products, other companies will. Companies must decide which functions are essential and which might be subcontracted outside. Aside from manufacturing jobs, even telemarketing, research and development, technical support and distribution are steadily moving overseas. Work with the supply chain to lower costs. Outsourcing can create significant cost advantages by reducing overhead and administrative expenses. A firm's long-term success depends on its relationship with its suppliers, as it regularly depends on its suppliers for materials, services, good credit terms, quick delivery, etc. Hence, the quality and cooperativeness of a company's suppliers have a large impact on the company's success. Suppliers are partners and allies and therefore should not be manipulated.

Good suppliers may not be in abundance. Be on guard against powerful suppliers and subcontractors who erode profitability out of buyers. On the other hand, your firm can become a powerful customer, driving down prices, demanding higher quality or more services by comparing one competitor with another. Competitive pressures frequently force suppliers to reduce prices. One method is to engage partnering contracts in which firms make volume purchase agreements with suppliers in exchange for a reduction in inventory possession time and payment. A manufacturer must also manage the risk of ceasing production in case a supplier fails to deliver required materials at the promised time with acceptable quality. There are savings to be garnered from the threat of competition. The willingness to switch suppliers and publicize the implicit threat to take your business elsewhere may prompt your current suppliers to generate better terms, provide creative approaches that were not previously offered and prompt attention regarding pressing needs. Suppliers who ship low quality products, deliver late and are hard to reach are a bane to a company's existence. Yet, many companies end up with such suppliers because they accept the lowest bidders and do not develop long lasting and satisfying relationships with suppliers. Companies must keep themselves informed with their suppliers' capacities, performance and problems. By managing an early warning system to detect supply and quality problems, the company can avoid failure to meet its marketing commitment. Increasing inventory turns, simplifying work through improvement in design, manufacturing, service and other processes can substantially lower costs. Inventory is a conversion from cash. Inventory is used as a buffer against failure of people, machinery, materials or process. Institute tight inventory control, just-in-time production, and constantly monitor and pare down inventory levels constantly to minimize carrying cost. Low inventory levels force problems to the surface and increases pressure for managers and workers to resolve the problems. On the other hand, excess conversions from cash to inventory result in undesirable cash flow. Analyze capacity versus forecast and actual demand on an ongoing basis. Cost analysis must include evaluation of fixed, mixed and variable costs allocated to the unit of output: product or service. Fixed cost cannot be changed. Elimination of discretionary costs is the highest and most effective form of cost improvement followed in order of effectiveness by cost reduction and postponement of spending. Apply cost-cutting measures with their effects on future profitability in mind. However, remember that cost-cutting efforts must not affect customer satisfaction. It does not take an expert to cut costs without consideration to long-term consequences. Cost cuts in one area will provide opportunities by investing in another area with greater profit potential. In the drive to reduce cost now, managers may relegate future profits as a concern for the next generation of managers. Though cost containment is vital, one should differentiate between competitive cost and low cost. A company's cost structure must also be competitive enough to make a sale. As Norman Korbett (1995) aptly described it: "No one will question cutting fat, but future profitability is at stake when you cut into muscle, bone and nerves."

Build quality into the design phase and carry-forth continuous quality improvement into production. Work done correctly the first time is far superior to work achieved only after multiple attempts. Achieving this requires a system of monitoring and feedback. The key is to find and eliminate defective products, processes or services at the early stages. Build quality into the process and operators' functions.

9.5 Indicators and Measurement of Corporate Performance

⌘ Like loves like. Fortune begets fortune. ⌘

It is essential to keep score in business. Measurable indicators of success with reliable financial reporting allow people to be accountable. Indicators and measurements are formulated in ways that drive the needs of the corporation that includes monitoring plan implementation of corporate strategies, goals and objectives. They provide reliable antennae for spotting business trends. As Kirk Cheyfitz (Thinking in the Box, 1990) clearly stated that management theory holds that results are more important than processes. He further noted that it is a good thing to have processes – established ways of doing things. But disaster is waiting for any manager who forgets that the sole point for having a process is to help ensure some degree of management control and the replication of good results. Obviously, there are qualitative and quantitative dimensions in assessing corporate performance. As Don Peterson, former Ford President asserted with a word of caution: "Managing for profit is like during a tennis game, the player looks at the scoreboard instead of the ball." It is essential; therefore that one must looks at the scoreboard as well as the ball.

There need to be a complete menu of measurement strategies with collection of key indicators to accurately measure corporate performance without consuming excessive resources in time and money. According to Mark T. Czarnecki (1999), measures should be simple and easy to understand, clearly defined, meaningful to stakeholders and customers, economical to collect, verifiable, measurable, repeatable, can demonstrate a trend, drive the right action and accomplish the stated purpose. It is only logical to deal with issues that have clarity of purpose and are easier to measure. Measures and indicators are tool of management though no company can afford to measure everything it might find useful. Information system helps to measure costs, expenses and estimated profits in order to determine operational efficiency.

Measurement provides feedback to keep a system on track or that higher targets can be set so as to raise the level of performance. Measurement must be an ongoing program with full employee engagement through constant communication and feedback. We compare when we measure. It includes initial reference point from which to measure; past and present performance; and an estimate of future performance and comparison with competitors in the industry. Measurements include those relating to financial performance, public/investor perception, quality, productivity, cycle time and control. There need to have a systematic process for analyzing data.

There are four groups of financial ratios relating to profitability, activity, liquidity and leverage. Profitability and activity ratios measure the returns generated by the assets of a firm. Example of profitability ratio is net earnings over sales, net earnings over total assets or net earnings over net worth. Return on Investment (ROI) is net earnings over total assets. Example of activity ratio is asset turnover that is sales divided by total assets. Fixed asset turnover is sales divided by fixed asset. Inventory turnover is sales divided by inventory. Accounts receivable turnover is sales divided by accounts receivable.

Liquidity and leverage ratio measure the risks of a firm. Example of liquidity ratio is current ratio that is current assets divided by current liabilities. Quick ratio is current assets minus inventories divided by current liabilities. Leverage ratio is total debts divided by total assets or long term debt divided by equity.

Other indicators are revenue growth, rate of growth, whether growth is increasing at a decreasing rate, profit, estimation of future profits, cash position, cash generating qualities, operating margin, return on investment, short and long term debt, P/E ratio, market value, change in market value, inventory turns, market and technological position, market share, customer satisfaction, customer loyalty, customer retention, rate of material return and so on. Market share is one of the key measures of competitive success. All these indicators measure near term and long-term financial and operational performance and provide a degree of objectivity when measuring performance. They provide tools to self-monitor our performance for comparison and improvement.

One way is to compare a set of corporate performance measurements with a cluster of industry average to determine if there is a breakout from the pack. Another is to measure, analyze and fix the gap between customer expectation and corporate performance. In addition to quarterly, yearly indicators and trends, there should be daily, weekly and monthly measurement of operational efficiency. Indicators spell out the objectives and focus attention on specific aspects of the corporation and individuals. They communicate the special importance of a particular dimension of business. Since indicators direct one's activities, there should be a guard against overreacting. Indicators can be paired so that the effect and counter-effect are measured. Joint monitoring is likely to keep things in the optimum middle ground.

Customer value is becoming an increasingly important measure, though it cannot be measured with exactitude. Customer value is based on the projected earnings of current and potential future customers. Customer satisfaction is the leading indicator for predicting future revenue growth. Forms of dissatisfaction include taking the customers for granted, relative high prices of products and services, poor quality and delivery and significant gaps between customer expectation and actual performance.

9.6 Constant Technological Innovation and Aggressive Sales/Marketing

⌘ **Science commits suicide when it adopts a creed.**
                                          - Thomas Huxley ⌘

Society is increasingly celebrating innovators. Innovators are trailblazers. Technology, a bastion of the US economy, is growing in strategic importance to corporations. As Peter Drucker asserted in his book, Management Challenges in the 21st Century (HarperCollins, 1999): "An entrepreneur who does not learn how to manage, will not last long. A management that does not learn to innovate will not last long," Many companies are gaining competitive advantage through technological superiority. As long as the company remains at technology's cutting-edge, technical application can be exploited for a company's growth. The core activities in high technology companies are technical expertise. For good or for ill, technology undermines conventional practices and brings change to society. It was once said: "The way to predict the future is to invent it." With few exceptions, breakthrough technology and market pioneer typically wins and keeps leadership though it is risky to pioneer a new technology. Adequate funding is necessary to open the door for new technologies. It has to be weighed against financial merits. While necessity is the mother of invention it may not automatically produce innovation. It is also important not to confuse novelty with innovation; novelty creates amusement. However, innovation will have no relevance if it does not meet business fundamentals. Innovations are usually long-term investments with few short-term prospects. Suffice it to say that the financial arguments about the merits and demerits of investment in innovation are complex.

Search for ground-breaking innovations to increase corporate wealth and well-being. Dominate through wave after wave of technological innovation and aggressive marketing, even if it requires departure beyond existing good practices. Companies that outperform their competitors in product innovation have the driving force and strategic capabilities that they excel. It places major emphasis on R&D that drives reconfiguration of existing markets to the advantage of the driver. It provides the sparks that fire the imagination for innovation without being clouded by preconceived notions or ideas. It provides the locomotive that enables mind-stretching adventure of discovery and application. It encourages the diffusion of innovation throughout the company by supporting champion innovators. Innovation is potent and carries a premium in the battle for your customers' wallets. Companies that have insatiable appetite for profound and continuous innovation differentiate from those that are not. It is a bulwark against the threat of substitute products. These companies provide their people with excellent conduit for creativity and innovation by nurturing fledgling ideas. They possess spectacular engineering prowess and provide environments that foster a culture of continuous innovation.

Production efficiency by itself is not sufficient. Though the last buggy whip factory was a model of efficiency, it could not survive the onslaught of modern technology. If history is any guide, continuous innovation and organization remodeling account for the prosperity of most great companies. Business, technologies and products that are mired in deflating profit potential eventually cease to exist. Companies must develop superior ability to introduce new lucrative products faster and cheaper than competitors; developing products and services in anticipation of the needs of the marketplace. Lead times between product concept and practical applications must be drastically reduced. Cycle time to get products off the drawing board to the hands of customers must be drastically shortened. Develop products and make simple as well as complex innovations based on customer feedback, product features and short development times by providing a mechanism to incorporate customer inputs, set priorities, complete the most important parts first and change or cut less important features. We must not be trapped in a technology that is great for fun but does not serve legitimate business purpose.

As new products are introduced, buyers and sellers cannot possibly have complete information on potential markets. Many new products die prematurely. Many organizations practice product innovation in a haphazard manner (Michel Robert, 1995). Many opportunities failed because the degree of difficulty in implementation was underestimated. Products become obsolete very fast in fast-growing industries. Product investment may not be recoup before replacement can be developed. Product innovation should be part of a deliberative process with marginal, incremental streams of new products though occasional quantum leaps are appreciated. No producer can make claim that no product will ever be late or free from defects due to unrealistic pressure and impediments to deliver products in a short period of time. There is increasing demand for product reliability. To stimulate wide-scale adoption, make products and services reliable and simple enough for novice consumers to understand.

The domain of marketing is broadening as its significance for business success is being recognized. Marketing is the art of creating or finding, satisfying, retaining profitable customers and building relationships. It is about systematically and thoughtfully coming up with plans and taking actions that get more and more people to buy more of your products and services more often so that the company is profitable. Generally the sales force knows how to push product and services, which is a good thing. Good marketing goes beyond achieving sales objectives. It involves careful research into opportunities and the development of strategies to meet the company's broad financial objectives. It includes broad market knowledge, content coverage and deep working relationship internally and with customers and suppliers. It includes understanding consumers. Consumption is primarily determined by income. The propensity to consume is also closely related to population size, age, ethnic, education and other characteristics. Companies should have a dual focus on market sharing and market creation. Market sharing involves taking market share away from your competitors, step by step, victory by victory. Market creation involves getting into emerging markets with new ideas and innovations. Due to salesmanship and advertising, "want" becomes more dependent more upon supply instead of demand.

Firms must decide whether to lead or follow in the marketplace. Exit markets that are not making money. Market leaders are pacesetters that read the market well, constantly revamp their marketing and sales processes to respond quickly to changing market demands. Gathering of market information and using vast store of customer information for marketing purposes should be routine. While it is important to take a marketing advantage by tapping into existing customer base, it is equally important to gather information on non-customers to potentially increase business opportunities or redrawing the map of the marketplace. Most companies place more efforts and money surveying those customers that they do business with instead of those who are not. Evolving market preferences have radically altered long-established relationship among price, cost, feature, availability, maintainability, quality and reliability. Marketing managers must undertake constant assessment of customer needs, measure their extent and intensity and determine whether a profitable opportunity exists. Inherent changes in demography can transform markets. Marketing continues throughout the product's life cycle: finding new customers, improving of product performance and appeal, manage feedback from customers for repeat and new sales. It is marketing that positions products. It requires management creativity to position their products in tune with the marketplace. As Sergio Zyman, former head of Marketing at the Coca Cola Company pointed out, "I have approached every new campaign, every new promotion and every product as an investment that has to pay a return. Any company that intends to stay in business and grow has to market." Companies will pay a hefty price if they ignore basic market rules. Understand what and why and figure out how to market and produce what the customer wants. Added William Fulmer (2000): "We have all seen large companies whose executives, far remote from the day-to-day world of the customers decided what the customers want, when people much closer to the customers had a very different and more accurate view." Selling solutions to customers need more than intimate knowledge of products and services. Shift the focus of the organization from product-centered to customer or market centered.

Without substance, there is a hollow ring to marketing. Deliver more than what you promise. As someone once said; "You can shear a sheep every year, but you can skin it only once." In every market you serve, combine low price in combination with high level of performance and quality. As Jack Welch, former Chairman, General Electric clearly pointed out: "The value decade is upon us. If you can't sell a top quality product at the world's lowest price, you are going to be out of the game; the best way to hold your customers is to constantly figure out how to give them more for less." Imagination, quick market intelligence, market instincts and practical judgment are called upon to fashion technology through efficient manufacturing process into finished products. Technology should not operate in a closed system, obeying no laws but its own. Acknowledge your customers' power in the marketplace and bow to their demand. People buy not because you are selling, but because they see a benefit to their needs. Provide solutions, not just products. Preference is perishable. Unless there are new ways of reestablishing that preference, they will disappear. Never take your constituencies (customers) for granted. It is important for marketers to spend a lot of time in the field interacting with customers than in the office. You have to look around, to see what is going on. The marketplace changes every few years. Learn to nurture business relationships, create effective advertising, and conduct market research and improving selling skills. With good business relationship and goodwill, your customers will be more forgiving when you make mistakes.

Insightful ways are called upon to combine people, money, equipments and materials efficiently to earn a profit. The challenge of management is to differentiate and select opportunities with the greatest potential benefit within the companies' basic business plan (Michel Robert, 1995). Once you have convinced someone to buy your product or services, you do not have to spend again all the money that you spent to get their attention in the first place. You can reduce the amount of marketing and sales dollars you are spending on customers once you have them so that you can spend your marketing dollars on getting incremental volume. While you still need to give existing customers a reason to continue to purchase from you, you should be more efficient in doing it. In order to grow, you need to build on base volume. New customers are expensive; they need a lot of convincing. As Philip Kotler, world-renowned guru of marketing aptly stated: "First time customers are of varying profitability. Some make an expensive purchase and have the means and interest to buy much more. Others buy a small amount and may not buy again. The marketers then will focus on the best first-time customers to the effect to convert them into repeat customers." Kotler cited four reasons why repeat customers are more profitable:

1. Retained customers buy more over time if they are highly satisfied.
2. The cost of serving a retained customer declines over time.
3. Highly satisfied customers often recommend the sellers to potential buyers.
4. Long-term customers are less price-sensitive in the face of reasonable increases by the sellers.

Do not bundle your products and services. The more you bundle your products and services, the more you risk losing your sale entirely.

While all customers are important, some customers are more important than others. It is important to identify these customers and control the efforts and energy in servicing them. Having too many difficult and high maintenance customers can place excessive pressure on profitability and overstretch the organization. A diversified customer base reduces vulnerability to the ups and downs of any business sector. Customers can be classified by their recency, frequency and monetary value.

Demand management in marketing deals with the level, composition and timing of demand. One should search for fresh outlets in high growth businesses in areas with high population growth and evolving markets to smoothen imbalance in supply and demand. Companies must be skillful at spotting trends. Demographic trends are more predictable. Age and composition data can be accurately projected. Migration data are useful; some areas lose population while other places gain population. Areas of high growth are attention getters.

One of the fast growth areas is in technology convergence. Technology converges when two or more technologies start to merge. The convergence of telecommunications, computers, video, audio disks and internet provide major opportunities to be exploited. Each of these technologies, by itself does not present substantial opportunity.

How broad a market can a company profitably serve?

Companies may decide to create separate business units to market their varied products. Mass marketing is where companies offer products or services to the whole market, especially in areas with burgeoning population. Product standardization changes the basis of competition. The locus of competition shifts to product costs. The way a commodity business can be profitable is low price. Market segmentation deals with designing and dividing mass markets into targeted segments. Marketing determines the appropriate market segmentation to improve market strategy. Management must decide which segment of the market to pursue. Transaction customers do not remain loyal to one supplier. They consider one transaction at a time depending on the alternatives. These customers typically base their purchasing decisions largely on price. Relationship customers are loyal and see the benefits that come with being loyal. Marketing managers can choose wisely by relating its core competencies to the success requirements to the target segment. The disadvantage of market segmentation is that it leads to generic products with generic prices. The advantage is that it provides the producer with volume production runs that enable them to attain production efficiency. Firms that enjoy low costs can best practice aggressive pricing. Competitors can easily duplicate a system that stresses volume production runs and commodity products.

It is difficult to establish product differentiation. Differentiation strategies appeal to customers who are especially sensitive to a particular attribute of product or service. The base for product differentiation is that customers will pay a little extra for things that solve his/her problems. This comes from enhanced products and services that add value for the customers. It is not differentiated until the customer understands or perceives the difference. It is to create, splinter products and services that change the rules in your favor and allows for premium prices. However, differentiation strategy comes with a fixed cost: product development, advertising, marketing and sales service, maintaining service network, etc. Also, the distinctions will gradually blur.

The key to prevent products to become commodities is to practice market fragmentation. Fragmentation strategy is to identify large commodity driven markets and fragment them to smaller pieces to the fragmentor's advantage. Market fragmentation results in a wide variety of customized products and services, each differentiated to suit a unique set of requirements. This makes it difficult for competitors to emulate. It requires production versatility without lowering efficiency. Note however, that customization is profitable for some companies, but others may find it unprofitable.

Inculcate better public image, better operational and developmental processes. Improve ability to deliver products in a predictable timeframe. Key dimensions for differentiation are value, uniqueness, innovation, reliability, speed, availability and so on.
From another vantage point, business is full of nooks and crannies into which entrepreneurs have been able to wedge them. Niches are common in many markets today. Companies may have to serve niche markets or be hurt by nichers. Successful small companies thrive because they focus on limited market niches. Focus on niches allows small companies to compete on the basis of rapid response, differentiation and low cost against large companies with far greater resources. Identify a niche that you can successfully exploit and thrive. Select the niche that larger corporation do not see, whose potential is underestimated or cannot successfully exploit. Start as a niche, dominate and then

188

shape the landscape. A niche has to serve an unmet need. Another niche strategy is to build on innovation. Apart from product and technology niches, other niches include cost, quality, flexibility, convenience and scale.

Market shapers introduce technology where there was initially no need for it and suddenly everyone began to use it. Market shapers are companies that revolutionize business.

Questions to ask to reveal depth of business understanding:
- ➢ What is your business?
- ➢ Who are your customers?
- ➢ Who are your competitors?
- ➢ What is your marketplace?
- ➢ What are your strengths and weaknesses?

⌘ Everybody says you can't make money off small cars. Well, you better damn well figure how to make money, because that's where the world is going.
- Alan Mullaly ⌘

1. Branding

⌘ A brand for a company is like a reputation for a person. You earn reputation by trying to do difficult things well.
- Ray Kroc ⌘

Marketing requires relationship building and brand image development requires more time to deploy and change in comparison to others. A large part of marketing is building and sustaining brand loyalty. Brand innovation must have a purpose. A brand name must communicate what you represent in a believable manner and be consistent with the product's value positioning. Values are those things people hold dear. A good brand is powerful. It can enhance pricing power. Dominant companies may become quasi monopolies (Airbus, Boeing, Comcast, and new AT&T). A brand is a differentiating factor in customers' decision-making. The reason for creating a brand is to get customers to identify a number of desirable qualities with your products and differentiate as to why they are better and special than other ones. Once the perception of a brand is established it is hard to alter. People prefer brands they can clearly identify and are comfortable with, including brand that promotes group identity. The brand is supported by product quality, customer service and overall business behavior. The brand will be wasted if the behavior of the company is not congruent with it.

When you move into new territories, make sure that the customers will allow you to play in the new space. Entering new segments of a business can come with a price tag. The best-known brand names carry unique and positive associations: they are brands people believe in and trust. Some strong brands may even have diehard loyalists. In situations when customers already have a negative preconception, products and services may need to be repackaged with a new brand and message. This may involve positioning and repositioning your brand message.

A commodity is not a brand. For commodities, price is essential; thus, the low cost producer wins. Some companies can have low cost by dint of their size and economic muscle.

On the other hand, a product with a brand that customers favor will retain the advantage of product differentiation. Such products can be sold at a higher price than others in its class, and thus, companies with a successful brand image will garner larger revenues. While branding is very important in a crowded marketplace, the economic performance of some powerful branded products may not necessarily distinguishable from mundane commodity businesses.

2. Image

⌘ Branding is what you do for cows. There's nothing original about your product. I prefer the Disney name to Disney brand.

- Roy Disney ⌘

Although one might find it hard to believe, customers are going to have an image of your company and your products, even if you do not intentionally create one. Creating and maintaining a good image in an atmosphere of cynicism and suspicion is challenging. Product image is the overall impression of your product. The good news is that image branding is to some degree, under the marketer's control. It is important to present a good public face through effective advertising and public relations. An environment of message discipline and control helps foster consistency. Product packaging, rudeness or politeness of your employees, distribution channels or whatever purchasers hear about your company will create an image of your company that will influence a customer's decision whether to purchase from you or your competitor. A good example of successful brand imaging is Apple Computers. By emphasizing the user-friendly aspect of their products and creating a trendy and stylish image in well-designed print advertisements and commercials, Apple has made products like the IPod and PowerBooks seem both useful and fashionable. It is a way to maximize the inherent value in image, real or cosmetic. By being media smart and public opinion sensitive, they have created a positive brand image that continually stays in customers' minds. Coca-Cola has done something similar, although their image is one of longevity and traditional excellence. Because Coca-Cola marketers emphasize that it is America's "classic" beverage of choice, the brand has become imprinted upon customers' minds as reliable, classy and outstanding. Similarly, use your product or company's strong suits to your advantage by underscoring them in your message. Brand builders articulate and strengthen the brand image through word, slogan, color, symbol, message and service actions. It must be developed with energy and pizzazz. Remember, too, however, that a brand manager needs to assure that the brand experience matches the brand image. Poor quality and customer service will be harmful to a company's image. Mediocre image is a result of management failure. In such situation the firm's position must be reviewed, necessary actions are to be taken to renew the company's image for the better. As the saying goes, we have seen the enemies and it is ourselves.

3. Competition

> ⌘ We throw all our attention on the utterly idle question whether A has done well as B, when the only question is whether A has done as well as he could.
>
> - William Graham Sumner ⌘

Business globalization and expansion present growing opportunities but also attract competitive engagements. Competition can inspire you or immobilize you. Competitors can help create or expand markets. Competition keeps you on your toes and sharpens your wits. To compete you have to improve. You must do what rivals do and doing it better. Because business is so multifaceted it requires approaches from different directions. Assessing threats and anticipating pitfalls is essential. What companies need is a competitive strategy to combat contest and weaken the appeal of competitors. Winning companies monitor not only their customers, but their competitors as well, including their beach-heads. A hyper-competitive climate and rule of engagement have fundamentally shifted the basis of geo-industrial rivalry. While protectionism is occurring in some places, the trend is shifting toward free competition in open markets. In this jungle, companies will undoubtedly face new as well as entrenched competitors lurking in the background to take customers away from them. As the stakes are high, competition will be intense and we cannot totally see the competitors' cards or how the game will turn out. New products and new competitors arrive daily and therefore markets must be defended with eternal vigilance with application of the fine arts of business combat. Competitors can drive a crowbar to gain a foothold. They will then use it as a springboard to attack your main line causing ripple effect. Companies that under-rate their competitors are skating on thin ice.

Every business has different fundamental economic and technical characteristics that give rise to different sets of competitive forces. This is complicated by myriad of different global, regional and local business conditions. Highly successful businesses and products inevitably invite a proliferation of new competitors, both foreign and domestic. Companies face varying levels of vulnerability to challenges. Your competitors will emulate some of your successful policies. Therefore, you must incessantly stay ahead the cycle of innovation and imitation. It is easy to be squashed by giants. Companies must have accurate information about their competitors and respond quickly to market forces in order to blunt the force of competition. It includes understanding the psychology and capabilities of your competitors' leaders. You have to set your company apart from your competitors, pick your fights and then put your energy into winning them. Gauge the likely response from competitors whenever you introduce new initiatives. Avoid battling too many fronts. You have to draw on the resources and strategic strengths that your competitors do not have. Instead of engaging in old-fashioned competition, companies must establish serious short and long-range preparedness to identify threats, understand the nature and complexity of competition and learn to outflank, outfox and outperform competitors.

Apart from direct competitors, companies must deal with potential impact arising from emerging technologies, keeping in mind that such companies may have an enlarged capacity to generate ingenious defenses. Companies prefer the devil they know to the one they don't.

Market leaders, especially first movers and fast followers must preempt, block or leapfrog competitors' moves and prevent them from gobbling your customers and destroying your margins. Products and services with a long learning curve assume greater significance when a competitor enters a field earlier than others. Incumbents have more time to prepare their defenses and construct barriers that make difficult for competitors to copy. Do not make frontal attack on a leader's strong position or against competitors with high exit barriers as they will be staunchly defended. Most insurgencies start from the edge and move into the center, chipping away at the armor. New players and low barriers to entry can change the scale of competition. Knowledge acquired through experience and refined via utilization of diverse skills and processes create barriers to imitation. Established strength can be leverage into a portfolio of related competencies including superior quality and lower cost substitute products. In other words, combining quantity and quality can be a powerful competitive advantage. In order to position themselves against new and long-standing rivals, companies need to secure accurate information about competitors, especially their strategies, objectives, strengths, weaknesses, cost points and response patterns. Information regarding the number, size and relative strength of competitors is central in defining the area in which a firm competes. Established firms are at a disadvantage because of their lack of momentum and dogged commitment to old models. However, there are certain advantages to incumbency against competitive squeeze – well-known brands, global distribution, portfolio of patents, established infrastructure and deep pool of talents – and companies should not squander them.

Coming to push and shove, new competitors usually use low price, discounts and capacity to make inroads into entrenched markets, driving down profit margins. If the leading firm has a strong position in the industry it can charge high price to maximize its profit. Operational effectiveness and efficiency can make one company more profitable than its rivals. Priced competitive assets are managerial know-how and proprietary technology. Companies can build strength by acquiring competitors. It is valuable if a firm possesses resources that few others do. Resources that are readily copied cannot generate long-term competitive advantage. Competitive analysis should be viewed in the context of alternatives available to customers. Good competitive analysis must be preceded by good analysis of customer needs and expectation.

While it is highly advantageous to have access to customers that rivals cannot match, high commitment and performance are necessary to be competitive over the long haul. While it is fine for a company to track the activities of its competitors, to remain competitive, its central objectives should be self improvement. The ultimate competitive goal is to get maximum rate of return. Some industry players alternate between competition and cooperation.

9.7 Building Superior Manufacturing System and Logistics

As William Abernathy, Kim Clark and Alan Kantrow aptly described in their seminal work entitled *Industrial Renaissance, Producing a Competitive Future for America* (1983); "To speak about the linkage between technology and competition is to acknowledge, but understate the all important means by which that linkage is accomplished. The skills, systems and organizational resources that together comprise a production system are in a word, the means by which technical change becomes competitively visible." US companies have often paid dearly for treating technology management and production management as if they are separate and mutually exclusive systems. In combination with applying proven and successful formulas, companies must grapple manufacturing issues by reframing the approach toward manufacturing system with new mindsets and placing careful attention to cost and operation. Hyper-competitive situations may require breaking the rules of the game in manufacturing, raising the playing field to a higher plane. The manufacturing plan and implementation should be purposeful instead of accidental. It should not operate with just grandiose statements, exhortations and awards which are only fit to be framed on the wall near the receptionist area while the factory remains unproductive.

The competitive markets place continually provides strong incentives for manufacturers to improve the efficiency of manufacturing existing and new products by using their imagination to harness their capabilities. Technological innovations continue to be fueled by the upturn in the computer, handset, electronics gaming and internet industries that have brought costs to within reach of mass consumers. To

197

excel, companies must turn technological innovation and manufacturing operation into rapid-fire marketing weapons. What matters most is manufacturing agility and productivity by high performing satisfied employees. Satisfied employees will make significant difference in ensuring manufacturing efficiency and effectiveness. Manufacturing agility to respond to varied and changing customer requirements and high productivity are the only means to maintain high profits. An appreciation for the methods of production is a useful asset for people in marketing and design whose interests are in essence inextricably intertwined. Companies can outrun the competitors by operating more vibrantly and managing with a clear and unmistakable global perspective. It includes being able to navigate through the turbulence of globalization. Essentially, success means making manufacturing run like a Swiss timepiece. These require qualified people who understand and will take orders and respond to manufacturing requirements with agility, accuracy and timeliness. Make the necessary changes to improve your manufacturing system with considerations based on the calculus of costs and benefits. It includes understanding the workforce landscape, configure and deploy a manufacturing system that is leaner, faster and work harder. For it to thrive, it is essential for companies to hire hands-on managers with operational experience who can translate innovative design based on marketing guidance into low cost high quality products with customer-centered services.

There is accumulated evidence that established production systems are deeply rooted in every company. The way in which they are rooted will significantly impact the way production systems adjust to the fluid nature of business, inter-industry variations; competitive situations and as the markets beckon. Improved competitiveness is highly reliant on the mastery of rapid new product introduction, labor productivity, product quality and reliability. Mass production method is more suitable for volume production and job shop manufacturing is suitable for small business. To remain competitive, a company's manufacturing system must be able to accommodate diversity of products via concurrent actions, performing several activities simultaneously rather than sequentially. This includes quick prototyping, rapid manufacturing and a flexibility that allows process modification for diverse products. As products are perishable or become obsolete, it is essential to keep products and materials inventory to a minimum or maintain a sound first-in first-out (FIFO) system that supports high-velocity of inventory movement. However, it is important to keep products in stock. Efficient manufacturing system must go hand-in-hand with efficient inventory control and logistics. It is necessary to invest in efficient inventory management system and to simplify logistics to assure accurate and on-time delivery of products and services without generating oversupply. This involves flexibility in managing production capacity ramp-up and ramp-down in mass production and short cycle time scenarios in response to often unpredictable market changes. To be out of stock is to have planned poorly, and is unacceptable. On the other hand, when inventories exceed demand, production must be cut. One way to track product status and movement is to use radio frequency identification. Manufacturing and inventory storage decision must also take into consideration the advantages and disadvantages of centralization versus localization of manufacturing, inventory storage and distribution with respect to market location. There are situations when it is beneficial to manufacture onsite to meet local demands, serve customers better and save shipping cost.

Business circumstances do change. Therefore, it is essential to garner useful insights and provide effective and efficient responses to these changing requirements. At times, it may require breaking from the confines of conventional wisdom, freeing from vestiges of the past. A paucity of orders may lead to the decision to take a product off the market. It is necessary to reduce the processing of defective parts, keep waste low, use high-volume machines often and maintain low absentee rates in order to shave the time and cost of production. These could obviously be directed at delivery of better products and services. This is possible with detailed management and control of the production system that converts raw materials into finished products while guarding against the plague of overcapacity. One tip is to standardize as well as reducing the number of parts and suppliers: this can simplify manufacturing. Unfortunately, a loss of flexibility is inherent in standardization.

There is universal recognition that treating the work force as a competitive asset is one aspect of the efforts to fuel mega producers. Prosperity results only where there is high productivity derived from harnessing human and capital asset, with focus measured in value terms. It is important to masterfully balance competing goals of various departments and avoiding "them versus us" mentality. It includes establishing an environment that foster transparency and cooperation instead of relying on control freaks. One the other hand, employees who are by nature, non-conformist, will not fit well in a production environment. The production people want to make products fast. The quality control department is probably more interested in perfecting a product, even if that process is slow. Placing a high premium on fulfilled leaders, advancing product and process technologies, removing barriers between manufacturing and other functions and improving communication at all levels are some of the requirements for revitalizing manufacturing. Manufacturing and quality instructions need to be expressed with clarity, courage and consistency.

9.8 Prudent Application of Information Technology as Commercial Tools

During the past decades, we have witnessed a paradigm shift from the industrial age to the information age. In an ever-increasing media driven society, much information is universally available. Information technology has flattened organizations at breathtaking pace by simplifying hierarchy and reducing layers of bureaucracy. It has enabled structural changes and productivity gains, bringing industry from the back-waters to the age of Oracle, Google and Yahoo. Increasing numbers of companies are investing in information technology and other business infrastructures to power growth and to increase competitiveness. Managers are utilizing computers and IT-enabled business processes more to improve productivity. For example, today, customers and suppliers for every business across the planet are interacting more electronically. The electronic linkage among suppliers and manufacturing create a beneficial extension of the enterprise. Electronic linkup of the supply chain slashes lead-time by facilitating process flows in terms of material, product, financial movement and accuracy. Computers can spit out data; keep track of what something costs and the results it is producing. New and versatile software systems help companies manage business better by reducing the cost of global distribution, providing extensive, detailed and timely customer information, thus increasing overall customer satisfaction. Software for financial applications, customer care applications, inventory and procurement systems, human resource packages and myriad EDI implementations has boosted productivity. Information technology will become even more commonplace with increased utilization of mobile phones and electronic gadgets. The intranet can be used to

202

disseminate information to be shared among marketing, sales, technical support, customer order entry, etc. For the astute IT-enabled company, the payback can be enormous in terms of user satisfaction, improved customer service and increased revenue. However, it is important to be cognizant of the fact that IT and MIS people should be in the role as cast members rather than superstars.

Digital communications cut through layers of bureaucracy, neutralize hierarchy and propel widespread global communication. They are the enablers of globalization and prosperity. IT managers must open to new and unfamiliar technologies. Reliability, scalability and manageability are key requirements for IT applications. As Charles Wang, former CEO of Computer Associates stated (Techno Vision, 1994): "Everyone must learn to take information responsibility. This means asking what information do I need to do my job, from whom, in what form and when. And you are going to ask what information do I owe to whom, in what form and when – not only so that others can do their job, but so that they can enable me to do my job."

Many commercial applications have failed because of crashed servers, information overload or unacceptable response time. However, there are notable successes in information technology such as American Airlines SABRE reservation system and Federal Express GLOBX delivery tracking system. Companies must establish favorable climate for successful deployment of information technology.

1. Strengthening Your Internet Presence

The Internet and information highway is no longer a secret. The dot.com bubble may have burst but the impact of the internet in our business and daily living is incalculable. By its nature, the Internet is inherently global, widely accessible, instantaneous and free of boundaries. The Internet enables the convergence of an amalgam of disparate technologies, including but not limited to text, graphics, audio, video, animation and telephony. It is a vast and powerful resource that connects information seekers with information providers and vastly extends a company's geographical reach. The Internet has made communication and transactions immediate, transparent and ubiquitous. It provides a real solution for connectivity and interactivity. The aggregation of web-based services empowers companies of every shape and size. The vast amount of information readily available on the Internet has catapulted it to new levels of significance and sophistication, influencing global and market trends and customer expectations. The cost of ownership, ease of use and ubiquity of web access makes this technology essential to all businesses, large and small. Companies must learn how to leverage Internet access to business access and integrate it into a multi-channel strategy that is commensurate with the scale of growth. The web has provided customers unparalleled access to products and services. By providing ease of adaptation and customization, your products and services are a mouse-click away from your competitors'. Using the Internet to gather competitive intelligence is a must. The Internet can no longer be ignored.

2. Low Cost Web Presence

Many companies today have web presence, thereby taking advantage of easy access and low cost. To a large extent, it has bridged the wide chasm between small and large companies in terms information access. More and more companies will be able to afford full-time web publishing and connectivity as prices for Internet access and competitive pressure increase. Though the World Wide Web is the heart of the Internet and is in vogue for quite some time, many companies have yet to establish a web presence or use it effectively to garner business benefits. Many companies have lost Internet credibility, as the contents of their websites have fallen into decrepitude, in large part due to an absence of regular maintenance. A major reason is that in many companies, no one is assigned the responsibility and authority to keep the website up-to-date. This peripatetic effort may be due to lack of commitment, attention or competing demands. A company must properly present and maintain its information to build and sustain user trust. Doing so will give an inestimable boost to business activities. There is no reason not to keep web information up to date and wide-ranging: financial savings are substantial with minimal upfront cost for implementation. Moreover, because services are hosted and maintained offsite, there is no cost associated with hiring, training and retaining IT personnel.

3. Harnessing Web Power for Business

Companies with financial wherewithal and internal skills can integrate complex hardware and software components to create a powerful internet presence that is multi-purposed in scope. As time progresses, an endless parade of companies will be soliciting customers in varied locale or providing services on the internet. The task of developing, implementing and maintaining that presence becomes more complex. The need for secure transaction and transmission of confidential information will increasingly be felt. The number of tools to enable customer ease-of-use and to satisfy the needs of demanding customers will also increase. The convenience of anytime, anywhere availability of on-line transactions will gain increasing popularity with a healthy infusion of technology. The internet will also be a popular medium for burgeoning commercial information and transaction such as pricing, order catalog, purchase orders, shipping status, notices, etc.

A setup screen can define how clients who are permitted to access your web can be identified. An important feature should be an extensive set of statistics on users. These statistics can tell how many people are accessing your site, identities of visitors, whether they are repeating visitors and which pages are being accessed most often. These will help you update your site to optimize access. You can utilize the information and update your content to attract more visitors.

9.9 Continuous Improvement

⌘ In every discipline, progress comes from people who make hypothesis, most of which turn out to be wrong, but all of which ultimately point to the right answer.
                                                    - Milton Friedman ⌘

1. Learning, Training, Branching and Pruning

⌘ It is not the strongest of the species that survive, or the most intelligent, but the one most responsive to change.
                                                    - Charles Darwin ⌘

Nothing is more important than education. Continuous organizational improvement and transformation require the capacity for listening, perpetual learning and never ending supply of ideas and information to do things in better ways. This is a time-honored formulation. In the words of Peter Senge (The Fifth Discipline, 1990), "these organizations that will truly excel in the future will be the organization that discovers how to tap people's commitment and capacity to learn at all levels in an organization." It depends on ceaseless efforts and attention, verification and extension. It takes time and enormous commitment. It involves learning by experience, continuing education, intuition, instinct and instruction. It includes hard work, planning, improvisation and not bound by conventions. Experience and continuing education is getting more and more important as the world is getting more complex. It is important to recognize the strengths and core competencies of a company in order to develop measurement and improvement programs.

Learn from misses as well as hits. There is much to be gleaned from successes and failures of companies and apply what have been learned in improvement programs. This includes learning from the best that other countries and corporations have to offer. Achievers watch and learn enormously from the successes of others and from their own mistakes. Successes and failures can become the subjects of some superb accounts. There is no substitute for knowledge gleaned from work experience, learning the ropes, learning through iterative fashion from failures and successes. However, past afflictions do not provide future immunity. Provide a platform to learn good ideas and Best Practices from others, including competitors and develop training program and support system for the entire rank and file. Learning is acquisition of new knowledge and skill to improve now and in the future. Skill building comes from planned approach to learning, managing the learning process and building on the work of achievers. Lifelong learning is being accepted as part of personal and work philosophy. We need a penchant to learn continuously because human beings, practices and environments are dynamic. Ideas and technology become obsolete with time and have to be rejuvenated with new doses through learning. Be cognizant that great ideas cannot be defended logically during their nascent stage and therefore can easily be suppressed. By learning, we may discern new ways to do things and solve problems. Continuous discussion is part of continuous improvement. Mistakes can often be a good teacher as success. Proper application of knowledge, acquired through learning is wisdom. Wisdom involves applying what we learn and turning it into something useful. In order to become wise, we need to have the drive to learn, but also the humility to know how little we know and the curiosity to learn more (James K. Lucas, 1999).

Top companies recognize the importance of high quality and well-trained managers. Employees should be cross-trained to increase the scope of their capability and know-how. Provide employees a great deal of coaching, training and suggestions from experienced managers. While corporate human resource development department plays an important role in training, the ultimate responsibility for training should be the manager's. However, training is ineffective in high employee turnover companies. Provide people opportunities to teach others what they have learned. Recognize those who mentor passionately and mentor many. People may confuse coaching and mentoring with command and control. Care must be taken to assure that employees do not feel being proselytized instead of being trained. A method of developing managers is to provide them with challenges.

The key to continuous improvement is through a monitoring system that reports the continuation of practices that worked and measures progress against new moving targets. Keep those ideas that work and discard those that do not. Alternatives that do not fit into predetermined structure must not be ignored.

2. Internal Role Models

> ⌘ When you look at the leaders around the world – whether they're running countries, businesses, churches, educational institutions, or what have you – too many people are choosing to be self-serving rather than serving – why is that? Because they don't have a different leadership role model.
>
> - Ken Blanchard ⌘

The role model of a manager is a time-honored and influential factor affecting employee performance. A mentor is someone whom you hold in high regard. He/she shares what he knows with those who are less experienced. He/she can serve as a sounding board before ideas and plans are tested. Employees learn from a plethora of insights and through observation of the actions of role models. These are less obvious but more important. Several companies that I've associated with, to their credits, have role models who are unsung heroes. These people are able to maintain balanced approach and sound business sense despite obstacles thrown in its way. Some managers have an uncanny ability to command loyalty and inspire employees. Others are resolute in making sound policy decisions. A successful role model fascinates. He can provide a benchmark to emulate. By observation and listening, we can learn the lessons from living exemplar on what has worked and what has not worked. Good role models can show employees the inner workings of sound business practices. They can pass along lessons of lasting value. As Charlie Munger, Vice Chairman Berkshire Hathaway used to say; "There's no reason to look at just the living. Some of the best role models have been dead a long time."

3. Using Common Sense

⌘ Use your intellect to inform you instincts, but trust
your instincts.
- Observer Unknown ⌘

We need an enormous infusion of common sense to tackle
problems we face daily. It is fundamental to use common
sense in every situation and learn from experiences by way of
cumulative wisdom and analogy, capturing the old and the
new. It means avoiding being drawn into obsession with
management fads touted by high paid consultants. Nowadays,
it is not uncommon to witness a herd mentality that can lead
people off the cliff. Common sense, intuition, lessons learned
from anecdotal evidence and gut level understanding are
wisdom shared by everyone. They are versatile and are
developed through life experience. They can take diverse
forms in different settings. They can be vivid and powerfully
resonant. Everyone is imbued with it, so use it. It is easy to
forget and squander it. It is following simple logic and
performing simple acts. Another important aspect is to
recognize and take advantage of the winds of change. Skills
can be learned and developed by everyone by thinking in new
and ever-evolving ways. Temper grand vision and lofty goals
with common sense and wide-angle perspective. Do not forget
the basics.

4. Prejudices Limit Improvement

⌘ A prejudice is a vagrant opinion without visible means of support.

- Ambrose Bierce ⌘

The reality in today is that prejudices still exist in many forms and plaguing businesses. It is by no means the exclusive province of a few. The truth is that it even infects people with respectable credentials who themselves bear scars of prejudices. It touches everyone, everywhere, widening chasm and is anything but reassuring. Prejudices may be the result of cultural, social and religious and biases. Other prejudices are due to people who are unable to tolerate the "unpleasant peculiarities" of people of other cultures who have different view of life, cultural baggage, activities, habits, etc. For good or ill, our experience with prejudices in large measure shapes our views of life and work. For some, bad experiences with prejudices give ground for skepticism and causes negative psychological effect. It is defined by parochial interests, jaundiced view and simplistic stereotype. It is ill-suited for today's diverse global settings in which people are more aware of prejudicial issues and perpetrators. It is petty and in a way caused by fear. It must be unapologetically and fulsomely rejected. The swirling undercurrents of prejudice de-motivate and precipitate non-cooperation. It is an embodiment of ignorance, short-sightedness and an anathema. It manifests itself in other ways, relying more on brute strength and brutality rather than mental processing power and open minded-ness. Though archaic, it can easily infect people who take superficial view of things. It is a bête noire created by ugly stereotypes that are factually wrong. It is widely acknowledge that prejudices limit improvement by creating invisible boundary that impedes cross-pollination of ideas, causing suboptimal results. It belonged to a certain historical moment that has passed. Companies are burdened by bias and hidebound preconceptions which contribute to a calcifying effect on operations. Unfortunately, many companies appear to take a laissez faire approach to these problems. Even managers may be nonchalant and leave it to employees to bear the brunt of prejudices. If prejudices are rampant, there will not be a sliver of hope for the company to succeed.

There should be no return to the old system. We should open the doors, clear the paths and not let prejudice define the parameters in which we operate. All stereotypes contain some elements of truth. Shed prevailing biases. High achievements are considerably derived from forward thinking, open minds and accepting a rich texture of fresh ideas, free from prejudices and warped beliefs. In one way or another, treat everyone decently.

Chapter 10
Studies on Productivity Improvement and Human Motivation

⌘ Education makes people easy to lead, but difficult to drive; easy to govern, but impossible to enslave.
- Lord Brougham ⌘

It is appropriate to pause at this point and review seminal studies on human motivation and productivity improvement that are integral to reinvigorating businesses. Unlike fads or cookbook approach, they are included here as they have significantly influenced and shaped the progression of management thinking for the past few decades, though they were established predating the internet and information period. Each of these studies, in various settings, is appropriate for its times and situations. Some of these studies still hold considerable sway in management thinking today. Singly or in combination, they can be effective when applied adroitly under current business scenarios. Yet others would fade away giving way to fresh managerial initiatives. Companies must be in the forefront in overcoming the orthodoxy of a particular system and be selective in utilizing the arsenal of approaches in productivity improvement. It is useful to recognize marked shift in productivity improvement and human motivation theories and visualize how these studies play out in actual practice. It is important to recognize that every employee is at a different level of maturity, capability, experience and development.

1. "Hawthorne Effect" and Productivity Improvement

The Hawthorne studies offered insights into motivation of employees. The "Hawthorne Effect" was orchestrated at the Hawthorne Plant of Western Electric Company in Cicero, Illinois (1927 – 1932). The study encompasses the influence of physical, environmental and psychological aspects on employee motivation and productivity. These included "brightness of lights, humidity, breaks, work hours, supervision, etc on worker efficiency. There may be frequent need to re-design workflows that will help companies pulsate with activities. It was observed by Professor Elton Mayo, Harvard Business School and his associates William J. Dickson and F.J. Roethlisberger that, in essence, productivity of the workers was improved because workers were pleased to receive the attention of management. The act of showing people that managers care about them usually encourages them to do a better job. There is psychological importance that workers' behaviors may be altered when workers are aware that they are being studied. Among other conclusion it was pointed out that the workplace is a social system of interdependent functions and the way the workers perform is highly influenced by their relations with their supervisors. The work groups tend to arrive at norms of what they consider as "a fair day's work." The study showed that productivity is significantly impacted by social and psychological dynamics of workgroups. The finding shows that the need for recognition, sense of belonging and security is more important than the physical workplace conditions. Poor productivity is symptomatic of the monotony of the work itself. To this end, it appears that this experiment treats workers as pawns to be manipulated, though it has been a decisive factor in the success of production management during the middle part of the 19th century.

2. Frederick Winslow Taylor and Scientific Management

Frederick Taylor – time-and-motion study, for which he was famous, was a foreman at Philadelphia's Midvale Steel Company who laid the foundation that revolutionized scientific management. He pointed out that the remedy for inefficiency lies in systematic and scientific management based on clearly defined rules and principles. Employees pay special attention to their work when under the spotlight. He favors scientific measurement of productivity and setting quotas. This includes managing time-and-motion studies on workers in functional departments. The fundamental interests of employers and employees are not necessarily antagonistic. He emphasized that the principle of management is to achieve maximum prosperity for the employers and employees. In other words, long-term prosperity of the employers cannot be sustained if it is not accompanied by prosperity for the employees. Greatest prosperity for employees can only occur if the employees have reached their highest level of efficiency, achieving highest output. At the same time, greatest prosperity for the employer can be achieved only when the lowest combined expenditure of human labor, material resources and cost of capital such as buildings, machines, etc. However, his solution of systematic watching and measuring employee performance appears to be dehumanizing. It generates the routine of dull work and underutilizes the creative capacity of employees.

3. Maslow's Hierarchy of Needs

Maslow developed his theory with high level of practicality based on the recognition of human experiences. He determined that people are basically trustworthy, prefers to be self-governed and love. People can grow and actualize their potential when given the opportunity to do so. People tend to be violent or evil when their lower needs are not achieved. As lower level needs are satisfied, higher needs take its place.

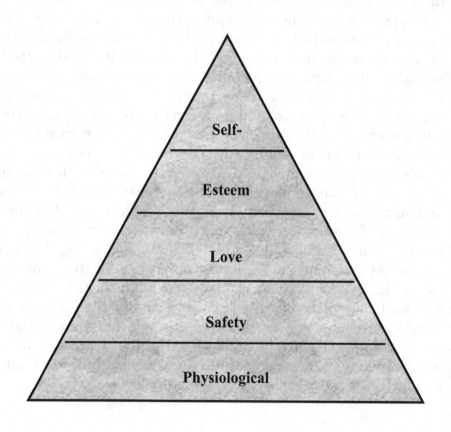

The establishment of a hierarchy of needs by Abraham Maslow brought forth new theory that people are motivated by unsatisfied needs. At the bottom of the hierarchy are Physiological Needs such as air, water, food, sleep, etc. Once these needs are satisfied, then people move on to other needs. The next level is Safety Needs such as those related to family and home. A good home and a loving family provide stability in an unstable and insecure world. Love Needs are the next level on the pyramid. Human beings are social creatures who have inbred desire to belong of groups: family, religious groups, clubs, gangs, etc. There is a need to be loved or accepted by others. At the next level are Esteem Needs relating to self-recognition and attention and recognition by others. These people take on an energetic role to take the company to new heights. This represents a key aspect of seeking self-attention and recognition by others. At the top of the hierarchy is Self-Actualization. People who have everything look to maximizing ones potential by seeking knowledge, peace, spiritual experience and other forms of self-fulfillment. They embark on an enchanting mission to achieve the crowning glory of what they seek.

4. McGregor's Theory of Motivation

In his book "The Human Side of Enterprise" written in 1960, Douglas McGregor presented his theories on employee motivation. McGregor developed a theory based on two opposing but interweaving views of worker attitudes which he named Theory X and Theory Y. Fundamentally, Theory X is more applicable for employees who have not reached the level of maturity and Theory Y are suitable to mature employees. By taking initiatives that recognize and are in tuned with employee needs and how they can be motivated, managers can create an environment that will render in high motivation and productivity. By recognizing the maturity level and the flaws of Theory X employees, managers can develop actions to motivate these employees based on what make them tick. Managers must be careful not to take on an arrogant and oppressive attitude towards these employees, whether they are of Theory X or Theory Y attitudes. Effective managers use a combination of command and control and a policy of judicious empowering of mature employees to take initiatives in fulfilling their duties.

Theory X Assumptions

> Work is inherently distasteful and workers are inherently lazy.
> People prefer close supervision
> Most people are lazy and their work must be carefully structured
> The principle worker incentive is money
> Typical workers are uncreative
> Workers need to be coerced, controlled, directed or bribed in order to get them to increase their efforts to meet their organizational needs

Theory Y Assumptions

> Work is as natural as play
> People like to work
> Self control is oftentimes essential
> Workers at all levels are creative
> Workers respond favorably to mature, favorable treatment

> Recognition and self-fulfillment are as important as motivation and money

5. William Ouchi: Theory Z (1981)

Theory Z was presented by William Ouchi in his 1981 book, Theory Z: How American Companies Can Meet the Japanese Challenge. It was popularized during the Japanese business boom in 1970s and 1980s. It was a relevant response to examine the successful practices of Japanese corporations with respect to US corporations. The theory is based upon the capitalizing the benefits of Japanese tradition of collectivism and the advantages of United States tradition of individualism. It is based on employee motivation via concerns for employee welfare including their social life, decision by consensus, high quality, informal slow promotion, and commitment to the company and lifetime employment. It was focused on the theory that employee loyalty will be increased if employers take special care of employee welfare both on and off the job.

It is important to understand the historical context in the development of Theory Z in order to have a better appreciation of its underlying principles. The obsession to lifetime employment is not easy to sustain in prolonged economic downturns nor is it viable to cocoon from the harsh reality of modern times. Therefore, many Japanese companies no longer consider it as sacrosanct. A new order will emerge, little by little on how Japanese employees will be motivated and managed. Slow evaluation and consensus driven decision-making, though promote employee engagement and are informative, they are implicitly risk averse. It stymies ability of employees to make bold decisions when such decisions are urgently warranted. Many Japanese corporations are grappling to respond to these dilemmas. The innovative of these corporations are trying to graft the advantages of Western system with the Japanese system and will continue to mutate with trend setting management practices.

6. Chris Argyris: Bureaucratic/Pyramidal Value System versus Humanistic/Democratic Value System

Though it was widely acknowledged that Theory X is no longer suitable in the modern era, nonetheless there is still a fixation. Many companies still treat employees as immature human beings. On the other hand, democratization isn't necessarily good for managing a business even though managers should be open minded and treat employees humanely. In his analysis, Chris Argyris of Harvard University attribute this situation to a management system with bureaucratic/pyramidal value based on similarity with Theory X assumptions as opposed to a humanistic/democratic value system akin to Theory Y assumptions about people.

a. Bureaucratic/Pyramidal Value System

Chris Argyris' research reveals that following bureaucratic/pyramidal value system leads to narrow and distrustful relationship. The focus on such value system is in carefully defined authority, direction and control and "getting the job done." There are hierarchies and set boundaries. It is hard-edged and has higher exposure to disgruntled employees. Decisions are made from top-down, essentially not from the choosing of people down the pyramid. Offenders are not tolerated. Resources are rationed. Ideas and opinions starve or fall by the wayside. In such a system, personal development is inhibited and generally related to work. It diminishes the capacity for employees to grow. The evidence is overwhelming that such simplistic system has significant shortfall, especially in information and knowledge based economy. It is another lesson of tunnel vision, superficiality and will lead to indifference, isolation and cycle of mediocrity. It obscures that fact that people can be thoughtful, brimming with great ideas and can contribute collaboratively to the organizations through their actions.

In the same vein, the negative aspects of the Bureaucratic/Pyramidal Value System must be understood in the context of management control versus general human aspirations to have control of their own lives and actions. It is important to note that in certain work environments, particularly in manufacturing and giant corporate (bureaucratic) scenarios, a level of employee discipline and obligation must be instilled. From the vantage point of discipline and order, it may be necessary to have structure and less debate. This may explain the reason why an appreciable number of US corporations are less successful in manufacturing due to lack of discipline and excessive tolerance for debates in decision making. In many situations, debates and tolerance for ambiguities lead to inefficiency and ineffectiveness. It is sad to note that this is part of the contributing factors why US and other developed countries outsourced manufacturing to less developed countries which have the distinction to be pliant, though labor costs have often been mainly touted as the primary reason for outsourcing.

b. Humanistic/Democratic Value System

On the other hand, humanistic/democratic value system leads to more trusting and cooperative relationship. People are treated like human beings and are acceptable to have divergent views. It emphasizes human relations and collaboration in people development. Success and failures have a human dimension. Organizations are believed to stand in the way of people reaching their full potential. Times have changed. This system goes further by encouraging flexibility in adapting to environmental conditions and makes work more challenging and deriving commitment through authentic relationship. The system is less insular. There is a common thread that facilitates human interactions without being adversarial. Such relationship provides opportunity and excitement for individuals to develop to fuller potential. It makes the organization sparkle if managed adroitly and in turning the right theory into practice.

The Bureaucratic and Humanistic systems, both with virtues and drawbacks coexist in strange harmony with each system having their unique features that can be applied efficiently and effectively in management practices. Proper mixture and application based on the strengths of these individual systems can be a winning combination, even under arid business environment.

7. David C. McClelland: Achievement Motivation

David C. McClelland and his associates at Harvard University observed in their studies that some people have an intense urge to achieve while the majority does not seem to be concerned about achievement. The urge to achieve was a study that intrigued McClelland and his associates for over twenty years. One of the keys to human motivation is the need for affiliation. People who are achievement motivated prefer to work on a problem instead of leaving the outcome to chance. Achievement motivated people are optimistic, self-directed and driven by the satisfaction of accomplishments. They stand out. Rewards and money are valuable in as much as they are measures of their performance. While achievement motivated people are more concerned with personal achievement than the rewards of success, they generally get promoted faster and get bigger raises. To achievement motivated people, money and acclaim that goes with it are valuable in as much as it is a measurement of their performance. McClelland further discovered that when people set high goals and think in achievements terms, they tend to be less tiring and the jobs get accomplished. Because of extraordinary vigor, it is not surprising that companies with many achievement-motivated people have vigorous growth and are more successful.

According to McClelland, achievement motivation can be developed. Achievement motivated people, though great producers may not necessarily be the best managers unless they develop human skills. Managers depend not only on the success of their own work but also are highly dependent on the activities of others. Achievement motivated people are usually more strident, want to know how well they are doing on the job instead of how people feel about them. Because they constantly think about doing things better, they get good results, albeit in a way that may not be diplomatic. In other words, stellar achievers may during communication, at times, deliver barbs without some accompanying balms. As they oftentimes are terse, pushy and work in a frenetic pace, they may not realize that what they say or do may offend people. In contrast, low achievement motivated people are more interested in how people feel about them instead of how well they are doing. People with low achievements can be trained to be high achievers. Quite naturally, achievement motivated people are more likely to be developed from families who have high expectations from their children. Some may be appear to be renegades who will defy expectations that are considered low by their own standards.

8. Frederick Herzberg: Factor Hygiene and Motivation Theory

Frederick Herzberg (1923-2000), a clinical psychologist, a pioneer and a great thinker of the twentieth century contributed to management theory by his Hygiene and Motivation theories. His work continues to be of fundamental importance to the study of employee motivation. He was basically bringing humane and caring management efforts into the workplace. Herzberg asserted that basically, people have two sets of needs. One: as an animal to avoid pain and two; as a human being to grow psychologically. The Hygiene Theory, first established in the workplace provided practical solution which includes factors that are needed for basic employee job satisfaction, not necessarily leading to higher level of motivation. He showed that satisfaction and dissatisfaction at work often happen from different factors and not simply opposing reactions to the same factors. These are environmental factors that include the company, working conditions, policies and administration, supervision, interpersonal relations, personal life, status, salary, company car and security. This tapestry is integral to satisfying employee self and shared interest. Hindsight reveals starkly that callousness and disregard of hygiene factors lead to dissatisfaction. The level of hygiene factors present is a gauge of how well developed a company's human resource department is. From the benefit of hindsight, it is unmistakable that hygiene factors play a large part in aiding and abetting employee motivation. As people are more educated and aware, the roles and importance of hygiene factors have expanded in significance. However, it does not deflate the importance of other theories of motivation expounded in this and other books. Companies can and should do more to provide satisfying hygiene factors. The motivational part of the theory concerns job interest, responsibility, achievement, recognition, nurturing work environment and potential for advancement. Simultaneous implementation of these hygiene and motivational factors contributes to higher levels of employee relations and motivation. People lacking "hygiene" needs strive to achieve them and the effects soon wear off once these factors are satisfied. In other word, the satisfaction is temporary.

9. Rensis Likert – Management Systems and Styles (The Human Organization, Mcgraw Hill, 1967)

Dr. Likert's research on human behavior within organizations was conducted under industrial setting. Based on his examination of various organizations and leadership styles, he concluded that organizations must make optimum use of its human assets in order to thrive.

Likert identified four main management styles:

a. The Exploitative – Authoritative System where decisions are imposed on employees. It gives primacy to command and over-control. The cardinal rule is employee motivation by threats. Lower level employees have virtually no authority and responsibility. There is little communication, no teamwork and employee welfare is neglected. People may be coerced to do something in ways that may be against their natural inclination. It fosters a sense of underclass where employees' hopes and expectations remain unexpressed and unfulfilled. Employees are discouraged to sound the alarms, even when situations warrant. This system undermines collaboration and is ill suited for a knowledge-based economy. In modern times, management systems have undergone radical departure from Exploitative-Authoritative system, yet it is no less essential to understand some of the positive aspects of this system; an example being short-term efficiency with narrowly defined objectives.

b. The Benevolent – Authoritative System where leadership is a form of master-servant relation-ship and motivation is via rewards. There is little communication and little teamwork though there are well defined parameters. There may be a manifestation of personal concerns for employees who may be encouraged to grow and flourish. In recent times, the influence of Benevolent-authoritative System has waned. One of the reasons is that this system undermined collegiality that is necessary for people who requires respect and self-determination in doing things.

c. The Consultative System where leaders have significant but not complete trust of employees. Motivation is via rewards and some participation. There is moderate communication and moderate teamwork.

d. The Participative-Group System provides the optimum where leaders have complete confidence in their employees, where rewards are based on achieving goals that are set with employee participation. Employees at all levels have real authority and responsibility and where there is substantial communication. Decisions are usually made after fulsome discussion. Through these discussions managers will have a better finger on the pulse of the situation. However, care must be taken to assure that the workplace do not become undisciplined including display of indiscretion.

Likert recommends the fourth system to be adopted in order for companies to attain optimum effectiveness. His study indicates that modern management principles and techniques must be applied for employee motivation and that employees' self-worth must be respected. Employee participation and empowerment must be encouraged and are conducive to supporting relationships. There should be high degree of loyalty and mutual trust. This system is more resilient to weather downturns, though autocratic leaders were at times accused of being domineering and democratic leaders were accused of being soft.

Chapter 11
Dealing with Uncertainties and
Formidable Challenges

⌘ Nobody looks at the sun except at an eclipse.

- Seneca ⌘

No discussions will be complete without delving in how companies deal with uncertainties and redoubtable business problems. Though it may be difficult to forestall, nonetheless we must learn to recognize early signs of impending trouble before they fester and spin out of control. Some setbacks may be serious while other may be minor and temporary, causing you to lose a step or two. It is amazing that some managers have almost clairvoyant sense of impending problems. These managers have weathered and evoked by the hardships of life. A rocky economy requires companies to save as much as possible. Companies that are deficient in skills and financial resources will not survive, let alone prosper.

How do companies stay in existence instead of being extinct? People who are self-confident will weather the storm. Dealing effectively with uncertainty is crucial for managers. It is not an easy task. Some challenges beckon whilst other problems threaten. Companies and managers face profound choices daily. Managers must make radical shift in their strategies and priorities when dealing with changing needs and conflicting demands both with and without the benefit of hindsight. There is no end to problems a company might face, as the future is as unpredictable as it is precarious. This is an immutable rule of business whether during boom time and bust. Management decisions and actions may have unintended consequences.

While there exists a commonality to the challenges all companies encounter, yet many of the challenges IBM faces might be different from those faced by Bank of America or Yahoo. Treat challenges skillfully and promptly with swift and steady hands. Indifference to the concerns of customers, employees and stakeholders, will leave the company beleaguered. Executives fail due to business ineptitude, reliance on outmoded business concepts and lacking the tact and discretion that are essential to succeed. Human artifacts don't last forever.

1. The Dilemma of Management

⌘ A slave who has three masters is a free man.
- **Roman Proverb** ⌘

Companies must constantly seek new approaches to solving age-old dilemmas. There are no easy answers. Business management cannot be defined in a simple equation. In business, there is no such thing as certainty. Sooner or later most businesses will fail. This fact makes it more important that managers exercise caution when they take quick and decisive actions daily. At the same time, they must be on the prowl to find out how to make business better. They must navigate effectively in order to survive the vicissitudes of turbulent years. When companies catch the flu, the flu need not develop into pneumonia. A good manager must overcome resistance to progress, as progress involves changes that may produce disrupt equilibrium and entrenched standards. Changes are at times gradual, sometimes rapid. While managerial policies should be based on sound principles, management can be an inexact science: at times to be principled may deny reality, be ineffectual and constricting, particularly with regard to the manipulative aspects of marketing. Corporations must set their priorities. They may need to decide pay raises for employees or price cut for customers, depending on business situation. Efforts to stretch the envelope of accomplishment must be balance with caution; that resources are not overextended, especially when you have to deal with problems from multiple fronts. There is no substitute for grits and dedication.

2. Managing in Rocky Times

⌘ When written in Chinese, the word crisis is composed of two characters. One represents danger and the other represents opportunity. ⌘

In the world of business, it is familiar to have a period of prosperity followed by recession when opportunities are few and far between. An often repeated adage: When the storms come, the eagles fly. The small birds run for cover. The penalty for incompetence is obvious. Some ancién regimes are unable to cope with economic hardships and receded into history. It's not hard to see why. Prime examples are American Motors, De Lorean Motors, Eastern Airlines, Pan

231

American Airways and Wanglabs. Others such as Microsoft, IBM, Apple Computers and Cisco Systems, to name a few, are able to weather the storm, reinvent themselves, survive and prosper either independently or merged with other successful companies.

In rocky times, it is imperative to take decisive steps that are departure from the norm. In a crisis, people look to the leader and the leader must clearly be in command. Quick actions must be taken. Leaders must be sure footed, projecting a sense of security and reassurance even as the crisis is looming. Crucial, painful and far-reaching organizational and operational changes may be required. There is no time for deliberation in an environment that is insecure and unpredictable. Companies in such situation cannot afford to be laissez faire - doing little to change the current state of affairs, less they be vanquished. You have to face grim reality and take decisive actions regardless of the sting of criticism before the situation turns chronic. Otherwise, your company may end up in the corporate graveyard. Pare the budget thinly and do it quickly. Stretched every resource as far enough as feasible. You need to have measured but decisive response coupled with courage and chutzpah. Some of these actions may help you or hold you back. Failure to comprehend and act decisively will have disastrous and unrecoverable consequences. False optimism and hoping that things will get better without taking actions is a costly form of procrastination in today's fast-moving business environment.

The only survival strategy is constant innovation and overcoming attitudinal and financial obstacles. It is crucial to monitor vital signs in order that preemptive measures can be taken to forestall impending problem before they arise. There are disturbing and concrete signs that point to companies in decay. Some of the problems dogging beleaguered companies are rapidly slowing economy, slow growth, depleted income, fierce price erosion and a struggle as margins keep dropping. Telltale signs of profitability decay are declining margins, rising debt to asset, downturn in customer spending and insufficient cash to survive the slightest economic, industry or business downturns. When in a hole, the first thing to do is to stop digging. Conserve cash to avoid expected or unexpected cash crunch. The wages of not controlling cash is death. A company facing too many challenges can run out of cash quickly. The cash situation becomes serious when the cash flow drops to a negative value over extended period of time. In times of cash crunch, cut operating expense (hiring/salary freeze, curtailing travel, stop executive bonuses, temporary wage reduction and reduce non-essential personnel/spending), speed up collection of receivables, sell non-essential assets and cancel or postpone spending on capital items (new buildings, tools and equipments). Controlling expense is the most important job and growing revenue is the second most important. Ongoing trend in operating margins should be tracked, rejecting occasional blips while analyzing the causes of continuing downtrend. Develop debt payback scheme as a realistic possibility of returning to sound financial health. Companies can be blindsided by competitors. As the market pie gets smaller, your competitors may try to penetrate your customer base. A wildly successful product can vanish within a few years.

One thing is clear. It is easier to manage a business in an expanding market or robust economy and quite another to manage during shrinkage in overall market demand. There are substantial advantages of scale and scope. Look at IBM, Microsoft and Cisco. Big players are often bettering equipped than small business to ride out rocky times. They are in better position to withstand financial strains from downdraft in the economy. They can negotiate better prices from suppliers because they buy in big volume. They can spread costs over a larger operation. Small businesses do not have much wiggle room. A company on the rocks can only think of survival. If customers are scarce or when supplies far outstrip demands, locating customers is a problem.

When sales level off or decline, there is a tendency for managers to have corporate liposuction: lay-off, deep budget cuts in hours and available capacity. While it is necessary to keep a tight rein on the purse strings during hard times, managers must be cognizant of new problems these actions might generate compounded by the fact that such as imbalance in services rendered to customers and poor equipment maintenance will result in frequent machine breakdowns. Managers need to have high sense of ethics and integrity in order to confront decline in moral standards in the company during hardship. Avoid making changes that are ineffectual like rearranging the deck chairs in the Titanic. Every plan must include options to be exercised if the outcome does not align with expectation. Encourage counter cyclical investments during economic downturns if they are financially supportable.

3. Managing Corporate Transition

The fortunes of many companies are made or lost during periods of booms and bust. Every business stage, cycle and sector copes with different forces and has its own sets of concerns. During business transitions, corporations will encounter political, bureaucratic, business and resource barriers. Organizations must manage business at different stages of growth and face the challenges at each stage of the journeys. This includes operating at a different pace and rhythm. There are important strategic properties associated with each phase of corporate transition. At every stage they must make sure that they do not go through cash faster than they are earning it. As organizations change from one stage of the life cycle to the next, they develop problems. Some of the problems are transitional in nature and arise during formative moment. These problems can block a company's advance to the next stage or in the worst scenario; a company can be swept under by the tide. Therefore, companies must adjust appropriately to the changing phases. There are times when there are changes in company leadership and new leaders must be good stewards of the legacy that was inherited from the predecessors, including founders. Understanding, perseverance and the ability to cope with various requirements and challenges at each stage of the growth process will help companies make successful transition. As market preferences shift, strategy, product, organizational and business parameters shift as well. This requires development and implementation of new business models as old models no longer work. At different points in the corporate evolution, focus may shift from acquisition of funding, market evaluation, and product feature to size, reliability and cost. This places a burden on a company's established production competence due to painful adjustments necessary to fulfill changing requirements.

i. Startup to Growth Stage

Generally, startups are singularly focused. Their success in many ways rests firmly on the capabilities, energy and force of personality of the founders. They typically are built around a great idea and enjoy technological advantage that can exert competitive pressures on large corporations. This is a critical stage for a startup to decide whether to enter high growth markets or focused markets. Startups have two fundamental priorities: cash flow and employees. A startup is established after adequate financing is available to begin the enterprise. In a new enterprise, cash flow matters more than profit. It gets you in the game until the well begins to run dry. Although a startup benefits from a successful start, it requires more capabilities to survive and grow. Nascent companies are usually cash-strapped unless they are well financed. Therefore, such enterprises cannot survive for long if they are under-funded. They usually have negative cash flow and experience losses, especially during the early years. Substantial cash is necessary to finance expansion. Thus, startups have little tolerance for non-performers. Problems must be quickly fixed or you go out of business. Fledgling enterprises are more susceptible to shocks. These enterprises need to absorb the various strains that are inherent in the growing process. A startup is usually propelled by the founder's imagination. Every entrepreneur is driven by optimism. During the embryonic stage and infancy, the founder's commitment is paramount follow by high level of fiscal austerity and prodigious work ethic. Nascent companies must build market share and building customer confidence in order to successfully move to the next stage. In startup and early stage, entry and exit are fairly easy to accomplish. Also, at this stage, there is a strong impetus for unique and leading edge products with high engineering content. These companies need a good takeoff.

ii. Growth to Mature Stage

Companies must grow in order to survive. Different companies take different growth trajectories. Growth may be attributable to one or a blend of several success factors: Product or service sales achieved critical mass, sales of star products, sales take-off or caught the wave, special sales contracts, expanding markets, competitors stumble, booming economy; among others. At this point, companies must be equipped to handle the frustration of growth and development. Many companies are struggling in their own ways with the problems of growth. These problems may include shortages of products or personnel. Growing pains are a natural consequence of a growing company. Unsurprisingly, companies may appear to be in an anarchic state, especially when growth is at a manic pace. Work habits need to change as the company grows. An ascendant enterprise needs profitability and growth to attract talents; create opportunities for job advancement and satisfy stakeholders. There is a need for discipline during times of growth. High profits are temporary as competition will copy the innovation, causing prices to fall.

A mature stage is characterized by a change from uncertainty to stability, from standardization to intense competition and razor thin margins. Its growth rate occurs less than at its peak, at a decreasing rate or none at all. Successful companies in mature industries concentrate on cost reduction by pressing suppliers to lower prices and by improving operational efficiencies to lower overhead and administrative costs. Mature companies need a core base of long-term employees with frequent injections of new blood. Product maturity is the process by which competition becomes progressively immune to changes in technology. At this stage, companies tend to streamline their product mix by dropping unprofitable product models. When a company reaches its mature phase of development, it is in full bloom, with relatively minor innovative activity. However, mature industries must be wary of the threat of catastrophe if business conditions radically change. On the other hand, if external changes are moderate, mature industries will adjust via incremental adaptation.

iii. Private to Public Stage

While there are financial advantages for a company to go public, there will not be without bumps. The company will face challenges on a variety of fronts. First of these is to be mindful of the speculative mania following the initial public offering. The excitement is generally media driven. Initial euphoria may be detached from the realities and the prospects are usually exaggerated. To sustain and grow the stock price, the company needs the oxygen of continuing revenue and profit growth. The company must assure that the shift continue to gain traction. Investors must be satisfied from time to time. Since public companies are subject to high expectation, close scrutiny, pressure from the investment community and public disclosure requirements, it will be a challenge to ensure continuing good stewardship of the legacy that was inherited from the founders.

iv. Aging to Stagnant Stage

At this stage, the corporation becomes fat and happy. The capabilities are diminished and declining, however much were wished otherwise. Revenues may increase but at a decreasing rate or reached a plateau. There is a level of equilibrium or perhaps there is growing weariness. There are people who are too free spirited for bureaucratic routine and they are most likely to depart from the company. Corporate culture is becoming increasingly feudal. It is easy to fall into the trap of lethargy as the corporate fortune slowly and insidiously wanes. Profits dwindle. Companies at this stage are hobbled by lack of renewed energy and an obsolete product lineup. Sales of certain products evaporate. Not surprisingly, there is a tendency to squeeze profits out of sunset products. This includes managing cost reduction, quality and service improvement.

4. Fixation to Longstanding Practices/Resistance to Change

⌘ **A living thing is distinguished from a dead thing by the multiplicity of the changes at any moment taking place in it.**
- Herbert Spencer ⌘

No individual or company can achieve peak performance without change. Embracing change has become a cliché for management and with good cause. Forces of change are inevitable and change is a journey that never ends. It is a clock whose hands cannot be turned back. As they say, what we can't prevent we must embrace. Improve and be in touch with modern times, or watch your company slowly decay. Companies need to be weaned from long established assumptions, which have not proved successful. They must reorient business thinking away from the past and towards the future. By and large, there is difficulty of changing traditional ways of doing things. In a way, we are all prisoners of our past experience. It is true that change is never easy: creatures of habit, we are prone to cling to familiarity and routine. In fact, even when attempting to implement change, you can expect some element of resistance to protect fragments of the past. Even if change is progress, well run companies can have difficulty adapting to swirling currents of changes due to forces of habit or fear of failure. Other companies are plagued with so many constraints with a fortress mentality that discourage people to change or adapt. Such companies should be firmly nudged into the twenty first century before they experience a reversal in fortune.

History does not treat kindly companies who cannot adapt to change. For example, the building of railroads upsets all calculations within its radius of influence. Unfortunately, most people are content with the way things are, and show little inclination to change because of a lack of incentive or motivation. Some people do not change due to convictions based on shifting foundations. Others cling rigidly to decrepit business model that has proven unworkable. Moreover, introducing change will impact those involved, whether positively or negatively. Some people may feel threatened while others may see the shift as a promising new start, an opportunity for positive renewal. Companies must adapt to the impact whenever there are changing rules in business or risk becoming obsolete. The same assumptions that helped the company prevailed in the past may prove to be its undoing in later years. For example, the replacement of cardiac medicine by the pace makers represented a major shift in the pharmaceutical industry. Companies that quickly responded to this shift prospered, while those that stubbornly stuck to old practices and beliefs fell behind. Clearly it is in every business' best interest to anticipate changing business trends. In his earlier work, Drucker wrote, "Every product, every process, every technology and every market eventually become old." The reluctance to adopt new mind-set limits options, hinders performance and may result in serious ramifications. At the same time, however, one must avoid change for the sake of change.

The corporation will not change unless those involved have the far-sight to perceive the vitality and intellectual under-pinning of what needs to be changed. People must see the value of change in order to buy into it. They must understand that while we cannot change the past, we can change the future. Initially, senior managers must lead a major change program. Those who view change as a threat can create formidable roadblocks that cause impasse, stagnation and wasteful friction. Unfortunately, they can bind managerial scope, coasting along with ingrained practices based on old assumptions, thus significantly limiting business potential. Watch out for such hindrances when implementing change.

5. Complacency and Arrogance

⌘ It's ain't what you don't know which gets you; it's the things you know which ain't so.

- Will Rogers ⌘

In the world of business, nirvana typically does not last long. Companies must guard against the pitfalls of complacency, while carefully guarding the enthusiasm and vitality that helped them first gain success. No firm, however successful can take itself and its market for granted. Any business, however well crafted is never good enough to run on autopilot. Some companies are successful as long as they monopolize the market. When conditions change and they lose the monopoly, they falter precipitously. Business conditions, especially for high technology industries can change practically overnight. Companies must then move forward and keep with the times instead of orbiting around the dying sun of habit. The adage: "If it ain't broke, don't fix it" no longer applies today. Models must improve through perpetual interactive learning and an embracing the process of discovery. There is a tendency for business leaders to be lulled into a sense of complacency when the company is number one, especially after many successful years as an established institution. Managers may be working in an insulated environment where questions, gripes and feedback are discouraged, where the company's growing problems are overlooked.

But cautionary tales persist: many failed companies did not see incoming problems until it was too late. These problems will invariably occur. They unwittingly fall into fire due to lack of vigilance, distracted by pageantry and proclamations. Companies must take corrective actions before they fall into such a predicament. Pay attention to the clues and slippery slopes. Recognize the beginning of a downward slide and take immediate action to forestall it. Do not wait until your competitiveness has slipped before taking action. Avoid being over-confident, "like mosquitoes dancing before the frost." Do not bask in the success for too long. Avoid cultural arrogance that closes one's mind to accept new views. A dose of humility helps. Many successful companies and leaders forget that times have changed, and living in the past, forget that past success does not translate into a promising future. It is not enough to recognize problems when they occur or when there is fast erosion in your business position. There must be a system to recognize signs of impending problems in order to avoid serious repercussions. Just as good ideas and projects often die from inattention, negative signs go unrecognized because companies are not on careful watch. Recognizing and devoting a considerable amount of time to solving problems early on will ultimately save the company from long-term problems and expenses. Many businesses fail or regress due to a lack of attention to early warning signs. The signs are almost always there. There is a need to have the willingness and ability to face failures, accept reality and deal with the problems immediately.

6. Be Cautious of Success

Success, like everything else, must be managed. One must cope with success as well as failures. This principle is just as relevant today as well as time in memorial. Success can be an intoxicating experience. You have to come to grips with it.

Jack Welch of GE had seven successful deals until he bought Kidder Peabody, an altogether ill fated acquisition. At the time, he has reached his personal pinnacle of success, having successfully negotiated seven straight solid deals in a row. This likely created a sense of invincibility and thus, the Kidder Peabody deal caught him off-guard. Success breeds success, or so they thought. Even the sage of Omaha, Warren

Buffett failed to foresee the problems at GenRe, a colossal reinsurance company he had purchased that subsequently experienced billions of dollars in underwriting losses. The near financial meltdown of 2008 provides many ample examples of failed financial institutions (Lehman Brothers, Washington Mutual, Wachovia, Merrill Lynch and many more). As beautiful as success is, memories of past successes and bravado have often handicapped corporate renewal. One can easily fall victim to one's own success. It is not uncommon to witness tabloids of successful people making extravagant claims of success, resting on laurels and artifacts of the past. Business success and popularity is not normally seen as a reason for self-appraisal. Success has its virtues and its flaws. It encourages a wrongful belief that the existing formula will always be successful. Beware of a culture of arrogance rooted in record of economic successes and scientific superiority. Though it is said that success breeds success, the more experience one accrues the more arrogant and insulated one may become. One can easily fall into the trap of success and bask in reflected glory. Peter Drucker warned of the new "mandarinate" of the credentialed. Smart and successful people can easily degenerate into arrogant and fiercely independent people, neglecting to share information with their team, becoming unresponsive to customers and others. Simply put, one can easily be carried away with success. Eating some humble pies once a while helps.

Arrogance built up over years of success blinds new ideas and opportunities and may ultimately lead to a reversal of fortunes or at best, achieve minor and periodical gain.

7. Low Motivation and Morale

⌘ If you want to gather honey, don't kick the beehive over.

- Dale Carnegie ⌘

It is common for companies to motivate employees by offering reward or threatening livelihood. As it was once said; "You can lead a horse to water, but you cannot make it drink." Motivation ultimately comes from within the person. When a person has lost the zest, is aimless and adrift - not doing or loathes his job there can be only two reasons: He/she cannot do it, or is not motivated to do it. A manager has two ways to improve performance: training and motivation. A manager's top responsibility is to elicit peak performance from his/her subordinates by effective application of a variety of ordnance in the management arsenal. There no single approach or style to motivate employees and buoy the morale. There is a direct correlation between the way people view their managers and the way they perform. Employees may be extrinsically and intrinsically motivated. Extrinsic motivation relates to pay, recognition, promotion, etc. Intrinsic motivation relates to personal work ethics, interest on tasks, job excitement, etc. The approach and theory of motivation change with time including how performance-incentive levers are utilized. In certain situations, in order to broaden their experience or recharge, it may be beneficial to rotate responsibilities of groups with similar background.

245

Absenteeism is a serious problem because of its negative effects on morale, productivity and teamwork. Another problem is silence and careless passivity.

One should not be confused with one's employee's general competence to his/her task relevant maturity. As Andy Grove, retired Intel CEO succinctly described in his book - High Output Management; if the task relevant maturity of a subordinate is low, the characteristic of an effective management style should be structured telling "what," "when," or "how." If the task relevant maturity of a subordinate is medium, the characteristic of the effective management style is individual oriented with two-way communication, support and mutual reasoning. If the task relevant maturity of a subordinate is high, the characteristic of the management style is towards minimal involvement by the manager with establishment of objectives and monitoring. A person's task relevant maturity may change with change in work environment. A manager is ultimately responsible for the output of those who report to him.
It is important to assess performance based on real output, not good form. Rewarding a manager on good form would signal that to do well you must "act" like a good manager, "talk" like one, "look" like one but you do not need to perform like one. The decision to promote should be linked to performance review. When we promote the best, we are saying that performance counts. Reviewing the performance of a subordinate and providing positive measures are formal acts of leadership. Preparing and delivering a performance assessment is one of the most difficult tasks.

You need not look far to know that job insecurity and corporate weaknesses are on the rise. Companies on the wane are hobbled by lethargy, indifference, and negative forces of tradition and low trust. It leads to fissures and fractionalization. When a company or its leader is meandering, its managers will be demoralized. Demoralized workforce saps an organization's vitality. Workers with low spirit do not perform well and can turn a company into a land of the living dead - fossilize in their jobs. Such workers may appear to be working but they do so reluctantly and resentfully. At best, employees will do their job but nothing more as they do not resonate with their work activities. Companies can fuel confusion and disillusionment by giving conflicting messages. There need to be clarity in direction and rekindling of spirit through massive doses of activities that boost employee morale. Remember that when facing challenges focus on the solutions rather than the problems.

Drive those who lack direction and initiative. Understand their motivation and purpose in life. In some companies, a culture of leniency tolerates mediocre performance. Managers often fail to fire people, preferring to adopt a policy of tolerance. When people fail to respond to financial and other incentives to improve performance, the problems need to be discussed with the individual. People who fail to perform or lost the determination to do so should be given opportunity to improve via additional training and counseling. If performance remains poor they need to be let go. Usually, people who under-perform at one job will do likewise wherever you place them whereas those who are committed to superior performance continue to do so no matter what the assignment. People with fatal flaws must be terminated promptly. Fatal flaws include dishonesty, untruthfulness, dishonorable, does not keep promises, lack of accountability, unable/unwilling to change and unable and unwilling to learn from mistakes.

247

8. Bounce-back Capacity

There is an abundance of stories that chronicle the seemingly insurmountable failures of great leaders and how they overcame them, demonstrating the admirable quality of perseverance. No company and leader have perfect and unblemished records. This is an oft-repeated adage. No success exists without occasional failures. When hard times hit some people may go down. Providence may not come to the rescue. It may be easy to be like a cat which jumped on a hot stove and thereafter would not jump on any stove, hot or cold.

Successful leaders must be as tough as linebackers, with the fortitude to press against insurmountable odds. These leaders learn from mistakes, and are able to regroup and get going again, even from the brink of failures. They draw inspiration from the phoenix that rose from the ashes.

Long time AT&T's CEO Mike Allen's acquisition of NCR was a dismal failure though his acquisitions of McCaw Cellular and spin-off of Lucent Technologies were notable successes. At $700 million, he sold AT&T's 19% of Sun Microsystems too soon (AT&T's share of Sun Microsystems would be worth $35 billion in 2000, though it has drastically declined since.) Similarly, AT&T's Mike Armstrong's ill-fated purchase of MediaOne, Nortel's poor purchase of Bay Networks and Wachovia's purchase of World Savings were by far some of the most serious mistakes committed by CEOs. However, while leaders may commit mistakes, missteps and missed opportunities, successful ones realize that they represent lessons that must be learned again and again. Dealing effectively with uncertainty and risk (however bleak and perplexing) is crucial to success. Making tough decisions involve risk and daring, even though the risks may be calculated. Even very successful leaders sometimes make bad calls. There are both mistakes and triumphs: some ventures will tumble or stall. Successful leaders are able to wrench the company out of its tailspin, regain traction and achieve resurgent success. As Stephen R. Covey (The 8th Habit, 2004) said: "Setbacks are inevitable; misery is a choice. There are always reasons, never an excuse." After energies have been sapped, the ability to pick up the pieces, bounce back and reconstruct under adverse conditions build endurance and tenacity. Companies will experience difficult times. Managers may face situations that yield no obvious answers but nevertheless require resolution. Financial trouble may be dire, and lethargy difficult to overcome. The company's fiber will be tested. Some may feel cheated when what they expect does not pan out. There is a choice either to wallow in self-pity or step out to the warm sunshine when situations are dismal. Successful people learn how to gain control of situations that are out of control and out of dogged persistence, rebound quickly from setbacks. They persevere and restore the luster instead of giving up as others might have. According to Andrew Shatte who taught corporate clients on how to stay resilient in the face of adversity at Adaptiv Learning Systems (a consulting firm based in King of Prussia, Pennsylvania), some of the key principles are:

➢ Dealing effectively with setback starts with how you explain it to yourself and others around you. Many people tend to have negative or helpless ways of thinking. Some people tend to explain setbacks as temporary while others view them as permanent. Some cast blame on themselves while some tend to blame others. Each style needs to be offset with logic and perspective.

➤ People tend to overreact. Most of the time, things are not as bleak as they appear.

➤ It is important to be honest when you run into trouble and to be sure to understand what is really going on. Armed with accurate facts, understanding and analysis the problem can be worked out.

➤ Keep it in perspective. Determine the probability of the worst and best outcome and take proper steps to remedy the situation.

9. Move On

People and businesses do fall on hard times. Whether we surmount them is up to us. Given the realities of the business world today, you must face the truth when dismal conditions prevail. We are, in one way or another, prisoners of our past experience. Do not indulge in despair and self-pity when things go wrong no matter what the circumstances. Do not dwell on the problem and feel helpless when flying into heavy headwinds. You waste your time and energy from dwelling in negativity. There may be a sense of lassitude and isolation to a point where you feel like buckling under the pressure. Take a break, then bounce back, be resolute and get on with life. You have it within your power to do it though the comeback may be long and slow. Explore new vistas with your fertile brain. Then extract the necessary resources and rebuild brick-by-brick.

Begin anew. Be ready to pull the plug and move on when highly touted investments turn sour with no recovery in sight. Although certain times call for perseverance, you must exercise common sense and judgment when projects fail and show no signs of reawakening. Know when to end a deal, and more importantly, how to learn from the failure and churn the experience into future success. Once you determine what may have led to a project's end, think about how to avoid such missteps. Regain your equilibrium. If business conditions are to blame, what can be done to extricate from failures, to improve them, to circumvent them? Is there any link in your company's chain that is to blame? How can it be improved? Explore for other opportunities for which there will be many.

10. You can't judge a book by its cover

⌘ A hen lays one egg, the whole village hears her cockles; a turtle lays eggs by the hundreds, not a sound is heard.

- Malay Proverb ⌘

In complex and multifaceted situations, it is easy to be deluded by specious arguments that look good on the surface but are flawed underneath. In today's sophisticated environment, especially in the field of sales, marketing and public relations, it is common to couch thing into respectable language. We often equate wealth and opulence with success

251

and image with leadership. In an era where time is a precious commodity we look up to appearance and sound bites, style over substance. It is easy to be deceived by colonnaded façade, pomposity and pretensions. Some leaders use surface charm to mislead and manipulate. Such leaders are astute at presenting urbane exterior and maintaining a glamorous façade. There is a blanket default presumption to judge people by the image they convey rather than character and competence. Character and courage are inseparable. Celebrity is not leadership. There is a tendency to confuse activity with progress and passivity with lack of initiative. Don't confuse language ability to capability though some people may have both. People can be easily impressed by amalgamated quasi-economic ramblings. There are nonetheless good reasons to be skeptical of such claims. Arguments may be theoretically elegant, but lack substance in actuality. Sometimes, things are not what they seem, and a jazzed up exterior may hide an unsubstantial interior. Big egos and grand ideas are not sufficient. In other words, false solutions are often more hot air than real action. People may be impressed by methodological elegance over insight. Issues can be sugarcoated. High sounding impressive words and exhortations are overused but under-practiced. Do not confuse motion with action. A down-to-earth manner can mask abuse of power. There is often a disconnection between how well you think you do and what is actually in the minds of your customers. Remember that public posturing can be mistaken for true commitment. Unfortunately, errors of human judgment can infect even the smartest people. People who looked promising at the start may turn into liabilities later on. These people may get high marks on paper. At times their business acumen may not quite necessarily match their rhetorical gifts. They have to earn their stripes as someone who can deliver on the promises. On the other hand, there may be people who work quietly for transformation. There are people who are low key and abhor the spotlight. They are the backbones of the company.

A company's growth and prosperity can be misleading. Care must be taken to not mistake information for reality. Human beings are complex and managers must learn to cut through the fog and distinguish between hot air and inaction. Pressure and stress can accentuate the true and troubling aspects of one's character. Job applicants may have impressive resumes and appear charming in chitchats but can turn out to be duds.

Another example of dangerous misleading appearances is that of false unity; an outward appearance of unity may actually conceal undercurrents of bad feelings. Anger may not be immediate and sometimes may not be articulated. Organizations will be well served if they can pierce the veil of opaque systems, process, procedures and practices.

Chapter 12
What is wrong with Wall Street?

⌘ In the short run the stock market is a voting machine
but in the long run it's a weighing machine.
- Ben Graham ⌘

Simply, the stock markets provide a source of corporate
funding and vehicles for people to participate in corporate
growth. To this day, among all financial markets, Wall Street
poses the greatest challenge to investors and regulators.
Insider stock traders, short-term traders, momentum-driven
day traders, financial speculators, corporate manipulators,
frauds and born-again group of financial pundits are eroding
public confidence in this important financial institution. The
Securities and Exchange Commission (SEC) has oversight and
fiduciary responsibility to look after the interest of investors.
They are charged with keeping the system honest. The
Federal Reserve (Fed) is responsible for monetary policy and
behavior of financial institutions. Strictly speaking,
regulations and enforcement, thus far have not adequately
accomplish policy goals. William H. Donaldson, since
becoming chairman of the SEC in February 2003, said his
biggest eye-opener is how much wrongdoing at Wall Street he
saw and was surprised three months later to see how
prevalent it was in the economy. This is sad, disturbing but
true. Company's directors failed badly in upholding
shareholder interest. Many reckless Wall Street promoters
are capitalizing on the greed of unwary speculators
(specialists and neophytes alike) with sleazy research and

promises of bumper profits. Many theories expounded by Wall Street analysts, snake-oil merchants, investment bankers and venture capitalists by means that are self-serving, superfluous, deficient in concept and implementation have devalued public trust. The problem was compounded when executives took advantage of stock options back-dating to the detriment of stock holders. Credibility is shattered. The financial fiasco of 2008 has once again proven that regulations, thus far are ineffective.

Wall Street has its fair share of shady characters. Hypes, artful languages, accounting gimmickry and incomplete information are often clouded with small grains of truths. Corporate executives are adept at making well-planned speeches that disguise ailments. Though swayed by highly touted values, transient results and the "herd effect," the aura of success is eventually dissipated by the cold wind of reality. The inevitable always happens, but not always when it is most convenient. The misfortune of some became bonanzas for others. It is not surprising that for the average investors, profits are elusive and slippery. The business plans of many startups, notably during the stock bubbles, were to launch initial public offerings (IPOs) or be purchased. During the heyday, founders and initial investors in these companies were preoccupied with fast growth and cashing out for considerable personal gain within a short time with scant regard for the interest of other stakeholders. Unscrupulous entrepreneurs misled unsophisticated investors with manipulated financial measure. Some peddle vague and generalized predictions. Financial predictions and calculations based on warped figures were disappointing to say the least. These masquerades led to wrong decisions and buying frenzy that were detrimental to investors and consumers. These wrong doings have resulted in many investors badly bruised, disillusioned and parting with their hard-earned wealth, causing disruptive bouts of public indignation during the period following the stock market debacle of March 2000. Disenchantment with the performance of mutual funds was heightened with an injection of realism. And the rest on the e-business wave of year 2000 – so goes the cliché – is history.

Left unchecked, these wrong doings bode ill for corporate America in the years ahead as the fates and fortunes of many people are affected. While this chapter appears to be a litany of Wall Street failures, there is no silver bullet to address this longstanding malady. While there is no clear answer, free financial markets should be protected and encouraged to flourish, it should be counter-balanced with toughened enforcement and punishment against activities that are outright illegal or bordering on illegality. The centerpiece of policy and legislative initiatives should provide a distinction between free market principle and runaway abuse of the system by those in superior vantage points. In the wake of significant investor loses and dampened enthusiasm, appropriate regulations should be enacted and have teeth. There should be enough funding for the SEC to address the weaknesses that underlie Wall Street. Legal loopholes should be plugged in order to bolster investor confidence, in a market that is largely unpredictable. As Federal Reserve Chairman Alan Greenspan stated on April 16, 2004: "Sinners on Wall Street should be *expeditiously punished*, less they erode the foundation of trust on which U.S. financial markets are built. I couldn't agree more. However, in rewriting rules and practices that are no longer effective to address the recent run of Wall Street scandals, rule makers must be careful not to inflict *collateral damage*. In spite of progress significant doubts exist. Laws and regulations must address the underlying issues that affect speculative price movements, exacerbated by exhortations from pundits of all stripes. There should be more demanding accounting whenever valuations are unreasonably high or when executive compensations are outlandish. The SEC should focus more on the surveillance of stocks with surging price rises and declines beyond or below the levels justified on economic grounds. The SEC should carefully look out for professional collaborative traders trading for and among them to manipulate price movements. Although some steps in this direction are occurring the tasks remain formidable. The web of complicity must be exposed and abuses curbed. A concerted selling effort could plunge a stock to low level, even with the up-tick rule. Analysts are under constant pressure to deliver favorable reports about companies they track. There should be more public scrutiny and publicity to educate and caution investors when newspapers, magazines and televisions are pumping hot air with public proclamation and great fanfare to float a blimp. Many of these proclamations are woefully narrow in scope though they are influential in swaying investment decisions, more so during market craze. It is hard for investors to tread above the market madness riddled with inaccurate financial data. Punishment for violators in this shark-infested ocean must be severe enough to make the costs far outweigh the benefits of risking a violation. Investors must learn to cut through the fog, the hype, patterns of suspicious activity and other financial misconduct and public deception. The public must learn more about the malady on how accounting and statistical models can be manipulated. They must learn to separate the facts from the hypes. Prudence dictates that we must learn how to spot balance sheet and financial statements that is window dressed. There should be more preventive actions to forestall illegal, debilitating, and unsavory acts. You don't want to let the horse out of the barn and then give yourself a medal for bringing it back. Notwithstanding the fact that many investors are gullible as ever, there should never be justification for fraud.

According to Jim Huguet (Great Companies, Great Returns, 1999), most Wall Street money managers buy stocks for the short-term. Wall Street is reinforcing a narrow preoccupation with short-term gains and public relations hypes, coupled with impatient stockholders, including continuous influx of pension and mutual funds, lured by the prospect of easy wealth and succumbing to greed and wishful thinking. When prices reach silly levels, they eventually will come down fast. This concern was further described by Alan Greenspan in his recent book (The Age of Turbulence, Penguin Press, 2007): When markets are behaving rationally, as they do almost all the time, they appear to engage in "random walk:" the past gives no better indication than the flip of the future direction of the price of the stock. But sometimes, that walk is a stampede when gripped by fear, people rush to disengage from commitments and stalk will plunge. And when people are driven by euphoria, they will drive up prices to nonsensical levels.

Investors are giving companies less time to prove themselves. Gambling mentality predominate today's stock market. Investors are demanding continuing growth for each and every quarter. A company's stock gets clobbered when earning that is below analyst expectation or when corporate results headed south. As such, companies are pressured to stretch the numbers and accounting rules. It turned out to be a delusion. Against the backdrop of skullduggery, these situations should evoke serious concerns. Some companies will ultimately pay a high price with tainted reputation and financial retribution when they resort to accounting devices that obscure potential adverse results. There is no escape from reality of greatly diminished corporate balance sheet and investor confidence.

In order to fend off potential takeovers, especially when valuations are low, corporate leaders may resort to self-serving activities by mortgaging the future through poison pills and golden parachutes.

Investors are unable to decipher what is being said on the surface and underneath, as languages used in disclosure documents are typically full of jargon, buzzword, legalese and complex sentence construction. Jargon may be puzzling to people. For reasons not entirely evident, Wall Street sharpie has demonstrated ingenuity in generating buzzwords coupled with hype and inaccuracies. Buzzwords can be deceptive. As Arthur Levitt, Chairman, US Securities and Exchange Commission said: "The legalese and jargon of the past must give way to everyday words that communicate complex information clearly." Indomitable as it is and in the face of compelling evidence: the Office of Investor Education and Assistance of the SEC should do more to strengthen requirement and promotion of disclosure documents with more information and clearer English, improving the fog index. The public should be provided with well-informed and credible information to sooth nerves frayed by the continuous credit trauma.

There will always be renewed search for Holy Grail of financial success. Many money making ideas sound deceptively simple. Making money, even in the land of milk and honey is trickier than anyone expected and justifiably so. In a sense we learn a lot from experience through up and down economic cycles. There is always an element of risk, even during halcyon years beside the recrudescence of stock market gyration. Without shareholder pressure for regular short-term profits, companies can take time and money to develop products, gain market share and long-term profits without jettisoning the entrepreneurial spirit. Unfortunately, many companies are using stock prices as the compass for managing their business, leading ultimately to less than desirable results. Even best run companies are subject to the vagaries of economic cycles, shareholder-management divide and the emotions of fear and greed. Higher stock prices may be due to the industry high growth period or short term maneuvers. There is tremendous pressure from the investment community to meet elevated expectations quarter after quarter.

By most measures, building total business value is the way to create and sustain enduring market valuation. Company reputation is one of the most important contributors to the market value of a company. Wall Street is too preoccupied with revenue growth versus real cash earnings. Sustaining revenue and earnings growth depend to a very large extent on the qualities of the business the companies are engaged in, their financial capital and market presence. A substantial number of companies were on shaky ground, generating revenue in un-sustaining ways with stock prices at dizzying heights. Eighty percent of efforts should be devoted to real cash earnings and twenty percent to revenue growth over the long haul. There should be renewed emphasis on earnings growth and quality of management rather than relying on the tempo of the stock market. Low price to earnings ratio should be a general favorite. Well-run companies grow sales and profits at rates that are higher than industry average. Key factors for evaluation should take into account a number of dimensions including actual value of the company's customer franchise derived from basic, predictable trends instead of headlines. The financial data should be viewed within the context of prevailing economic conditions. All marketable securities should be valued at cost, not at market value. Corporate chieftains should find ways to unlock hidden values in the companies. Indicators of past performance should be weighed against potential future performance. In large measure, stock investment is an aleatory activity.

Chapter 13
Sarbanes-Oxley

⌘ Many of the scandals that I have seen has began from glossing over unpleasant facts.

- Lord Chandress ⌘

The Sarbanes-Oxley statutes, Section 404 or SOX as it is known: was enacted by Congress in 2002 in the wake of colossal scandals concerning Enron, Worldcom and other corporations. It was instated as a rational response to accounting control failures in which the true state of a business' corporate financial position was disguised. During the course of investigations, ethically unsound operational procedures were uncovered, a battered testament to human frailties and excess. In these cases, revenues, profits and other financial projections were significantly inflated. The fallout from these scandals has strong repercussions on the confidence of business enterprises. In the case of Enron, it was the biggest bankruptcy at that time and 400 employees lost their jobs. (As it happens many years before, a young trader stationed in Singapore (Nick Leeson) through concealed trading losses ultimately brought down Baring Brothers of London, a long established British institution. Just prior to the collapse of Enron, the company bankers and academics had call Enron the model of the 21st century success. A more recent news reported history's biggest fraud by 31 year old French rogue trader Jerome Kerviel, who caused a $7.1B trading losses to France's Societe Generale Bank). Disappointment was inevitable when flaws were uncovered. It tarnished the image and undermines the underpinnings of

American business, and in some cases, jolting companies to the core. The aftershocks linger long after the scandals are consummated. It lessens the trust by employees and people at large regarding the safety and security of their investments and jobs. It demonstrates the failure of self-regulation. The concept of meaningful "old fashioned" oversight has essentially being forgotten.

It is not uncommon for companies to put the spin on the numbers to manipulate results and create a certain public impression. These are some of the key reasons why, nowadays, corporate leaders and numbers are held in such low esteem. The statute provides measures to check avaricious appetites of the unscrupulous and their compliant associates. It provides latitudes to fix such problems making it harder for corporate leaders to claim ignorance as reason for negligence. It subjects business leaders to insider trading and anti-fraud rules of the SEC. The statute provides different arrows in the quiver as antidotes to check the excesses. It requires certain accounting best practices to be enforced but the company auditors who in turn are overseen by Public Company Account Oversight Board (PCAOB) which is irreverently referred as "peek-a-boo." Other key provision requires independent audit committees. Companies cannot purchase Consulting Services from the same accounting firms that do their audits. Loans to officers are prohibited and executives must personally certify financial statements. In spite of these efforts recovery of trust will be long and slow.

While the period since the infamous Enron scandal reveals starkly the need for rigorous financial control, laws by themselves will not guarantee good governance as there is significant limit to what regulation can accomplish. There should be continuing vigilance to forestall the chicanery of unscrupulous business leaders. Otherwise, market reaction would be ugly and demand for compensation from those who are hurt will be colossal. Companies can learn from others who are models of good governance. Companies must assure a culture of integrity and maintain rigorous internal financial control, one that can stand up to fair minded scrutiny.

Since the introduction of SOX six years ago, it and other regulations and controls have failed miserably as demonstrated by the financial turmoil of 2008. There are costs to Sarbanes-Oxley some of which are wasted. Sarbanes-Oxley may go too far to create waste, duplication and dilution of corporate resources. It decreases US competitive flexibility. If not carefully exercised, Sarbanes-Oxley post-Enron reform can become "regulatory overreach" that helps build bureaucracy – i.e. checking the checkers who check the checkers. The army of auditors that are needed to maintain surveillance on the financial processes and procedures would by their actions undermine financial flexibility so essential in today's fast-moving business. As Tom Perkins, legendary Silicon Valley venture capitalist asserted (The Education f Tom Perkins – Valley Boy, 2007): "Unfortunately, the compliance aspects of SOX can, if permitted, come to dominate everything that the board does. In my view, it is bad news for the shareholders if a chairman's proclivity for SOX that is form over substance becomes ascendant. What's more important is creating rising shareholder value." There need to be a balance between arduous financial record keeping and rules for investor protection, les; one end up oscillating between modernity and regressive tradition. Because policies and procedures are set to protect against a small percentage of unethical people, they miss servicing the honest majority. Corporate executives might find themselves consumed by red tape and paperwork rather than devoting more time for real management. It creates a pool of investigators, testing groups, watchful guardians and monitors running around rather than doers actively performing work. This will eventually sap the time, energy and spirit of innovation of public companies. Also, the costs of installing safeguards, auditing and financial reporting increase sharply and have proven prohibitive for smaller companies. In many cases, the payback does not justify the cost invested. Because of these vexing problems and high risk of litigation, many companies may be forced to list in London, Hong Kong, Canada or other stock exchanges instead of listing in the US. Another danger is that foreign companies may decide to de-list or drop new listings in the US. In 2007, only 5% of the value of global initial public offerings was raised in the US compared to 50% in 2000. The irony of this is that Sarbanes-Oxley creates more jobs and profits for accountants and auditors, the professions that are at fault in the original scandal.

The genie has been out of the bottle and SOX should be scaled back. However, this does not mean that corporate financial controls should not be exercised. The battle for corporate financial integrity is far from won. Corporate thieves who break the law must not go unpunished. There is no doubt that disclosure standards must be improved by establishing clear rules. A system of check and balance against negligence must be fortified at the corporation, even though fraud and malfeasance may not be totally prevented despite all precautions. However, regulators must stay clear of dictating business practices, making rules as tight as a drum and cause unnecessary fear of making mistakes. Regulations must not be defined in narrow terms which might be more suitable under more static business conditions. Regulators must find ways to reduce unnecessary regulations that will stifle creativity and innovations. It is impossible to legislate integrity and sound moral.

Chapter 14
Protection of Environment, Intellectual Property Right and Privacy Right

⌘ It's easier to stay out of trouble than to get out of trouble.

- Warren Buffet ⌘

It is essential that governments and businesses across the globe do more to address the issues of environmental protection, intellectual property rights and privacy rights. Politically, socially and morally, the average customer believes in the need for companies to protect the environment as well as intellectual property and privacy rights. The reasons should not be new to anyone. It runs the gamut from compliance to local laws, sound business practices, commitment to environmental concerns, international obligations and mitigation strategies and so on. It is not too great a stretch to say that the allure of profits has contributed to the neglect of the environment and other irresponsible and damaging activities. It is becoming important to comply with federal, state and local provisions regulating carbon emissions and discharge of materials into the environment. The public is increasingly aware of environmental and energy conservation issues though these still constitute only a fraction of what need to be addressed. Leaders must be in the forefront and efforts must be intensified to do more than what the law requires to optimize energy consumption, cut emissions and reduce pollution. Tackling these gargantuan issues involve welding economic concerns with environmental issues. They require governmental and corporate resources and ingenuity on a global scale.

Clearly, however, there is still a long way to go toward addressing these environmental quandaries, as many companies in poor countries lack the resources to meet international standards and requirements. These problems have developed over the years on a scale the world has never seen before. They cannot be solved overnight. There is patchwork of competing disparities between rich and poor nations in combating disturbing deterioration in local and global environmental conditions. It should be recognized that 80% of people worldwide are still very poor. Environmentalists are clamoring for universal standards but poor countries cannot afford to adopt those standards. The question of how much does it cost and who will pay for it remains to be answered satisfactorily. Realistically, companies who can afford to do so should uphold these public and international obligations. It is understandable that environmental issues are at low priority for struggling companies as they are more concerned with financial survival. While attention getting statements are important, to be credible we need an objective and unbiased study regarding environmental and human impact, free from political maneuverings and herd behavior. It is a question that sparks further discussions. These issues will reach a roiling point sometime in the near future, if it is not addressed proactively by responsible corporations somewhere along the line.

The 1997 Kyoto Protocol, from the United Nations Framework Convention on Climate Change (UNFCCC) serves a broad purpose by taking the lead to solve the problems of global warming through controlling greenhouse emissions. The treaty ratified by more than 175 countries requires industrialized nation that ratify it to reduce emissions by 50% from 1990 levels. The cap will go into effect in 2008. Marching under the broad banner of environmentalism, many European nations have already ratified it. Environmentalists bemoan the fact that major countries such as US, China, India and Russia, to name a few, still fall short in these areas. By a vote of 95-0, the US Senate had rejected the treaty. The world expects more from the US. Environmental chiefs from the Group of Eight (G8) countries on May 26, 2008 pledged toward cutting greenhouse gas emissions in half by 2050 but is it aggressive enough? The European Union (EU) has agreed to cut greenhouse gas emissions by 20% from 1999 levels by 2020, The EU is leading the way to higher fuel efficiency standards with a goal of 48.9 miles per gallon by 2012. Japan, with a current standard of 40.9 miles per gallon aims to increase fuel efficiency to 46 miles per gallon by 2015. China currently under 35 miles per gallon is expected to reach 35.8 miles per gallon by 2009. This is part of the progression of improving fuel efficiency but will it be fast enough? Though the scope of undertaking is vast, companies must be encouraged to accelerate development of fuel efficient and low emission engines to meet or exceed automobile exhaust regulations. Efforts should not be spared for more research on consequences on global environmental change, energy and resource options. Much help and cooperation are needed to usher in the age where corporations and nations take their obligations seriously which require many years of sustained commitment.

Interspersed among these topics are intellectual property (IP) rights which have replaced mineral rights as drivers of success. The complexity of this situation and its economic relevance has no equal in history. And it is hardly news. Intellectual property protection raises the barrier of entry and will buy some time. Integrity aside, companies must remember that practically, business policy hinges on corporate accountability to the community and society as a whole. Otherwise, companies will be goaded by regulations to comply. Though intellectual property such as patents and copyrights can provide certain level of legal constraints, they are different from physical property in that they are more difficult to protect. Physical property can be easily protected by security forces. IP can be developed from old ideas that can be difficult to trace. For all intent and purpose; some companies may not always practice true to declared principles, with all talk but no action. This has contributed to the erosion in a staggering degree of ethics in business and education. In reality, good ideas will be copied sooner or later. It is important to remember that money is a by-product of a business, not an end in itself. While imitation is a way to learn, it is not an uncommon practice by unscrupulous companies to cut corners and pirate design and manufacturing technologies of other companies to circumvent development cost. IP violations occur when selling prices are high relative to manufacturing cost, when products are easy to manufacture and when they are available in the retail market.

While the US and key allies have narrowed the differences on the need to tackle greenhouse gases that were linked to global warming they remain far apart on how to do it. Industrialized countries should step up to the challenge and provide incentives to induce voluntary compliance to this ever wider range of environmental issues by granting or withdrawing market access. It is rich nations obligations to provide financial and technical wherewithal to help developing countries battle global warming, including sharing information and facility. The process will be long and slow. However, as Rajendra Pachari, Chairman of the intergovernmental Panel on Climate Change (IPCC) a UN Nobel-winning panel at a gathering of EU ministers in July 2008 noted: "We have till 2015 to meet target that is safe." Corporations, especially large ones need to make special efforts on public engagement with clear implementation both in form and spirit. It will be helpful if more countries including the US agree to designate CO_2 as a pollutant. To this end, power plants that emit CO_2 will be subjected to environmental regulation. Rule-based systems must be complemented by incentive-based system to discourage businesses from undercutting these cherished human values. Schemes that enriched some but impoverished many should be discouraged.

Interesting Quiz

1. What did McDonald and California has in common?

2. What did General George Patton, Jr. and California has in common?

3. What was the original business of Berkshire Hathaway?

4. What business was Nokia started out in?

5. What was the original business of Warner Brothers before entering the film industry?

6. What did John Chambers, CEO of Cisco and Wang Laboratories have in common?

7. What high profile company merger occurred one week before 911?

8. Which multi-billionaire was the creator of the hugely successful Computer Dealer Exhibition in the early 1990s (COMDEX) but eventually leverage his success by entering the casino business.

9. How did the brand "Adidas" came about?

10. Who started Sony?

11. Who started Ampex?

12. Who is the employee with the longest service at Fairchild Semiconductor, the pioneer of the semiconductor industry?

13. At what age did Alexander the Great died?

14. Who invented the incandescent light bulb?

15. When were DuPont founded and what was its original business?

16. Which well know person was the first Chairman of the Securities and Exchange Commission (SEC)?

17. Who collected Albert Einstein's Nobel Prize money?

18. What is YAHOO an acronym for?

19. When did Toyota Motor Company got its start?

20. What's an "inkfish"?

Answers to Quiz

1. Dick and Mac McDonald opened McDonald in 1940 as a small drive-in restaurant in San Bernardino, California.

2. General George Patton, Jr. was born in Lake Vineyard, California in 1885.

3. In 1965 Berkshire Hathaway was a struggling textile manufacturer in Nebraska.

4. Nokia's original business was in pulp and paper industry.

5. Warner Brothers started out as owners of a string of funeral parlors.

6. Prior to Cisco, John Chambers spent 8 years at Wang Laboratories and six years with IBM.

7. HP and Compaq. (Call that timing).

8. Sheldon Adelson created and sold COMDEX to Japanese firm Softbank for $ 862 million in 1995. He now owns Venetian and Sands Casinos in Las Vegas and other mega casinos in Macao.

9. "Adidas" is named after its founder Adi Dassler, an avid soccer player who spent a greater part of his life creating athletic equipments.

10. Sony was founded by Akio Morita and his friend Masaru Ibuka, an engineer. It started as a maker of electrical parts for the Japanese Navy.

11. Ampex was founded by Russian immigrant Alexander M. Ponniatoff in 1944. The name was derived from the initial plus "ex" for excellence. It started out by making entire motor for the navy

12. Harlan Lawlers who has been working for Fairchild, now named Fairchild Imaging, a direct descendent of the company that hired him as employee # 23.

13. Alexander the Great died at age 33.

14. The first incandescent light bulb was invented at the same time by Thomas Edison in United States and Joseph Swan in England.

15. DuPond was founded in 1802 and made gunpowder.

16. Joseph P. Kennedy.

17. Einstein's Nobel Prize money ended was collected by Mileva Manic, his first wife, many years after the divorce. It was based on a divorce agreement made long before Einstein won the prize. Einstein was highly assured of winning the prize that he promised that if Mileva would give him a divorce, he would be inclined to give her the prize money, to which Mileva collected many years later.

18. Yet Another Hierarchical Officious Oracle.

19. Toyota Motor Company was founded in 1933 by Kiichion Toyoda as Toyoda Automatic Looms Works, a manufacturer of weaving machines.

20. An agricultural vehicle in China that spew from its exhaust large amounts of thick black smoke.

Bibliography

1. Abernathy, William J., Clark, Kim B. and Kantrow, Alan M: "Industrial Renaissance: Producing a Competitive Future for America," Basic Books, Inc., New York, 1983.
2. Adizes, Ichak: The Pursuit of Prime,"Knowledge Exchange, LLC, Santa Monica, California, 1996.
3. Adler, Lou: "Hire with Your Head – Using Power Hiring to Build Great Companies," John Wiley and Sons, New Jersey, 1998, 2002.
4. Alletzhauser, Albert J.: "The House of Nomura – The Inside Story of the Legendary Japanese Financial Industry," Arcade Publishing, Inc., New York, 1990.
5. Amor, Daniel: "Internet Future Strategies – How Pervasive Computing Services Will Change the World," Prentice-Hall, New Jersey, 2002.
6. Assaraf, John & Smith, Murray: "The Answer – Grow Any Business, Achieve Financial Freedom, and Live and Extraordinary Life," Atria Books, New York, 2008.
7. Axelrod, Alan: "Patton – A Biography," Palgrave Macmillan, New York, 2006.
8. Barner, Robert W.: "Crossing the Minefield: Tactics for Overcoming Today's Toughest Management Challenges," American Management Association, New York, 1994.
9. Bartelle, John: "The Search – How Google and Its Rivals Rewrote the Rules of Business and Transformed Our Culture, "Penguin Group, New York, 2005.
10. Batstone, David: "Saving the Corporate Soul: Eight Principles for Creating and Preserving Integrity and Profitability without Selling Out," Jossey-Bass Publishers, San Francisco, 2003.
11. Beatty, Jack: "The World According to Peter Drucker," The Free Press, New York, 1998.
12. Beckwith, Harry: "The Invisible Touch," Warner Books Inc., New York, 2000.

13. Beckwith, Harry & Beckwith Christine Clifford, "You, Inc. – The Art of Selling Yourself, Warner Business Books, New York, 2007.

14. Bennis, Warren and Nanus, Burt: "Leaders: Strategies For Taking Charge," HarperBusiness Press, New York, 1985.

15. Benton, D.A.: "How To Think Like A CEO," Warner Books Inc., New York, 1996.

16. Bernstein, Pete W. and Swan, Annalyn: "All the Money in the World – How the Forbes 400 Make and Spend their Fortunes," Alfred A. Kopf Publishing, New York, 2007.

17. Bethanis, Susan J.: "Leadership Chronicles of a Corporate Sage – Five Keys to Becoming a more Effective Leader," Dearborn Trade Publishing, Chicago, 2004.

18. Blanchard, Ken: "Leading at a High Level – Blanchard on Leadership and Creating High Performance Organization," Prentice Hall, New Jersey, 2007.

19. Blanchard, K., Hybels B. and Hodges, P.: "Leadership by the Books," Waterbrook Press, New York, 1999.

20. Blanchard, Ken and Waghorn, Terry, "Mission Possible: Becoming a World-Class Organization While There's Still Time," McGraw-Hill, New York, 1997.

21. Blanchard, Ken, Carlos, John P. and Randolph, Alan: "The 3 Keys to Empowerment," Berrett-Koehler Publishers, Inc., San Francisco, 1999.

22. Bonner, William and Rajiva, Lila: "Mobs, Messiahs and Markets – Surviving the Public Spectacle in Finance and Politics," John Wiley and Sons Inc., New York, 2007

23. Bossidy, Larry and Charan, Ram: "Execution: The Discipline of Getting Things Done," Crown Business, New York, 2002.

24. Bossidy, Larry and Charan, Ram: "Confronting Reality – Doing What Matters to Get Things Right," Crown Business, New York, 2004.

25. Boyatzis, Richard and McKee, Annie: "Resonant Leadership – Renewing Yourself and Connecting with Others Through Mindfulness, Hope and Compassion," Harvard Business School Press, Massachussetts, 2005.

26. Bradford, David L. and Cohen, Allan R.: "Managing for Excellence: The Guide to Developing Performance in Contemporary Organizations," John Wiley and Sons, Inc., New York, 1984.

27. Bradford, David L. and Cohen, Allan R: "Power Up: Transforming Organizations through Shared Leadership," John Wiley and Sons, Inc., 1998.

28. Buckingham, Marcus & Coffman, Curt: "First, Break All the Rules – What the World's Greatest Managers Do Differently," Simon & Schuster, New York, 1999.

29. Buderi, Robert and Huang, Gregory T.: "Guanxi – Microsoft, China and Bill Gates Plan to Win the Road Ahead," Simon & Schuster, New York, 2006.

30. Bund, Barbara E.: "The Outside-In Corporation – How to Build a Customer-Centric Organization for Breakthrough Results," McGraw-Hill, New York, 2006.

31. Buzzotta, V.R., Lefton, R.E., Cheney, Alan and Beatty, Ann: "Making Common Sense Common Practice: Achieving High Performance by Using What You Already Know," St. Lucie Press, Boca Raton, Florida, 1996.

32. Carnegie, Dale: "How to Win Friends and Influence People," Pocket Books, NY 1981.

33. Case, Sheila: "Kaizen Strategies for Winning Through People," Pitman Publishing, London, 1996.

34. Cassell, Jonathan: *"Internet Box: Paradigm Shift or StepBackward?"* Electronic Buyers' News, Jan 29, 1996, pp. 14-16.

35. Cassidy, John: "dot.con – The Greatest Story Ever Sold," Harper Collins Publishers, New York, 2002.

36. Cauley, Leslie: "End of the Line – The Rise and Fall of AT&T," Free Press, New York, 2005.

37. Cepuch, Randy: "A Weekend with Warren Buffet and other Shareholder Meeting Adventures," Thunder Mouth Press, New York, 2007.

38. Champy, James and Nohria, Nitin: "The Arc of Ambition: Defining the Leadership Journey," Persus Books, Massachusetts, 2000.
39. Chan, James: "Spare Room Tycoon – Succeeding Independently, The 70 Lessons of Sane Self-Employment," Nicholas Brearley Publishing, Naperville, 2000.
40. Chang, Ha-Joon, "Bad Samaritan - The Myth of Free Trade and the Secret History of Capitalism," Bloomsbury Press, New York, 2008.
41. Charan, Ram: "Know-How – The 8 Skills that Separate People Who Perform from Those Who Don't," Crown Business, 2007.
42. Charan, Ram, Drotter, Stephen and Noel, James: "The Leadership Pipeline: How to Build The Leadership Powered Company," Jossey-Bass, San Francisco, 2001.
43. Cheyfitz, Kirk: "Thinking Inside the Box - 12 Timeless Rules for Managing a Successful Business, "Free Press, new York, 2003.
44. Cohen, William A.: "The New Art of the Leader," Prentice Hall, New York, 2000.
45. Collins, Jim: "Good to Great: Why Some Companies Make the Leap...and Others Don't," HarperBusiness, New York, 2001.
46. Collins, James C. and Porras, Jerry I.: "Build To Last – Successful Habits of Visionary Companies," HarperBusiness, New York, 1994.
47. Constantine, Peter (Editor and Translator): "The Essential Writings of Machiavelli, " Random House, New York, 2007
48. Cook, Susan Johnson: "Moving Up – Ten Steps to Turning Your Life Around and Getting to the Top," Doubleday, New York, 2008.
49. Covey, Stephen R.: "The 7 Habits of Highly Effective People," Simon & Schuster, New York, 1989.
50. Covey, Stephen R.: "The 8th Habits – From Effectiveness to Greatness," Free Press, New York, 2004.

51. Covey, Steven R., Merrill, A. Roger and Merrill, Rebecca R.: "First Things First," Simon & Schuster, New York, 1994.

52. Crainer, Stuart: The Ultimate Book of Business Gurus – 110 Thinkers Who Really Made a Difference," AMACOM, New York, 1998.

53. Cramer, James J.: "Real Money – Sane Investing in an Insane World, Simon & Schuster, New York, 2005.

54. Curtis, Donald: "Management Rediscovered," Dow-Jones Erwin, Illinois, 1990.

55. Cusumano, Michael A. and Shelby, Richard W.: "Microsoft Secrets: How the World's Most Powerful Company Creates Technology, Shapes Markets and Manages People," Free Press, New York, 1995.

56. Cusumano, Michael A. and Markides, Constantinos C.: "MIT Sloan Review: Strategic Thinking for the Next Economy," Jossey-Bass, San Francisco, 2001.

57. Czarnecki, Mark T.: "Managing by Measuring," AMACOM, New York, 1998.

58. Davenport, Thomas H & Prusak, Laurence with Wilson, H. James: "What's the Big Deal? Creating and Capitalizing on the Best Management Thinking," Harvard Business School Press, Massachusetts, 2003.

59. Davidson, Bill: "Breakthrough – How Great Companies Set Outrageous Objectives and Achieve Them," John Wiley & Sons, New Jersey, 2004.

60. Day, George S: "The Market Driven Organization," Free Press, New York, 1999.

61. DeLuca, Joel R.: "Political Savvy – Systematic Approaches to Leadership Behind-the-Scenes," EBG Publications, Pennsylvania, 1999.

62. Demma Translation Group: Sun Tzu the Art of War – A New Translation, Shambhala, Boston, 2001.

63. Deming, Edward W.: "The New Economics: Massachusetts Institute of Technology Center for Advanced Educational Services," Cambridge, 1994.

64. Dixon, Nancy M., "Common Knowledge – How Companies Thrive by Sharing, What They Know?" Harvard Business School Press, Massachusetts, 2000.

65. Drucker, Peter F.: "Management Challenges for the 21st Century," HarperCollins Publishers, New York, 1999.

66. Drucker, Peter F.: "Managing in a Time of Great Change, " Penguin Books, New York, 1995.

67. Drucker, Peter F.: "The Effective Executive," Harper & Row Publishers, Inc., New York, 1985.

68. Drucker Foundation: "Leader of the Future," Jossey-Bass Publishers, San Francisco, 1996.

69. Drucker Foundation: "Organization of the Future," Jossey-Bass Publishers, San Francisco, 1997.

70. Drucker, Peter F., "Managing in The Next Society," Truman Talley Books, New York, 2002.

71. Eberstein, Lanny: "Milton Friedman – A Biography," Palgrave Macmillan, New York, 2007.

72. Edersheim, Elizabeth Haas: "The Definitive Drucker – Challenges for Tomorrow's Executives; Final Advice from the Father of Modern Management," The McGraw-Hill Companies, New York, 2007.

73. Elashmawi, Farid and Harris, Philip R.: "Multicultural Management: New Skills for Global Success," Gulf Publishing Company, Texas, 1993.

74. Elster, Charles Harrington: "Verbal Advantage – 10 Easy Steps to a Powerful Vocabulary," Random House, New York, 2000.

75. Fingar, Peter: "Extreme Competition – Innovation and the Great 21st Century Business Reformation," Meghan-Kiffer Press, Florida, 2006.

76. Fiorina, Carly: "Tough Choices – A Memoir," Penguin Group, New York, 2006.

77. Firestien, Roger L.: "Leading on the Creative edge," Pinon Press, Colorado Springs, 1996.

78. Fishman, Ted C.: "China Inc. – How the Rise of the Next Superpower Challenges America and the World" Scribener, New York, 2005.
79. Franson, Paul: "High Tech, High hope – Turning Your Vision of Technology into Business Success," John Wiley & Sons, Inc., New York, 1998.
80. Frieberg, Kevin and Jackie: "Guts! Companies that Blow the Doors off Business-As-Usual," Doubleday, New York, 2004.
81. Fulmer, William E.: "Shaping the Adaptive Organization," AMACOM, New York, 2000.
82. Gallagher, Carol & Golant, Susan K.: "Going to the Top – A Road Map for Success from America's Leading Women Executives," Penguin Group, New York, 2000
83. Garten, Jefftrey E.: "World View – Global Strategies for the New Economy," Harvard Business School Publishing, Massachusetts, 2000.
84. Gasparino, Charles: "King of the Club – Richard Grasso and the Survival of the New York Stock Exchange," HarperCollins Publishers, New York, 2007.
85. Geisst, Charles R.: "Deals of the Century: Wall Street, Mergers, and the Making of modern America," John Wiley and Sons, Inc., New Jersey, 2004.
86. Geisst, Charles R.: "Undue Influence – How the Wall Street Elite Puts the Financial System at Risk," John Wiley and Sons, Inc., New Jersey, 2005.
87. George, Bill with Sims, Peter: "True North – Discover Your Authentic Leadership," Jossey-Bass, San Francisco, 2007.
88. George, Bill: "Authentic Leadership – Rediscovering the Secrets to Creating Lasting Value," Jossey-Bass, San Francisco, 2003.
89. Gerstner, Jr., Louis V.: "Who Says Elephants Can't Dance," Harper Collins Publishers, New York, 2002.
90. Giulian, Rudolph W with Ken Kurson.: "Leadership," Hyperion, 2002.
91. Gladwell, Malcom: "blink – The Power of Thinking without Thinking," Little, Brown and Company, New York, 2005.

92. Goffee, Rob and Jones, Gareth: "The Character of a Corporation," Harper Collins Publishers, New York, 1998.

93. Golin, Mark, Briklin, Mark, Diamond, David and the Rodale Center for Executive Development: "Secrets of Executive Success – How Anyone Can Handle the Human Side of Work and Grow their Career," Rodale Press, Emmaus, Pennsylvania, 1991.

94. Goleman, Daniel, Boyatzis, Richard and McKee, Annie: "Primal Leadership – Realizing the Power of Emotional Intelligence," Harvard Business School Press, Massachusetts, 2002

95. Gordman, Robert: "The Must-Have Customer – 7 Steps to Winning the Customer You Haven't Got," Truman Talley Books, New York, 2006.

96. Gottry, Steve: "Common Sense Business – Starting, Operating and Growing Your Small Business – in Any Economy!" HarperBusiness, New York, 2005.

97. Gratton, Linda: "Hot Spots – Why Some Teams, Workplaces and Organizations Buzz with Energy – and Others Don't," Berrett-Koehler Publishers, Inc., San Francisco, 2007.

98. Greenspan, Alan: "The Age of Turbulence – Adventures in a New World," Penguin Press, New York, 2007.

99. Greenwald, Bruce and Kahn, Judd: "Competition Demystified – A Radically Simplified Approach to Business Strategy," Penguin Group, New York, 2005.

100. Grove, Andrew S.: "High Output Management," Random House, New York, 1983.

101. Grove, Andrew S.: "Only the Paranoid Survive," Doubleday Dell Publisher, New York, 1996.

102. Gutek, Barbara A. and Welsh Theresa: "The Brave New Service Strategy," AMACOM Press, New York, 2000.

103. Hagstrom, Robert G.: The Warren Buffett Way – Second Edition," John Wiley & Sons, New Jersey, 2005.

104. Halpern, Belle Linda and Lubar, Kathy: "Leadership Presence – Dramatic Techniques To Reach Out, Motivate and Inspire," Penguin Group, New York, 2003.

105. Hamermesh, Richard G.: "Fad Free Management: The Six Principles that Drive Successful Companies and Their Leaders," Knowledge Exchange, LLC, Santa Monica, 1996.

106. Hammel, Gary: "Leading the Revolution," Harvard Business School Press, Massachusetts, 2000.

107. Harcavy, Daniel: "Becoming a Coaching Leader – The Proven Strategy for Building your own Team of Champions," Thomas Nelson Publishers, New York, 2007.

108. Harper, Steven C.: "The Forward-Focused Organization," AMACOM, New York, 2001.

109. Harrell, Keith: "Attitude is everything – 10 Life-Changing Steps to Turning Attitude into Action," HarperCollins Publishers, New York, 2000.

110. Harrington, Daryl R. and Horney, Nicholas L.: "Project Change Management – Applying Change Management To Improvement Projects," McGraw-Hill, New York, 2000.

111. Harvard Business Review (1980 – 1994) – Managerial Excellence, McKinsey Award Winners, Harvard Business Review Press, 1996.

112. Heller, Robert: "Managing for Excellence," DK, Publishing, New York, 2001.

113. Herman, Roger E.: "Keeping Good People," Oakhill Press, Virginia, 1999.

114. Hersey, Paul and Blanchard, Kenneth H.: "Management of Organizational Behavior, "Simon and Schuster, New York, 1993.

115. Hiam, Alex: "Making Horses Drink- How to Lead and Succeed in Business," Entrepreneur Press, Canada, 2002.

116. Hilton, Steve & Gibbons, Giles: "Good Business – Your World Needs You," Texere Publishing Ltd., London, 2002.

117. Hira, Ron and Hira, Anil: "Outsourcing America – What's Behind Our National Crisis and How We Can Reclaim American Jobs," AMACOM, New York, 2005.

118. Hoover, John: "Difficult People – Working Effectively with Prickly Bosses, Coworkers and Clients," Hylas Publishing, New York, 2007.

119. Hou, Wee Chow & Lum, Lan Luh: " The 36 Strategies of the Chinese: Adapting Ancient Chinese Wisdom to the Business World," Addison Wesley, Singapore, 1998.

120. Housel, Thomas & Bell, Arthur H.: "Measuring and Managing Knowledge," McGraw-Hill Irwin, New York, 2001.

121. Huguet, Jim: "Great Companies, Great Returns – The Breakthrough Investing Strategy That Produces Great Returns Over The Long-Term Cycle of Bull and Bear Markets," Broadway Books, New York, 1999.

122. Hundt, Reed: "In China's Shadow – The Crisis of American Entrepreneurship," Yale University Press, New Haven, 2006.

123. Hurd, Mark & Nyberg, Lars: "The value factor – How Global Leaders use Information for Growth and Competitive Advantage, Bloomberg Press, Princeton, 2004.

124. Iacocca, Lee with Whitney, Catherine: "Where Have All The Leaders Gone?" Scribner, New York, 2007.

125. Imparato, Nicholas and Harari, Oren: "Jumping the Curve," Jossey-Bass Publishers, San Francisco, 1994.

126. Jackson, Tim: "Inside Intel: Andy Grove and the Rise of the World's Most Powerful Chip Company," A Dutton Book, New York, 1997.

127. Jennings, Jason: "Less is More – How Great Companies Use Productivity as a Competitive Tool in Business," Penguin Group, Middlesex, England, 2002.

128. Johanson, Johnny K. and Nonaka, Ikujiro: "Relentless – The Japanese Way of Marketing," HarperBusiness, New York, 1996.

129. Jordan, Jr., Vernon E., with Gordon-Reed, Annette, "Vernon Can Read," Public Affairs, New York, 2001.

130. Joyce, William, Nohria, Nitin and Roberson, Bruce: "What (Really) Works – The 4+2 Formula for Sustained Business Success," HarperCollins Publishers, New York, 2003.

131. Juergen Daum: "The New Economy Analyst Report," January 26, 2002.

132. Juran, J.M: "Juran on Leadership for Quality," The Free Press, New York, 1989.

133. Kelley, Tom and Littman, Jonathan: "The Art of Innovation," Random House, New York, 2001.

134. Kanter, Rober Moss, "When Giants Learn to Dance: Mastering the Challenge of Strategy, Management and Careers in the 1990s," Simon and Schuster, New York, 1989.

135. Kanugel, Robert: "The One Best Way – Frederick Winslow and the Enigma of Efficiency," Penguin Group, Middlesex, England, 1997.

136. Kevin Knight: Translation of Summa Theologica of Saint Thomas Aquinas (1920), 2003.

137. Keyes, Jessica: "Internet Management," Auerbach Publications, Florida, 2000.

138. Khan, Riz: "Alwaleed – Businessman Billionaire Prince," William Morrow, New York, 2005.

139. Kobert, Norman: "Cut the Fat, Not the Muscle," Prentice-Hall, New Jersey, 1995.

140. Kotler, Philip: "Kotler on Marketing: How to Create, Win and Dominate Markets," Free Press, New York, 1999.

141. Kotter, John P.: "A Force for Change: How Leadership Differs from Management," The Free Press, New York, 1990.

142. Kotter, John P. and Cohen, Dan S.: "The Heart of Change: Real-Life Stories of How People Change Their Organizations," Harvard Business School Press, Massachusetts, 2002.

143. Krames, Jeffrey A: "Jack Welch Lexicon of Leadership," McGraw-Hill, New York, 2002.

144. Krames, Jeffrey A: "The Rumsfeld Way: Leadership Wisdom of a Battle-Hardened Maverick," McGraw-Hill, New York, 2002.

145. Krames, Jeffrey A: "What Best CEOs Know: 7 Exceptional Leaders and their Lessons for Transforming any Business," McGraw-Hill, New York, 2003.

146. Langenwalter, Gary A.: "Enterprise Resources Planning and Beyond – Integrating your Entire Organization," St. Lucie Press, New York, 2000.

147. Lee, Charles: "Cowboys and Dragons – Shattering Cultural Myths To Advance Chinese-American Business," Dearborn Trade Publishing, Chicago, 2003.

148. Levin, Robert and Rosse, Joseph: "Talent Flow – A Strategic Approach to Keeping Good Employees, Helping Them Grow and Letting Them Go," Jossey-Bass, San Francisco, 2001.

149. Lewis, David and Bridger, Darren: "The Soul Of The New Consumer," Nicholas Brealey Publishing, 2000.

150. Levinson, Jay Conrad: "The Way of the Guerrilla: Achieving Success and Balance as an Entrepreneur in the 21st Century," Houghton Mifflin Company, Boston, 1997.

151. Lichtenstein, Nelson (Editor), "Wall-Mart – The Face of Twenty-First-Century Capitalism," The New Press, New York, 2006.

152. Louis, Arthur M.: "The Tycoons: How America's Most Successful Executives Get to the Top," Simon and Schuster, New York, 1981.

153. Lowe, Janet: "Bill Gates Speaks – Insights from the World's Greatest Entrepreneur," John Wiley & Sons, New York, 1998.

154. Lucas, James R.: "The Passionate Organization," American Management Association, New York, 1999.

155. Lynn, Matthew: "Birds of Prey – Boeing versus Airbus, A Battle for the Skies," Four Wall Eight Windows, New York, 1997.

156. Marconi, Joe: "Image Marketing – Using Public Perceptions to Attain Business Objectives," American Marketing Association, Illinois, 1996.

157. Martin, Chuck: Managing for the Short Term – The New Rules for Running a Business in a Day-to-Day World," Doubleday, New York, 2002.

158. Maxwell, John C.: "Leadership Gold – Lessons I've Learned from a Life of Learning," Thomas Nelson Publishers, Tennessee, 2008."

159. Maxwell, John C.: "The 21 Irrefutable Laws of Leadership – Follow Them and People will Follow You, Thomas Nelson Publishers, Tennessee, 1998."

160. Maxwell, John C.: "Thinking for a Change," Warner Books, New York, 2003.

161. Maynard, Micheline: "Collision Course – Inside the Battle for General Motors," Birch Lane Press, New York, 1995.

162. McCraw, Thomas K.: "Prophet of Innovation – Joseph Schumpeter and Creative Destruction," The Belknap Press of Harvard University Press, Massachusetts, 2007.

163. McElroy, Mark W.: "The New Knowledge Management: Complexity, Learning and Sustainable Innovation," Butterworth Heinemann, New York, 2003.

164. Menkes, Justin: "Executive Inteligence," Harper Collins Publishers, New York, 2005.

165. Michael, Ed, Handfield-Jones, Halen and Axelrod, Beth: "The War for Talent," Harvard Business School Publishing, Massachusetts, 2001.

166. Michelli, Joseph A.: "The New Gold Standard – 5 Leadership Principles for Creating a Legendary Customer Experience Courtesy of The Ritz-Carlton Hotel Company," McGraw-Hill, New York, 2008.

167. Mills, D. Quinn, The New Competitors," John Wiley & Sons, New York, 1985.

168. Moore, James F.: *"The Advent of Business Ecosystems,"* Upside Magazine, December 1995, pp. 30-46.

169. Moser, Mike: "United We Brand," Harvard Business School Press, Massachussets, 2003.

170. Mullen, James X: "The Simple Art of Greatness – Building, Managing and Motivating a Kick-Ass Workforce," Viking-Penguin Books, New York, 1995.

171. Naisbitt, John: "Mind Set," HarperCollins, New York, 2006.

172. Nanus, Burt and Dobbs, Stephen M.: "Leaders Who Make a Difference," Jossey-Bass Inc. Publishers, San Francisco, 1999.

173. Neff, Thomas J and Citrin, James M.: "Lessons from The Top – The Search for America's Best Business Leaders," Doubleday, New York, 1999.

174. Nicholson, Nigel: "Executive Instinct," Crown Publishers, New York, 2000.

175. Ohmae, Kenichi: "The Borderless World – Power and Strategy in the Interlinked Economy," Harper Perennial, New York, 1991.

176. O'Reilly III, Charles A., and Pfeffer, Jeffrey: "Hidden Value – How Great Companies Achieve Extraordinary Results with Ordinary People," Harvard Business School Press, Massachusetts, 2000.

177. Orman, Suze: "The Courage to Be Rich – Creating Life of Material and Spiritual Abundance," Riverhead Books, New York, 1999.

178. Ostroff, Frank: "The Horizontal Organization," Oxford University Press, Oxford, 1999.

179. Pal, Nirmal and Ray, Judith M.: "Pushing the Digital Frontier: Insights into the Changing Landscape of E-Business," American Management Association, New York, 1999.

180. Pan, Eric T-S: "Perpetual Business Machines – Principles of Success for Technical Professionals," Meridian Deployment Corp., Fremont, California, 2005.

181. Pascale, Richard T. and Athos Anthony G.: "The Art of Japanese Management," Warner Books, New York, 1981.

182. Pascale, Richard T., Millemann, Mark and Gioja, Linda: "Surfing the Edge of Chaos – The Laws of Nature and the New Laws of Business," Crown Business, New York, 2000.

183. Pearce II, John A. and Robinson Jr., Richard B.: "Strategic Management – Formulation, Implementation and Control," Irwin McGraw-Hill, New York, 2000.

184. Pearce, Terry: "Leading Out Loud: The Authentic Leader, the Credible Leader," Jossey-Bass Publishers, San Francisco, 1995.

185. Perkins, Tom: "The Education f Tom Perkins – Valley Boy," Gotham Books, New York, 2007.

186. Perkowski, Jack: "Managing the Dragon – How I'm Building a Billion Dollar Business in China," Crown Business, New York, 2008.

187. Peters, Tom and Austin, Nancy: "A Passion for Excellence," Random House, Inc., New York, 1985.

188. Peters, Tom: "The Circle of Innovation," Alfred A. Knope, Inc., New York, 1997.

189. Peters, Tom: "Thriving on Chaos, Harper and Row, Publishers," New York, 1987.

190. Pfeffer, Jeffrey: "Managing with Power," Harvard Business School Press, Massachusetts, 1992.

191. Phalon, Richard: "Forbes greatest Investment Stories," John Wiley & Sons, New York, 2001.

192. Plunkett, Lorne and Hale, Guy A.: "The Proactive Manager," John Wiley & Sons, Inc., 1982.

193. Pollan, Stephen M. and Levine, Mark: "Turning No into Yes – Six Steps to Solving Your Financial Problems, Harper Business Press, New York, 2000.

194. Porras, Jerry, Emerry, Stewart and Thompson, Mark: "Success Built to Last – Creating a Life that Matters," Wharton School Publishing, New Jersey, 2007.

195. Posner, Kouzes: "The Leadership Challenge," Jossey-Bass, San Francisco, 2002.

196. Prestowitz, Clyde: "Three Billion New Capitalists – The Great Shift of Wealth and Power to the East," Basic Books, New York, 2005.

197. Price Waterhouse. LLP Change Integration Team: "The Paradox Principles – How High Performance Companies Manage Chaos, Complexity, and Contradictions to Achieve Superior Results." Irwin Publisher, 1996.

198. Primozic, Kenneth I, Primozic, Edward A and Leben, Joe: "Strategic Choices," McGraw Hill, New York, 1991.
199. Puris, Martin and Edidin, Peter, "Comeback: How Seven Straight-Shooting CEOs Turned Around Troubled Companies," Random House, New York, 1999.
200. Rogers, Jim: "A Bull in China – Investing Profitably in the World's Greatest Market," Random House, New York, 2007.
201. Rose, Charlie: "Transcript of Interview with Neutron Jack, # 3059. Neutron Jack in His Own Words," October 24, 2001.
202. Rosen, Robert H. and Brown Paul B.: "Leading People: Transforming Business from the Inside Out," Penguin Books, New York, 1996.
203. Robert, Michel: "Product Innovation Strategy Pure and Simple," McGraw-Hill, New York, 1995.
204. Robinson, Adam: "Word Smart II – How to Build a More Powerful Vocabulary," Princeton Review Publishing, New York, 2001.
205. Rubinfeld, Arthur & Hemingway, Collins: Built for Growth – Expanding Your Business Around the Corner or Across the Globe," Wharton School Publishing, New Jersey, 2005.
206. Rushkoff, Douglas: "Get Back in the Box – Innovation from the Inside Out," HarperCollins Publishers, New York, 2005.
207. Sato, Masaki: "The Honda Myth – The Genius and His Wake, Vertical, Inc., New York, 2006.
208. Sawyer, Keith: "Group Genius – The Creative Power of Collaboration," Basic Books, New York, 2007.
209. Schoenberg, Robert J.: "The Art of Being a Boss – Inside Intelligence from Top-Level Business Leaders and Young Executives on the Move," J.B Lippincott Company, Philadelphia, 1978.
210. Security and Exchange Commission: A Plain English Handbook, Draft revision, January 22, 1998.
211. Senge, Peter: "The Fifth Discipline – The Art and Practice of the Learning Organization, Doubleday, New York, 1990.

212. Sewell, Carl and Brown, Paul B.: "Customers for Life: How to Turn That Onetime Buyer into a Lifetime Customer," Bantam Doubleday Dell Publishing. New York, 1998.

213. Seybold, Patricia B.: "The Customer Revolution: How to Thrive When Customers Are in Control," Crown Business, New York, 2001.

214. Shenkar, Oded: "The Chinese Century – The Rising Chinese Economy and Its Impact on the Global Economy, the Balance of Power and Your Job," Wharton School Publishing, Pennsylvania, 2005

215. Slater, Robert: "No Such Thing as Over-Exposure – Inside the Life and Celebrity of Donald Trump, Prentice Hall, New Jersey, 2005.

216. Smith, Theodore A., "Dynamic Business Strategy: The Art of Planning for Success," McGraw-Hill, New York, 1977.

217. Solvi, Daniel R.: "The Smaterst Investment Book You'll Ever Read – The Simple Stress-Free Way to Reach your Investment Goal," A Preigee Book, New York, 2006.

218. Sonnenfeld, Jeffrey and Ward, Andrew: "Firing Back – How Great Leaders Rebound After Career Disasters," Harvard Business School Press, Massachusetts, 2007.

219. Soros, George: "George Soros on Globalization," Public Affairs, New York, 2002.

220. Soros, George: "The Bubble of American Supremacy; Correcting the Misuse of American Power," Public Affair, New York, 2004.

221. Spector, Robert: "Anytime, Anywhere – How the Best Bricks-And-Clicks Businesses Deliver Seamless Services to their Customers," Perseus Books, Massachusetts, 2002.

222. Stevens, Mark: "Extreme Management," Warner Books, New York.

223. Stewart, Martha: "The Martha Rules – 10 Essentials for Achieving Success as you Start, Build, or Manage a Business," Rodale, New York, 2005.

224. Taylor, Don: "Solid Gold Strategies for your Business," American Management Association, New York, 1996.

225. Tarkenton, Fran with Smith, Wes: "What Losing Taught Me about Winning – The Ultimate Guide for Success in Small and Home-Based Businesses," Simon & Schuster, New York, 1997.

226. Thompson, Vince: "Ignited – Managers! Light Up Your Company and Career for More Power, More Purpose and More Success," FT Press, New Jercey, 2007.

227. Thurow, Lester: "Fortune Favors the Bold – What We Must Do to Build A New and Lasting Global Prosperity, HarperBusiness, New York, 2003.

228. Thurow, Lester: "Head to Head – The Coming Economic Battle among Japan, Europe and America," William Morrow and Company, New York, 1992.

229. Tulgan, Bruce: "It's Okay to Be the Boss – The Step By Step Guide to Becoming the Manager Your Employee Needs," HarperCollins Press, New York, 2007.

230. Tomasko, Robert M: "Rethinking the Corporation, the Architecture of Change." AMACOM, New York, 1993.

231. Toogood, Granville N.: "The Inspired Executive – The Art of Leadership in the Age of Knowledge," Carrol and Graff Publishers, 1997.

232. Town, Phil: "Rule # 1 – The Simple Strategy for Successful Investing in Only 15 Minutes a Week," Crown Publishers, New York, 2006.

233. Tracy, Diane and Morin, William J.: "Truth, Trust and Bottom Line 7 Steps to Trust-Based Management," Dearborn Publishing, Chicago, 2001.

234. Treacy, Michael & Wiersema, Fred: "The Discipline of Market Leaders – Choose Your Customers, Narrow Your Focus, Dominate Your Markets," Addison-Wesley, New York, 1995.

235. Trout, Jack with Rivkin Steve: "The Power of Simplicity," McGraw-Hill, New York, 1999.

236. Trump, Donald J.: "The Way to the Top – The Best Business Advise I Ever Received," Crown Business, New York, 2004.

237. Trump, Donald J. & Kiyosaki, Robe T.: "Why We Want You To Be Rich," Rich Press, Scottsdale, Arizona, 2006

238. Wacker, Watts & Taylor, Jim with Means, Howard: "The Visionary's Handbook – Nine Paradoxes That Will Shape the Future of Your Business," HarperBusiness, New York, 2000.

239. Wagner, Rodd & Harter, James K.: "The Elements of Great Managing – Based on Gallup's ten million workplace interviews, the largest worldwide study of employee engagement," Gallup Press, New York, 2006.

240. Wakerle, Frederick W.: "The Right CEO," Jossey-Bass, San Francisco, 2001.

241. Wall, Stephen J., & Wall, Shannon Rye: "The New Strategists – Crating Leaders at All Levels," The Free Press, New York, 1995.

242. Wang, Charles: "Techno Vision: The Executives Survival Guide to Understanding and Managing Information Technology," McGraw-Hill Inc., New York, 1994.

243. Warren, Rick, "The Purpose Driven Life," Zondervan, Grand Rapids, Michigan, 2002.

244. Watson, Charles E.: "Managing with Integrity," Praeger Publishers, New York 1991.

245. Weil, Sandy and Kraushaar, Judah S.: The Real Deal – My Life in Business and Philanthropy," Warner Business Books, New York, 2006.

246. Weiner, Eric J.: "What Goes Up – The Uncensored History of Modern Wall Street as Told by the Bankers, Brokers, CEOs, and Scoundrels Who Made it Happened," Little, Brown and Company, New York, 2005.

247. Weismantel, Guy E. and Kisling Jr., J. Walter, "Managing Growth: Keys to Success for Expanding Companies, Liberty House Books, Pensylvania, 1990.

248. Welch, Jack & Byrne, John A.: "Jack - Straight from the Gut," Warner Books, New York, 2001.

249. Welch, Jack & Welch, Suzy, "Winning," Harper Business, New York, 2005.

250. Wiersema, Fred: "The New Market Leaders: Who's Winning and How in the Battle for Customers," The Free Press, New York, 2001.

251. Wilms, Wellford W.: Restoring Prosperity: How Workers and Managers are Forging a New Culture of Cooperation," Times Business, New York, 1996.

252. Worth, Robert: "What Lou Gerstner Could Teach Bill Clinton," Washington Monthly, September 1999 – Volume 21, Issue 8.

253. Zenger, John H. & Folkman, Joseph: The Extraordinary Leader – Turning Good Managers into Great Leaders," McGraw-Hill, New York, 2002.

254. Zhijun, Ling – Translated by Avery, Martha: "The Lenovo Affair – The Growth of China's Computer Giant and its Takeover of IBM-PC," John Wiley & Sons (Asia) Pte Ltd., Singapore, 2005.

255. Ziglar, Zig: "Top Performance: How to Develop Excellence in Yourself and Others," Fleming H. Revell Company, New Jersey, 1986.

256. Zook, Chris and Allen, James: "Profit from the Core – Growth Strategy in an Era of Turbulence," Harvard Business School Press, 2001.

257. Zyman, Sergio with Brott, Armin A.: "Renovate Before you Innovate – Why Doing the New Thing Might Not Be the Right Thing," Penguin Group, New York, 2004.

258. Zyman, Sergio: "Brand-Width – Closing the Sale Online," Harper Collins Publishers, New York, 2000.

259. Zyman, Sergio: "The End of Marketing As We Know It," Harper Collins Publishers, New York.

About the author

James Lim has been actively involved in high technology companies in Silicon Valley, California for over 30 years. These companies range from startups, mid-size and multi-billion dollar corporations. A seasoned leader and active participant with a successful track record with hard-won and varied experience, he has intimate association with numerous professionals in industries spanning automatic test equipments, defense electronics, computers, telecommunications, professional audio equipments, image sensors, graphics, core logic chipsets, programmable devices, semiconductors and component services. With unique combination of technical expertise and finely tuned business acumen and managerial experience, the author draws on his experience and endeavors in a lifelong study of high technology companies in the trough and belle époque of business and economic cycles. With equal or greater ardor, he blends key concepts with a worldview that are used to develop winning strategies, create products, shape the market and manage the creative energies of all employees today and tomorrow.

As a resident of Silicon Valley for 34 years, he has witnessed the inception of various high- powered companies, notable of which are AMD, Cisco System, Intel, Marvell Semiconductors, National Semiconductor, Nvidia and TSMC, to name a few. He has seen up close the rise of tremendous growth companies such as Intel, Marvell Semiconductor and Amgen; wobbly downs-and-ups of AMD, National Semiconductor and Apple Computers; the ill-fated acquisition of Bay Networks by Nortel and the poor fate and demise of Diamond Multimedia, Everex, S3, Televideo and Wyse Technology. In the global setting, he is a keen observer of foreign companies such as Nokia, Sony, Chartered Semiconductor, TSMC, UMC, Philips Semiconductor, etc. These companies reflect the triumphs and tumults of the modern high technology business era. He writes authoritatively on a subject with which he has great familiarity.

He lives in Silicon Valley, California with his family.

Second Edition

www.totalbusinessmanagement.com

Cover photo by Benjamin Lui

298